A NOVEL

MICHAEL GROSS

Cover Art by James Scott

Produced by Raab & Co. | raabandco.com

Designed by Brian Phillips | brianphillipsdesign.com

Library of Congress Cataloging information available upon request.

First Print Edition

ISBN: 9798865879305

Printed in the United States of America

For my family, friends,
and the city I love

CONTENTS

"For, you see, so many out-of-the-way things
had happened lately, that Alice had begun to think that
very few things indeed were really impossible."

. . .

LEWIS CARROLL,
Alice's Adventures in Wonderland

Part
ONE

1

A PROPOSAL

Eliot asks Joan to marry him.

"Oh, Eliot," says Joan. "You can't be serious."

"Dead serious."

They've lived together eight years. On the same day they signed the lease on their East Village apartment, the Yankees were mathematically eliminated from the 1968 pennant race. Joan and Eliot didn't plan it that way. As a couple, they never planned much of anything, and besides, at the time they didn't follow baseball. Baseball followed them.

The man who sold them their secondhand bed claimed that Lou Gehrig once slept in it on the way to Iron Man stardom. The set of dishes they bought at the Salvation Army depicted Great Moments in World Series Play before the pictures got washed out. Dugan Inc. manufactured the solid-state black-and-white television with the twelve-inch screen they bought; Admiral Dugan owns the Yankees. And before they came across the large wooden cable spool left by the phone company at the corner of St. Mark's Place and First Avenue (they live between First and Second), someone had scrawled on it, "Ya bums! Bring back the glory days!" They brought it back to their third-floor walk-up and installed it amidst the books, records, comics, and art magazines scattered everywhere, between their semblance of a kitchen and their dual-purpose living room/bedroom, eating their meals while seated on straw mats when they didn't eat them in bed. They spent a hell of a lot of time in bed.

While season after season the fortunes of the Bronx Bombers steadily declined, along with the Bronx, along with all of New York, along with all of the nation's cities, Joan and Eliot grew so close that in the twelve hours a night they clung to one another in sleep, they even started to share the same dreams.

This season though, while the 1976 Yankees have recaptured their former glory, Joan's been plagued by nightmares in which she's burned at the stake by the good people of Salem, Massachusetts. Crowds huddle together to watch, children shout, "She's possessed by the Devil!" What's worse, she half-believes in them, while dreaming and after. Eliot doesn't. He thinks she's watched too many afternoon horror flicks. Meanwhile, he dreams that he is Adlai Stevenson's running mate. They keep running and losing, running and losing.

Joan has no intention of marrying Eliot. In fact, she's felt so removed from him lately that she's started to wonder whether it is time to truck out. Where would she truck to? She has no idea.

Given that she rarely leaves their apartment except to visit the Welfare Office and the neighborhood bodega, it's not as though she's had a great many opportunities to make friends in recent years. Having one friend—Eliot—has satisfied her fine (she likes to concentrate her energies), and when it comes right down to it, she wishes she were still satisfied (she doesn't want to hurt him), but the facts, she thinks, are the facts, and the fact is that when she rolls out of the sag in the middle of the bed and he gives her a gentle tug she understands as "be kinder," what she feels like doing, instead of stopping and sighing, is elbowing him as though he'd accosted her.

The fact is that she wishes he *would* accost her, not physically so much as . . . yeah, well, physically. She imagines him in leather (enough of this corduroy), a whip in his hand that she's urged him to use. But Eliot would never lift a finger to hurt her, even if she asked him to.

Eliot's dark brown hair is as fine as a baby's; he parts it on the right and tucks it behind his small ears. Joan has never seen him without his beard, which she trims for him monthly when the moon is full. She used to be turned on by his delicate body, but now he seems too scrawny. And whatever happened to those soft-toned, offbeat questions his dark eyes once posed when she least expected them? Now, when she looks at him, they only seem to beg, and the sad fact is she's plumb out of alms.

He ought to know better than to propose. She feels like she's held a placard in front of his face, pointed out the inscription syllable by syllable: I Feel Alienated. She shouldn't have to speak the words aloud and she won't. This is precisely the kind of thing he should be able to figure out.

"I think it's time," he says, "we shook up our lives a bit. Explored some new territory, know what I mean?"

He runs his hand down her long back while she thinks how absurd it is that in the fourth quarter of the twentieth century a woman who fancies herself a free thinker could almost reach the age of twenty-seven having made love to only one man, even if she has done her fair share of lovemaking.

"I agree," she says, "that the time's come for something."

"Wouldn't kids be a trip?" says Eliot. "I mean their changes would be so visible, we couldn't help but see ourselves change with them. It'd be as though we had these mystical mirrors."

"You're talking in the plural?"

"Of course, I'd need a steady job."

"Of course."

"And finding one, you know, that could hold my interest . . ."

"Your options are limited."

She hopes he works nights.

"This damned depression is for the birds," he says, raising his voice. "But I've got faith." And he kisses a clump of her thick red hair. "You want to get dressed and find a judge?"

"Not really. Do you?"

"Maybe later, I guess."

She puts a pillow over her head.

. . .

"Yup," says the voice of the Yankees, Al Deep. "Today we got baseball as it's never been seen before, baseball as only Nick 'The Swan' Spillage can make it, and does he ever, yessireebob. The rookie sensation, he just beats all. Twenty-six times he's appeared on the mound since he came out of nowhere near the start of spring training to ask for a tryout, and good thing we gave him one. Might not have, you know, if we hadn't been so desperate. But we were desperate indeed, so we gave him one, and has he ever given us back!

"Twenty-six times he's gone the distance for the win with that unorthodox delivery you'd think would tire him out (he chants, in case you haven't heard, and races around the pitcher's mound before each release like some kind of whirling dervish), except he doesn't get tired because his games don't last long for the simple reason that the opposition can't touch him. Boy's something else again, got amazing stuff. All kinds of records broken—I won't bore you with the details—and hearts too, you bet. The big thing though is what he's done for this Yankee ball club, and I can sum that up for you in a word: he's done miracles.

"Now don't get me wrong. I love every one of the ragtag bunch of god-awful misfits who finished in the cellar in '72, '73, '74, and '75 like I love my own kids. But I'm honest enough with myself to admit, love 'em though I do and kills me though it does, that they stink. Or at least they stunk. Wasn't a knowledgeable baseball man in the country who had them pegged for anything but the cellar again this year.

"This Yankee ball club was about as bankrupt before Swannie came as the Big Apple itself is, and while the long-necked, golden-curled, nineteen-year-old kid pitcher hasn't solved the major-league problems still facing this woe-begotten metropolis, if he could make these bums the champions of the world, then I wouldn't put it past him to do just about anything."

. . .

Joan may be the last person in New York to hear of the Swan. When she does, through Eliot, it's déjà vu: in her dream of burning last night, she dealt her soul to Satan for him, and what a trade it was! All she gave up to seal the deal was a lock of her hair, while she would have cut off her whole damned head if she'd had to for just one embrace of the Yankees' young savior. Of course, there were favors to be named later that she'd have to perform, but these were too far down the road to think about, in another dream altogether. In the meantime, life was so perfect, so filled with wonders at every moment.

Tonight, Spillage goes against the California Angels and a victory could send the Yanks into the World Series. *The Mercury* is filled with pictures of his season-long heroics, pictures that will soon be plastered all over the apartment. Eliot, who'd brought the paper home so he could look for jobs, diligently circles ads while Joan works with scissors and tape. He'd been vaguely aware of the Swan's existence but didn't give him much thought until after his father died, a victim of random violence, and he turned to baseball as a kind of therapy. Save for looking at box scores, he hadn't read the newspaper in months. Once upon a time, he'd been a news junkie, but as those twin evils, inflation and depression, worked their ever-nastier magic on the streets of New York—and as rising crime struck too close to home—his daily dose of robbery, rape, rioting, arson, assassination, suicide, infanticide, and homicide finally wore him down and he decided to kick the habit.

Joan lifts a cutout close-up of the southpaw's sweetly smiling, sweating face with a banner head that reads, "Hope for New York?" She asks Eliot if he'd mind if she hung it up.

"You think it'd add anything?" asks Eliot.

She shrugs. "Something needs to be added. I'm tired of the spartan look. And besides, he's so pretty."

"I guess. If you like primitives."

"I was thinking we could swing these vines down, you know, from hooks in the ceiling; pick up some jungle incense, a couple of eucalyptuses, maybe a pet leopard."

She fools with the buttons of his clean white shirt.

"Whatever you're into," he says.

"You're much too tolerant."

. . .

The Viennese artist Gustav Klimt left his studio one day around the turn of the twentieth century to stroll through the netherworld from whence souls originate, and there, thinks Eliot, the lucky devil spied Joan. Her eyes were closed, her full lips parted as she curled in a fetal pose atop a silken blanket, overlaid with a stream of gold sperm-and-egg shapes. Her unpolished fingernails, bitten to the nubs, seemed almost to dig into the flesh between her breasts. That the right was hidden by her sturdy thigh made the left the more delectable. Klimt wanted to roll his tongue around it; he'd center it when he reimagined it. The pink of that nipple matched the pink of her naturally flushed cheeks. And the red hair acted according to its own laws, curving like sound waves across her chin, shoulder, and arm.

When she stood, she stood straight. A serpent wound around her ankles. Her left hand held a magnifying glass, pale blue and incisive like her widely spaced eyes. In profile she became pregnant. Her belly looked big enough to hold a battalion. It ruined her posture, made her arms and legs seem emaciated. Demons floated above and behind her. She dared them. She dared Klimt.

Eliot is upset with Joan for shaving her head. She only did it, he thinks, because he shaved his beard. But at the same time, he's enthralled; it's miraculously smooth, impeccably shaped. And he might as well be magnanimous since he did land a job. The Burger Boat on 23rd and Second (part of Admiral Dugan's chain) just hired a new night manager.

2

ENTER CHOICE

While Eliot works his new night job, Joan heads up to the East 70s in search of a bar with a supersized color tube that'll show her Swan in all his glory. She grew up in this part of town, near her father's office on Madison Avenue, but she hasn't been here in ages, so it feels like virgin territory.

The people on the street are dressed in their finest garb, looking expensive from head to toe. Not Joan. She's in rags by comparison, with her light blue turban and multicolored peasant dress, and quite likes the effect. She was never drawn to the current fashions her father promoted in the ads he created, even when he pretended to be a loving dad, and she completely turned off to everything she associated with him once his secret second family came to light.

It was October 1963, during the Yankees-Giants World Series that nearly thirteen-year-old Joan had zero interest in. She had zero interest in any sports at the time—that was her father and brother's thing, while she focused on art, music, and dance—but she remembers this Series because that's where her brother first made the discovery. At Game Three with Big Daddy in a superspecial field level box befitting his status as an advertising heavyweight (among other things, he put Burger Boat on the map, helping Admiral Dugan launch his fast-food empire), her brother was brazenly seated next to an elegant woman her father claimed was his client but whose canoodling with him suggested otherwise, and her strangely familiar daughter, whom he told his mother when he arrived home could pass for Joan's twin.

That started the ball rolling, and it didn't take long for Joan's mom to figure the whole thing out and give Big Daddy the boot. Of course, he wanted her to figure it out, Joan's always thought—otherwise why tempt fate by bringing brother, future stepmother, and half-sister together in the first place? He was ready to leave, and he got what he wanted, as he usually did, the macho asshole, though not without the pain of a bitter divorce. Joan never wanted to see him again and never did, despite her brother's attempt years later to broker a reconciliation.

They're probably at the game now, Joan thinks with a shiver. It's been a while since she's thought about either one, and she quickly banishes the thought as she enters a bar called Fantasia, where the screen's almost movie-sized. No way they're at the game. Big Daddy moved to L.A. years ago, Tinseltown, just the place for him, and while she doesn't know his current whereabouts, she doubts it's the town he ran away from. Besides, he was never really a baseball fan. He just faked it for business reasons, like he faked everything. His whole life was a lie, including when he feigned affection for you when you were young.

She accepts an offer of a seat at the bar, orders herself a double tequila, downs it without the aid of lemon or salt and laughs as it goes through her like fire.

In the top of the first, Nick Spillage goes through the fearsome Angel order like a buzz saw through plywood, which is what their bats appear to be made of when they manage to make contact. Back in 1963, the last time the Yankees made the World Series, the announcer points out that they did it with a cast of aging stars who were swept by the Giants and never the same after. That won't be the case this year, he says—no siree, not with Swannie—and Joan agrees. That was the end of an era, she thinks, and this is the dawn of a new one.

It was all downhill for the Yankees after their 1963 Series debacle, an unprecedented dozen-year decline for baseball's most storied franchise. And it was all downhill too for Joan's mom, a former model who met her father on a commercial shoot, then gave up her professional ambitions when she had her first child. A distant cousin of the Kennedys (or so she claimed), she was prone to drink, depression, and delusion even before her marriage dissolved. When JFK was assassinated a month later, the double whammy drove her completely over the edge.

She consumed herself with cosmetic surgeries, which gave her face a masklike quality Joan hated. Another big fake! And she gobbled up conspiracy theories, in her home life as well as the world at large. At home, she tried to get Joan to testify in the divorce proceedings that Big Daddy was a monster who abused her repeatedly. While admitting he could be creepy, Joan refused to go that far, which didn't do wonders for the already tenuous mother-daughter relationship. As for the world, Dear Mother insisted that the Russians, Cubans, and Chinese all had a hand in JFK's demise, as did the Mafia, the CIA, LBJ, and Big Daddy's client Richard Nixon. She joined wacko support groups and subscribed to even more wacko newsletters in a never-ending quest to prove her case, contending with ever-increasing ardor that it was all one big plot, and she was the ultimate victim. The fact that Joan couldn't make the connection (any of her connections, really) created an even greater rift between them, until they were barely on speaking terms. Mercifully, Dear Mother moved down to Miami Beach to perfect her face-mask tan with her plastic surgeon boyfriend and fellow conspiracist around the time Joan entered college, studying art downtown at the Parsons School of Design, so they could stop having to try.

And this, thinks Joan, is the wonderful world of marriage that Eliot wants to usher her into! With these screwed-up parents as role models, how could we possibly have a happy one? Eliot knows the story, but he just plunged right in. And it's not like his own parents, Mr. and Mrs. Geek, the professors, were any great shakes either, though they stayed together until the very end. Somehow, they found each other, while failing at every other social connection they attempted, including with their only child. The odds are so long against us having a happy marriage, she thinks, it's not worth betting. What's wrong with that man, anyway?

Nothing wrong with Spillage, who strikes out ten before giving up his first hit in the fifth inning. He's beautiful, Joan thinks, unbelievably beautiful, as she remembers back to her first crush, George Harrison of the Beatles.

Joan rebounded from her parents' breakup by throwing herself into Beatlemania. She was one of three thousand screaming fans who greeted them at Kennedy Airport when they first arrived in America in February 1964. A year later, she was one of fifty thousand screaming for them from the stands when they performed at Shea Stadium, the only time she ever went to a major league ballpark.

For Joan, the Beatles represented four distinct types of men. There was John, the Genius; Paul, the Beauty; George, the Soul; and Ringo, the Goof. She fell for the Soul—tall, dark, quiet, with an inner strength and calm that gave her peace. During her teenage years, she had many suitors including each of these types, but in real life, Big Daddy's actions made her deeply distrustful of all men and she never had a serious relationship until Eliot came along.

Eliot was a Soul, like George. A sweet, unassuming Soul, devoid of swagger and pretentiousness, the total opposite of Big Daddy, the Evil Genius. She trusted him from the moment they locked eyes under the arch at Washington Square Park, where they'd gone for a rally to protest the Vietnam War. She still trusts him, she thinks. She still loves him. But it's time for something utterly different. Time for a Beauty! She stands up and cheers as her golden-curled Swan escapes a bases loaded jam in the sixth by notching his thirteenth strikeout.

By the time she met Eliot, Joan had moved beyond the Beatles, though she still bought all of their albums and knew much of their lyrics. She developed crushes on more edgy rock and rollers like Jim Morrison of the Doors, Jimi Hendrix, Lou Reed of The Velvet Under-ground, Grace Slick of Jefferson Airplane, and her all-time favorite,

Janis Joplin. Eliot, a pretty good guitarist in his own right, shared her passion for music. Wrote poetry and dreamed at one point of being a songwriter. Together, they frequented the Fillmore East in its late '60s heyday, along with several Village bars and clubs where emerging talent strutted their stuff. They spent three glorious days and nights at Woodstock, tripping on magic mushrooms. And they even formed an act—with Joan doing lead vocals and the tambourine, while Eliot strummed away and harmonized—which they took to the subways to make some extra cash after the stock market crashed, the economy tanked, and Big Daddy's checks stopped coming.

We had some amazing times, Joan thinks, and who's to say they're over? They're just not in the here and now. She recalls a Beatles song they had fun playing, a little ditty called "When I'm Sixty-Four." She sings it under her breath as the Yankees widen their lead to 3–0 in the bottom of the seventh. They used to joke in bed about growing old together, like the couple in the song. But eight years is a long time to be tied to someone, she thinks, never mind the more than forty-five it would take to achieve the song's late-life bliss. People change, they grow apart, especially when they start living together at eighteen, she tells herself. You just need to go solo sometimes to find out who you really are. Even the Beatles, who made such awesome music together, broke up after eight years. It could happen to anyone.

Throughout the game, she's been fending off guy after guy butting up against her at the bar to make approaches. It feels like one an inning, at least. Uptown guys, she thinks, of no interest whatsoever. Mini Mad Men, she imagines, Hollow Men, Tin Men, trying to fake their way through life with their catchy slogans like Big Daddy. Go peddle your cigarettes, your sugary drinks, your deodorants, and your gas guzzlers. Go hook America on whatever destructive crap you can get away with. Just get out of my face. Take your hand off my turban.

But when Spillage finishes twirling his three-hit gem, sending the Yanks to the World Series with a 5–0 victory, a more intriguing fellow comes into view. As she raises her glass to toast Swannie's accomplishment, it clinks against the scotch of a tall, athletic-looking Black man who says, "I'd rather toast you, momma."

"You're on," says Joan.

He's an out-of-work Shakespearean actor who calls himself Choice and is brilliantly bald, with riveting green eyes and a megawatt smile. Joan likes his style as they make conversation. Now here's a man who's authentic, she thinks, a one-of-a-kind, who knows who he is, what he's made of, and how he comes across, which is powerful, yet playful. He's a Beauty . . . and maybe a bit of a Goof too. He's played kings and princes and looks the part, though a bit frayed at the edges. He's not trying too hard to impress, like Big Daddy; he's just naturally impressive, so much so he makes light of it. And he's not begging like Eliot; he doesn't need you, just wants you. Just wants a good time, as you do, to celebrate the Yankee win. Poor Eliot. He's working way too hard and it's not at all attractive. Slogging away in the bowels of the Burger Boat, his only wish to make you happy.

Screw it, she thinks. Can't let Eliot hold me back. If he were here, he'd understand (which is part of the problem). A girl's gotta do what a girl's gotta do, especially this girl, who's been through so much. Burn me if you want to. I don't give a damn. Got to find out what I'm made of too.

Giddy with victory and ready for adventure, she suggests to Choice that they find a new scene, and he gladly agrees.

"Your place or mine," she says with a wink.

"If you got one," Choice says, "you're one up on me."

3

STRIKE WITHOUT WARNING

Choice is in a hurry. "Always in a hurry," he explains to Joan as he hustles her out of the bar and onto the street, "except when I'm making love to stately mommas like you."

His whistle for a cab is executed with the first and fourth fingers of his right hand stuck in his mouth and man, thinks Joan, does it ever carry. "Should've warned me," she says, shaking her head, while a cab brakes, runs a red light for an illegal U-turn and races toward them.

"Like to strike without warning," says Choice with a grand smile. "It's my charm."

New Horizons Playhouse, where he last performed, is not, though he insists it is, near St. Mark's Place, where Joan resides. It's way west of Times Square in a section of Manhattan known as Hell's Kitchen, and as the cabbie—named Fahmi from Pakistan—points out as they make the detour, it abuts a string of the sleaziest massage parlors, "bottomless" bars, and pornographic movie theaters in the city.

Not that the neighborhood, according to Fahmi, bears any reflection on the theater, which he's sorry got closed because he attended regularly (though he doesn't recognize Choice) and he never failed to be pleasantly shocked. Still, with times as bad as they are, you can't, according to Fahmi, expect anything good to last. Fahmi's fed up with the way the world is going. In fact, just the thought of it has given him a headache, and he wonders if either of them could help him out with some aspirin, as he happens to have run out.

Joan gives him some Midol, which she almost wishes she needed herself since her period is overdue. "You know it's incredible," she says to Choice, "but I've never once been to a play in all the years I've been living in the city."

"Shame on you," says Choice. "Where've you been that's so important?"

"Nowhere." She hangs her head. "But I'm gonna make up for it."

The actor props a finger under her chin and raises it as the cab passes *The Groupies, Bizarre Ways of Doing It, Saints and Sinners, More Fun with the Groupies, They Want It the Most, Ways You Never Dreamed Of*, and *The Groupies Come Back*, before whizzing by the boarded-up, graffiti-plastered New Horizons theater and turning downtown.

"What I love most," says Choice, "is women with determination. And you've got good instincts too, I can see it. Knew exactly what I needed as inspiration for our private show was to take a little peek at where I did my last public."

"That was it?"

"So it was. But no more, sad to say, like my good friend Raoul Wo."

"What happened to him?"

"You truly want to know?"

"Sure."

"I love you more and more, momma." He kisses her cheek. "Raoul was like family to me, bless his soul. His baby's my godchild, his wife Mirlanda's my main squeeze. Only woman, aside from you, who has any power to hold my attention. She held it for years. She designed my costumes—we used to do it backstage. And Raoul . . . excuse me . . ." He removes a purple handkerchief from the inside pocket of his frayed suit jacket and dabs his eyes. "Raoul never suspected. Or if he did, he never said nothing. What's he gonna say if Mirlanda's made her mind up? She's only five feet oh, my West Indian warrior-princess, but oh is she fierce. Like you, I suspect."

"I'm flattered."

"Believe it."

He slips a hand up her dress.

"So Raoul is dead?"

"Alas, poor Raoul. Gunned down by cops. Exit, stage left."

"Too bad. Another actor?"

"Bad actor. But soulful."

They kiss.

"I would've liked to have met him," says Joan afterward.

* * *

Every square inch of flaking wall in Joan and Eliot's apartment now radiates with pictures of the Yanks' super southpaw. Since she began her collage two weeks ago, Joan's raided libraries, newsstands, bookstores, subways, buses, park benches, and garbage cans to get more images.

"Don't know if I especially like your taste in wallpaper," the actor says as he takes off his shoes.

"Don't know if I care," says Joan.

"Bet you don't. Mirlanda's into that hyped-up pitcher too, though if I knew how come I'd be king of the world."

"She has good taste in men."

"She has flashes of good taste."

He rips a picture of the Swan getting kissed by Sheila Dugan (the Yankee owner's niece and heiress to his fast-food fortune) off the wall over the kitchen sink, which is piled with Great Moments in World Series Play dishes.

Joan, who took acute pleasure in bestowing upon Ms. Dugan a curled mustache and pointy little beard, tries to grab the picture back as Choice laughs at it, but he pushes her off and then flicks out a switchblade.

"Don't mess with me, momma. I play the hot-tempered roles," he says. "And like my boyhood hero Jackie Robinson, the fieriest of all the Brooklyn Dodgers, I hate the Yankees with a passion."

"Touch that picture with that blade and you'll never touch me," says Joan. "I don't care who your hero is."

"It's nothing personal," says the actor. "Just the way I'm wired. No way I can hold my emotions back."

"Then you better just split."

"You win." He hands her the picture, folds up his knife, smiles his grand smile. "Don't make me go. It's dark out there, and the area's dangerous."

"Nick Spillage is my idol," says Joan, rehanging him. "And I like the feeling that he's looking down at me from all sides. If I had that bitch's money . . ." She points to Sheila Dugan. "You know what I'd do? I'd commission some starving young artist to make stained-glass windows out of each and every one of these. I'd commission some starving young carpenter to build me a mansion, and it would have an inner sanctum with a high arched ceiling, and . . ."

"Let me help you with this peasant dress. Take a look at those long legs," Choice says, pulling at her skirt. "Hot damn! Your patch is flaming red! That the color of your hair too? Take a look under this sexy turban."

He starts to unravel it.

"I won't let you in my sanctum," says Joan. "But if you're good I'll build you a theater next door. You know, it's kind of cute the way you can blow up all of a sudden and in the next minute be calm."

"Who's calm?" says the actor. "I'm trembling with excitement."

"Eliot—that's my boyfriend—he has trouble getting mad."

"Then he's *in* trouble."

"Yeah."

"And you're bald just like me! Double damned!"

In bed, Choice gives a commanding performance, maybe a little too commanding for Joan's taste, but good enough to overcome her guilt and demand an encore, which gets cut short when she hears footsteps on the stairs.

She hides him under the mattress when Eliot arrives.

. . .

All Burger Boat workers dress in white sailor's uniforms but only managers get to have a blue stripe on each sleeve and a gold bar on each shoulder. As an aid to those customers who do not understand the significance of these insignias, managers carry a message clipped to their shirt pockets. The message that Joan's rumpled, beardless boyfriend brings home reads: "Ahoy! I'm Ensign Eliot Howe. I'm in charge here."

Evidently not, thinks Joan, as she sits up on the sagging mattress. His uniform is so big it would hang on a sumo wrestler, and what man of any substance has absolutely no chin? She has the urge to say something crushing, but while the actor under the bed curses softly, she figures she can't afford the luxury. So she borrows instead some words her mother used, back in the days when Big Daddy deigned to occasionally come home. "What you must go through for me, dear. Was it hell?" she says. And she feels pretty darned pleased with herself for how solicitous she sounds.

Eliot looks pleased with himself too as he flips his cap at the hook on the closet door. Missing it doesn't curb his enthusiasm. "How much do you think I made tonight?" he asks.

"I can hardly guess."

"$50,000!" says Eliot, holding up a roll of bills. "More than twice as much as my father used to make a year back in the '60s." He sighs. "Too bad this hyperinflation has made it all meaningless."

"Not all meaningless," says Joan. "Enough to go to the bodega and get me some carob ice cream. I have a huge yen."

"I *wish* they paid in yen," muses Eliot. "Would go much further."

"Go. Go. Sayonara. Go now." She waves her arms.

"Wait. Don't you want to hear how I got the money?"

"Yes. With a carob-ice-cream-coated spoon in my mouth."

"But Joan . . ." He plops onto the bed. "I *really* have $50,000. Don't you want to know how I got it? I've been through a harrowing experience."

"You brought it on yourself. I take no responsibility," she says, as he gives her a little kiss on the neck. She has no idea how to value the hefty sum, if in fact it's real, given the way inflation has zoomed totally out of control. But she can deal with that later. For now, she just needs him out.

"I'm not laying any on you though," says Eliot. "I mean if I was to lay it on anyone, I would lay it on this girl Crystal, because she's the reason I was manning the lines when it all came down. According to the grapevine, she's recovering from a botched abortion, and you'll never guess who was responsible—our old neighbor from across the hall, Art Popov! Small world, right?"

"Screwed-up world," says Joan. "I always hated that fat slob."

"Me too, though I never thought the old walrus would stoop to robbing the cradle like that. From what I hear, Crystal is just sixteen, only she pretends to be older by wearing tons of makeup. But if it wasn't her, it would have been someone else, because the working conditions are so bad, one of the sailors is always AWOL. And since part of the ensign's duties is to see that all battle stations are covered when the ship's going full steam, I have to count on manning the lines for at least a part of every night."

"Please, Eliot," says Joan, as he unbuttons his shirt. "A quick run around the corner. You could make me so happy."

"We shouldn't splurge on little things," he says. "We've got to budget ourselves, got to think about our future. This money . . ." He fans the bills. ". . . was a gift. And you know where it's going?"

"Where?"

"Under the mattress."

"No."

"Every last dollar, yes."

"I don't think that's such a great idea."

"But you don't know the whole story. Otherwise, you would." He bends over the side of the bed. "There. It's done." He does it. "That'll show him."

She collapses backward. "Show who?"

"Raoul. The guy who gave it to me." He kicks off his shoes and starts on his pants.

"Is Raoul your boss?"

"Nah. He works for Satan."

"How's that?" She lifts her head, red eyebrows arched.

"It's like I started to tell you. I was manning the lines in place of Crystal, it was about 10:30, the place was packed, I was working my butt off, but like my mind was someplace else."

"How unusual."

"Yeah. I was thinking about Crystal and her situation, and you and me and our situation. I was trying to imagine what our baby would look like and thinking up names and hoping I wasn't sterile. I've always been paranoid, you know, that I fucked myself over with all the tripping I used to do."

"I know."

"Anyway, Raoul waited his turn. I caught a glimpse of him in his black beret and green fatigues standing about three people back when I was taking this nun's order and thinking about adoption. It wouldn't be so bad, I thought, though I'd love a red-haired little girl, but it'd take a while for us to be respectable enough. They screen you pretty carefully from what I hear.

"And then Raoul, who's this Cuban-Chinese guy, no bigger than you but I bet he could lift a house, he lays a gun on the counter, tells me his name and asks if I'm married. I said almost, but not quite, my girlfriend isn't ready yet; and he said that's nice, he hopes it works out. Now he wasn't even holding the gun. At the other four battle stations the guys were holding theirs, and they also had these burlap sacks open to give the sailors something to put the night's bounty into."

"They all looked pretty much alike, these guys—I mean I'm not being racist, they all wore similar outfits and Raoul said they were his brothers. He called them 'The Satanic Vanguard.' Then he asked if I knew where you were tonight, because *he* did if I didn't. I said you were home, that you were a Spillage freak, and that you were watching the game. He laughed, asked me who was winning. "Beats me," I said. "I'm not the freak, she is.""

"So then he leans over the counter, puts his arms on both my shoulders and pulls me forward so like we're cheek to cheek. It itched; he has maybe three days' worth of beard that's growing in splotches. And he says in this hoarse whisper, 'Sí, Señor Ensign. You're no freak. You're a first-class sap and when you go home, you'll find out. The guy she's screwing at this very minute will be under your bed, and if you don't believe me, stuff the money I give you under your mattress.""

"So I did. I mean, what do I have to worry about, right? You don't have a lover under the bed, do you?"

"Nah."

"Only in the bed." He laughs. "But maybe I should give a quick look."

Before he can move, Joan imagines Choice slamming his switchblade through the mattress, straight into her boyfriend's lumbar nerve.

"Aaaaagh!" screams Eliot, clutching his back. "I feel like I've been stabbed! Am I bleeding?" He rolls onto his side so she can see.

"Don't be silly. Of course not." She massages. "Does it hurt here?"

"Lower. It's killing me."

"It's just a cramp. It'll pass."

"Jeez, it really did feel for a minute like . . ."

"Shhh. You're so tight. Relax."

"You're so good to me."

"No, I'm not."

I'm wicked, man, she thinks.

4

WHERE TO WATCH

Mercury reporter Art Popov, who's made a name for himself mixing his personal story, political views, and cultural observations with the news and gossip of the day, writes in his typical gonzo style:

MAYOR LIGHTLY SWIPED BY SATANIC VANGUARD

Is anybody going to pay attention? With the Yankees, led by rookie marvel Nick "The Swan" Spillage, about to embark upon a near certain sweep of this, the 1976 World Series, it's not likely.

Spillage, the kid phenom whose 22-strikeout, two-hit victory over the Angels yesterday propelled the cellar dwellers of the past four years into the magic land of championship competition, was sighted on his day off today running his huge Dalmatian through Central Park, while presidential hopeful NYC Mayor Lightly was speaking at the "Save the Cities" rally his Communist supporters organized.

The 100,000-plus crowd was bored to death by the candidate's prissy prattle. Their ranks were swelled with young welfare chiselers attracted by the lure of free cocaine, which

Lightweight's henchmen were able to dispense because our lazy good-for-nothing cops were nowhere to be seen.

The effect of the cocaine that I snorted through a $1,000 note (I could not have refused or my cover would have been blown) was to increase my already healthy sexual appetite for a yet undiscovered starlet of extraordinary proportions, as well as potential, whom I happen to be dating. Her name, for those of you who are looking to produce a box-office extravaganza, is Crystal Belle, and va-va-va-voom is she a knockout! Her stats are unreal.

Crystal happens also to be the daughter of Sister Sabrina, the SoHo seer who predicted for this newspaper, as you may recall, the coming of Nick Spillage. The good Sister, who is also a wonderful mother, will be on Al Deep's pregame show tomorrow at 1 p.m., so don't you miss her, like I missed Lightweight's speech.

While the vagrants who are the backbone of the mayor's political constituency were coupling, tripling, and quadrupling on the grass, the wild animal noises they made drowned out the squeaky nonsense their radical leader sputtered. Then, the minute Nick Spillage and his Dalmatian were spotted, the entire crowd leapt to its feet and chased after them as though salvation itself were at stake.

When we returned, the mayor was nowhere to be found, and a note from the Satanic Vanguard was pinned to the spot where he'd stood, saying, "God's will be done. Done and gone. Going, going, going gone."

Don't be fooled by this nonsense. Just because a Lefty was kidnapped, doesn't mean it was the Right. I'd bet my bottom dollar the Vanguard is connected with that devil Castro. Let the venomous snake chomp down on its tail, let one Red faction destroy the other. Nixon's still my man. The only one who can keep us safe. The Yankees start the World Series at 2 p.m. tomorrow.

Joan wakes at noon on the opening day of the World Series and reads the note that Eliot has left atop the fruit crate that serves as her night table.

Doing a lunch shift. Money, money, money. Be back at 3. I adore you. E.

She crumples up the note and throws it at the fresh crack in her TV screen. Even though Choice did the damage two days ago with the heel of one of his spanking-new crocodile-leather shoes, she blames Eliot for forcing her back onto the streets in order to watch her Swan perform.

Eliot after all had enough cash in his klutzy little fingers to buy the kind of radio-TV console they give away on game shows, plus one of those videotape machines that let you play back your favorite no-hitters at whatever speed you want for as long as you live or aren't robbed. $50,000—whatever that means these days! Only sure thing is that it meant a lot more yesterday. Still, Eliot had it and she told him to give it to her, but no, he had to make a big show about how trusting he was, stuff it under the mattress to prove no one was underneath.

Of course, Choice didn't have to adhere so strictly to the finders-keepers principle; he could have kicked a little back since he was there on her invitation and they'd made such good love, but he at least never pretended to be doing what he did for her sake. "Being a bastard," he'd said, "on me it's sexy." And she had to give him credit: for her it was.

Almost as though he feared that if he held on to even the smallest part of the $50,000 for too long, he would break from character and spend on his "main mommas," he'd gone straight out and spent it all on a bold, blue, bespoke pin-striped Savile Row suit. Where he was going to shelter it, since he didn't have a place of his own, Joan didn't know, but she certainly wasn't into the idea of his using her closet.

He put the idea to her during the *Wonderful World of Sports* highlights of the Swan's amazing season and all she said was, "Out of the question."

She didn't even bother to answer when he asked, "Why can't I grace this space with my pretty duds? The closet's just about empty, save for these Popeye outfits."

All she did was spit out one nail and start on another, so he just stepped up to the television and cracked the screen. The last thing Joan saw was the twenty-second Angel swinging and missing on a Spillage screwball for the pennant-clincher's final out.

So where will she watch today's opening game? Maybe, if she goes early to Fantasia, she'll get a seat close to that big color screen; or maybe walking past the elegant brownstones by Gramercy Park she'll find a working portable on the street; or maybe, she thinks, putting on her peasant dress, she should subway up to Yankee Stadium alone to see if she can win a favor from a scalper.

She leaves the apartment still undecided, gets dizzy on the staircase, and almost falls. There's that to be considered too. But it's just nerves, she tells herself. It better be.

. . .

"Welp," says Yankee announcer Al Deep, "today's the day it all begins. Best out of seven for the World Championship of baseball, the Yanks of beleaguered Bronx, New York, and the Phils of almost-as-belea-guered Liberty Bill Creek (though that town don't have the Satanic Vanguard to contend with).

"They say the problems of the Big Apple are the problems of all the cities in this country rolled up into a big round snowball and given a push down the hill the size of Everest, and I'll tell you, I got to go with them on this one, the mayor being kidnapped and what-have-you, but there's one problem we don't have and that's pitching. Nick 'The Swan' Spillage on the mound for the Yanks today—you see him there warming up—and with us on the pregame show is the SoHo Seer who predicted his coming, Sister Sabrina. Good to have you here, Sister. I know you're not in the habit of making public appearances."

"That's right, Al. My health is not so great."

"Can't complain about mine, knock wood."

"But you do."

"From time to time, sure."

"Not from what I hear."

"Is that so?" He chuckles. "You must've caught my wife in one of her moods then."

"Your mother."

"Hey, well, talk about moods. But she's . . ."

"Five years in her cheap coffin with such a tacky headstone, I know. She's a *kvetch* too."

"*Kvetch*. That ain't English, is it?"

"Yiddish, Al. The language of communication."

"I thought all languages were languages of communication, depending on how you use them, of course. I don't pretend that in the forty years I've been broadcasting Yankee games I've given the folks everything there was to be given, I mean I sometimes get tripped up on my own words or just plain can't keep track of the action, but . . ."

"You need not apologize. Your heart's in the right place."

"I'm glad you think so. I get letters, you know—angry letters from schoolteachers and such who you wouldn't expect to get so angry except for what you hear has been going on in the overloaded classrooms these days—accusing me of subverting the logical reasoning abilities of all the children coast to coast who've been so taken by Swannie's exploits. Some of these letters—and this hurts, believe me—accuse yours truly, Al Deep, of paving with my syntax the way for Communism."

"You shouldn't let these *meshugenahs* bother you."

"*Meshugenahs?*"

"Crazies. You have a patriotic soul and in the clutch it will show."

"That's reassuring. But maybe I'd be better off if I was to learn this Yiddish."

"Far better, but you couldn't, because you don't have gypsy blood."

"Too bad."

"When I call Yiddish the language of communication, what I mean is communication with the beyond. Yiddish is a nearly dead language; from this does it derive its power. Only gypsies of my generation speak it regularly, and there are not too many of us still around."

"How old are you, if I might ask."

"Ageless."

"I shoulda known."

"There are other dead languages, to be sure, but Yiddish is the chosen language, as gypsies are the chosen people. The Book of Life is written in Yiddish, and in convoluted Yiddish I might add. This is why interpretation gives us such difficulty, but I would not have it any other way. If the prose were straightforward, what would happen would be all too clear. It's the vagaries which God in his infinite wisdom built into the text which give us our critical pinch of free will."

"You mean that God's Yiddish is—and I hesitate to say this—like my English?"

"No comparison whatsoever."

"Darn. But it was real enlightening talking with you anyway, Sister Sabrina, as we draw near to game time on this beautiful day to play ball. Just one more question before you go. Is New York going to win?"

"If I have anything to do with it."

"Well, I sure hope you do then."

"Thank you, Al."

"My pleasure."

5

HIT REAL HARD

On his way to Joan's place, Choice runs into a friend who asks where he's been hiding out. "Where *you* been hiding out is the question," says the actor. "I heard you were dead, Raoul."

"It's true."

"Don't kid me. Heard you were mixed up with this radical group and . . ."

"It's all true. Everything you hear."

"But you're here right now, right? Strong as you ever looked. And I like that new beard."

"You look good too, compadre."

"Clothes make the man, my man. And this . . ." He displays the lining of his new Savile Row jacket. ". . . is clothes."

Raoul removes two Havana cigars from the shirt pocket of his green fatigues and offers one to his friend, who accepts.

"Wish I had a lifetime supply of these gems," says Choice, running the length of the cigar under his nose.

"You've got a long life ahead of you," says Raoul. "I'm jealous."

"Got a light?"

Raoul snaps his brown fingers, and a small flame emerges.

"That's some trick," says Choice, puffing.

"Sí. I've got lots of them."

"You show any to Mirlanda lately?"

"No."

"I'm ashamed of you. Good woman like Mirlanda, she needs attention. And you're a father too, which means you're obligated. Can't just run away from your responsibilities, not now. Too much of that kind of stuff going around these days. Got to stand firm, pound on your fine chest and say, 'I may not look it, but I'm a family man. Provide for my wife and child the best way I can.'"

"Sounds nice. Just impossible."

"Nothing's impossible if you're determined. And I'm determined in my role as god-daddy to make you determined. We're going home right now."

"Not my home no more."

"Now don't you be obstinate."

"Your clothes are in my closet."

"That's just for convenience. See my girlfriend, she's muleheaded."

"Both of them are."

"Where'd you get these ideas?"

"I've been through hell."

"Well, it's no wonder, the way you fantasize. You trying to tell me the reason you ran out on the best wife a man could wish for was you thought she'd been messing with the best friend a man could wish for? I hope you're not trying to tell me that, cause that's below you."

"I've been through hell. There's nothing below me. But I don't blame you."

"You blame Mirlanda, that's worse. You do that and I'll bash you."

"I don't blame her neither."

"Then who you blaming?"

"I blame this damned system, and the vicious, self-serving God who made it. Compadre . . ." He loops an arm over Choice's shoulder and walks him south down Second Avenue. ". . . I can't begin to tell you how oppressive this God is. He throws us into his private enterprise like a pitcher throws a beanball at a batter's head. He wants us to get hit. I've been hit real hard."

"I'm beginning to see that."

"But don't let it bother you."

"No? You're still my best friend. I've got to."

"Listen. It's good for you, my fate. You'll be famous before you know it."

"I hear the old Raoul scheming."

"Not my idea at all." He walks him around the front of a pink Bentley parked by a delicatessen and opens the rear passenger door like a practiced chauffeur. In the trunk, the mayor is bound and gagged.

"Damn-nation!" says Choice, taking his seat. "You travel in style for a man who claims he's dead."

"I do a lot of traveling. And I figured you'd like this," says Raoul, walking around and getting into the driver's seat.

"You're some kind of puzzle."

"I try to be."

"Always did. But this is on a new level."

"Sí." He starts the car.

"And I'm with you, Raoul. Only I wish to God I could convince you to drive straight back to Mirlanda. This stuff you've been imagining between me and her . . ."

"Don't lie to me, Choice. I've got no imagination. And if you knew how much I love her . . ."

"I love her too. That's why I'm telling you."

"Let's go to your other girlfriend's. She lives on St. Mark's Place, right?"

"Right, but she's not there now."

"I know. That's her across the street."

"Talking to a dog. Now what's that all about?"

"She believes the dog belongs to that pitcher."

"Hate that pitcher."

"It's only natural."

"Maybe you're pregnant," she hears from behind her. The voice is high, almost as high as her own, and for a moment she thinks it is her own. She trembles as she answers, "Nah," and doesn't turn around.

"Micky O'Mann here," says the voice. "My stepsister Crystal had those same kind of syndromes, and she was pregnant, but she's not anymore. Art wouldn't marry her. But I bet you're married, aren't you."

"No," says Joan. "And I don't intend to get married either, unless the owner of this magnificent creature asks me, which I don't think is likely."

By this time, she has taken a chance and pivoted around to face her interlocutor. He's a twelve-year-old boy, skinny like Eliot and with the same penchant for what doesn't fit him, from the cracked-leather newsboy cap that just about covers his eyes, to the emerald-green sweatshirt (streaked with what looks to be tar) that just about covers his knees, to the baggy jeans that line the bottoms of his torn sneakers. His nose, like Eliot's, has a ski-jump curve, and his eyes, like Eliot's, are an animated brown, but the thick red hair that runs almost to his shoulders is all Joan's own, and it makes her nostalgic in spite of herself.

"I sure do know who the dog's owner is," says the boy. "Only I have the feeling you don't."

"He's the greatest pitcher in baseball history."

"Nope. He only wishes he was, because then you wouldn't be able to resist him."

"I can't resist him. I'm totally devoted."

"You look like he dreams his own mother must have looked, and he doesn't say that to every lady he meets. Believe me, you're the first, and the last thing he wants is to let you down."

"Don't tell me he's yours, squirt."

"Okay. But you don't tell me he's not."

"He can't be!"

"Duke," commands the boy, and the dog steps to him. "See if you can find the lady some flowers to condole her."

The dog runs off.

"That's console, not condole," says Joan, feeling faint as she stands. "And I bet he doesn't come back."

The dog returns with a spray of willow branches in his mouth.

"I make mistakes with words," says the boy, "because I gamble on the tough ones. But I know my dog."

He offers the willows, but she doesn't accept.

"Christ," she says. "I feel so rotten."

"Why don't you let Duke and me escort you home. We'll see to it that you get back okay."

"My TV's busted." Joan begins to falter.

"We'll steal you a new one. Just pick one out. Of course, the heavier models would be kind of tough, but when a lady like you . . ."

"I only want . . ."

"Watch it! You're losing your balance!"

"My angel . . ."

He catches her when she falls. "She lost it, Duke," he says. "But we'll bring her around."

* * *

The door to Joan and Eliot's apartment is unlocked, so Raoul and Choice waltz right in, arm in arm with the bound and gagged mayor. Before they can make themselves at home, though, they hear Eliot shout from the street.

"Joan!" Eliot calls. "Hurry up and get dressed! We're going to the World Series!"

He takes the steps two at a time, feeling like a soldier who's come to liberate his homeland. She'll fling open the door, his long-suffering fiancée, the most sought-after woman in the entire city, and the neighbors will cheer from their respective landings as he runs toward her with the tickets in his raised right hand like the rifle he'll never need again, but which served him so well when he fought in the trenches.

"Box seats behind first base!" he shouts from the stairwell. "You'll be able to reach out and touch the Swan when he comes back to the dugout each inning. Come on, if we hustle, we can get there by the third. We'll use the money under the mattress to take a cab."

When the dapper actor hid under the bed, he was none too comfortable with the dust balls and the poking springs. So now Choice advises his friend Raoul that the closet would make a better hiding place. Raoul doesn't disagree. He pushes the bound and gagged mayor in first, then graciously motions Choice to follow.

By the time Eliot reaches the second floor, he realizes that Joan is gone, but he continues to call to her, almost as if to stop would mean she was gone for good.

"Art gave me the tickets," he says. "Art Popov, do you believe it? Dropped by the Burger Boat to tell me Crystal quit and says here, take these, and tell Joan I love her. Heard you'd become a Spillage freak, from who I don't know. You haven't seen him lately, have you?"

When he enters the apartment, he lowers his voice. "I guess I haven't seen you lately, have I?" he says. The pictures of the pitcher which cover the walls assault him in a way they never did before.

"You're right to be suspicious, Señor Ensign," says Raoul, stepping out of the closet. "Your girlfriend cheated on you just like I told you. This man here . . ." He raises his hand and his friend steps out. ". . . he's an actor named Choice and he's the first who she slept with. Hope you like his new suit. He bought it with the money I gave you."

"Feel this material," says Choice, offering his jacket.

"Not bad," says Eliot, whose sailor suit is splotched with ketchup. He should hate this guy, he thinks, but he finds him hard to hate. The smile? He can see how Joan found him hard to resist, if in fact anything happened between them, but it's still possible nothing did, because who's to say he should trust Raoul? And even if the worst did happen, this guy is not the culprit. The real choice was Joan's, and whose fault was that? How could he not have seen this coming?

"It's all according to taste," says Raoul. "I hope you're working hard, Señor Ensign, for Admiral Dugan."

"Too hard," says Eliot. And not hard enough . . . for Joan. When was the last time we had sex? Last week? And who was she doing it with—me or the guy looking down from the walls? Her heart wasn't in it, he remembers now. Something was off, but he let it ride. Something's been off for a while.

"I know how you feel. I worked hard, too, when I was married."

"You're still married," says Choice.

Raoul sits down beside Eliot, puts a hand on his thigh. "We're in the same boat, you and I, cuckolded by the same guy. But don't blame him, and don't blame her."

"I blame myself," says Eliot.

"Don't blame yourself either."

"Who am I supposed to blame, this godforsaken bankrupt city?"

"You're getting warmer," says Raoul.

Choice takes the World Series tickets off the top of the television.

"Raoul's got some strange notions," he says. "These for real, my man?"

"Sí," says Raoul. "For you and Mirlanda."

Eliot's glad they're not for Joan. There's still a chance, he thinks, they can put it all back together. He's not going to give up until he can see her, talk it through. He can forgive her obsession with Spillage. She's had these kinds of obsessions before. It's who she is, and he loves her for it. And Choice, if in fact she made it with him, was maybe just to send him a message to wake up, pay attention. Or maybe it was just to prove that she has an identity beyond theirs as a pair, which she needed to prove before they paired for good. And maybe you need to prove you have your own identity too. Stand up. Be a man. Manage on your own, whatever comes at you.

"You for real?" Choice asks Raoul. "With what you think's going on?"

None of this is for real, thinks Eliot.

"Game's about to start," says Raoul.

"I know," says Choice. "And these are the kind of seats a Yankee-hater dreams about. I could blow poisoned darts at the back of that Swan's long neck with pinpoint accuracy. You wouldn't happen to have any darts handy, would you, bro?"

"Go," says Raoul, flipping his friend a set of car keys. The actor scoots off.

"Is Mirlanda your wife?" asks Eliot.

"She was. Our contract expired when I did," says Raoul. "Now she's my widow, but Choice don't believe it. I think he's afraid to have her all to himself. Cigar?"

"Don't smoke."

Raoul sniffs the length of a hefty Havana. "It's a bad habit," he says. "But when you're dead, you indulge." He lights it with a snap of his fingers.

"I don't believe he's making it with Joan," says Eliot.

"Yes, you do," says Raoul.

"You're right."

Maybe you should hate Raoul, thinks Eliot. He's the maestro of this nightmare, the one pulling all the strings. But he's got you in some sort of trance. Just how much power does he have? As a lover of superhero comics from the early days of Marvel when he was just a preteen, as a voracious reader of science fiction and fantasy novels, and as a student of classics during his years at the New School, Eliot knows a villain when he sees one. And this guy's definitely up to no good, he thinks, regardless of his attempts to buddy up with you. The question is this: is he a supervillain who can threaten the world, or is he just capable of playing mind games with you? He wants you to believe that New York City's collapse is somehow responsible for the collapse of your relationship with Joan, that the chaos in the air has become personal, but isn't he contributing to that chaos? Maybe he's the cause. Joan's been dreaming she's possessed by the Devil, Raoul leads the Satanic Vanguard, it all connects. Maybe he's got her in a trance too and she's not responsible for her choices at all. She's in trouble and you've got to save her, venture into the underworld and bring her back.

Looking at Raoul with his black beret and green fatigues, Eliot is reminded of the Che Guevara poster that used to hang on the wall before Joan plastered it with images of the Swan. A bit of resemblance in the lower half of his face—the nose, lips, and beard—though the eyes are strictly from the Far East. You told Joan he was Cuban-Chinese, but is he? Or was that just because you had Cuban-Chinese on your mind from the time a few weeks ago when you had a severe allergic reaction to an overdose of MSG seasoning at the Cuban-Chinese restaurant on Avenue A? Now Raoul's eyes bring to mind another revolutionary whose picture once graced the wall, the Vietnamese leader Ho Chi Minh. Love them or hate them, those were true revolutionaries, Eliot thinks, true believers in their causes. And there was a time when he really did love them, at least in theory; loved Trotsky too, and the whole concept of permanent revolution. Even hitchhiked down to Mexico City with Joan to visit the house where Trotsky was killed, along with the home of Frida Kahlo, an artist she admired.

Eliot was never a committed revolutionary, never much of a political activist at all, but he did go through a period where he was intellectually intrigued. We were all revolutionaries in those days, he thinks. We thought it would be easy to remake the world, change it for the better, but then the world took a big change for the worse and we got disheartened. Can't blame that on Raoul. Looking at him light his cigar, the flame from his fingers obscuring his face, for a moment he sees him as a kindred spirit, a fellow traveler. He sees the flames rising from the huge pile of draft cards he tossed his into during the massive protest at the National Mall in Washington, D.C., back in 1969. Raoul was there, wasn't he? He was at all those protests. And so it's tough for Eliot to hate the guy either, even as he senses he'll need to battle him for Joan. Besides, if you can accept that there's even a shred of proof to his claims, how can you hate someone who's been through the same relationship hell you're going through?

"You want to know who introduced them?" says Raoul.

"Who?"

"Your friend Art, that sick reporter," Raoul lies. "He thinks if he keeps doing her favors, eventually she'll sleep with him. And Choice is a big favor, believe me, he's some dude."

"Art." Now there's someone I can hate, thinks Eliot.

"I hate him too, the wicked things he writes." Raoul stands and rests a hand on Eliot's shoulder. "I pity you," he says, "because I know you're in love, like me."

"If I get hold of that fat slob . . ." says Eliot. It's much easier to hate Art, since you're starting with a strong reservoir of dislike. The way he always leered at Joan, jealous beyond belief. Whatever success he's had with the nonsense he writes, he envies what you've got. And he can't have her. No way.

"Mull it over while you sleep," says Raoul.

A puff of cigar smoke in Eliot's face, and he slumps to the floor. Raoul carries him into the closet like a groom approaching the threshold with his bride.

6

SOUND AND SENSE

Twelve-year-old Micky O'Mann doesn't think twice when Joan falls into his arms. First, he orders his dog to fetch her smelling salts from the nearest drugstore. Then he props her up against the display window of the Sound and Sense radio and TV store, choosing the television he intends to steal so he won't waste time when the moment's at hand. He's never stolen anything before, but then, up until today he'd never been stolen from. Joan, he feels, has stolen his heart, so stealing for Joan is divinely just.

Defying heavy traffic, Micky marches into the middle of Second Avenue and hails a cab. The dog returns. Joan responds to the smelling salts. Micky helps her to her feet and walks her to the cab, asking her address and telling it to the cabbie as he helps her in. The cabbie asks if she's on some kind of drugs because he won't take her anywhere if she is. Someone's got to draw the line in these decadent times; Arsen from Kazakhstan is that someone and he's not ashamed to admit it. In fact, he's proud, and he'd like Micky to know it, but Micky has already slipped back into the store to make his heist.

Arsen doesn't notice. He'd be surprised, he says, if ten decent young people could be found in all of New York, and that's ten out of millions. The baby boom was a bust, according to the cabbie; quantity's not quality if you know what he means. You'd know what he meant if you read *The Mercury*. He has a copy on the front seat if you want to take a look. He lifts the paper over the backrest. "This is what I mean," he says.

"Thanks," says Micky. He grabs the paper as soon as he's placed a portable television on Joan's lap. If only he could place his head there, he thinks, but there's a time and place for everything and a boy can only go so far on his own.

In the meantime, he makes sure that Joan's peasant dress is tucked inside the cab, closes her door and runs around to the other side while Arsen tells him he should read Art Popov. Best damned reporter in the entire city; Popov *knows* what the rest can only guess. That's because he has vision, what Arsen calls moral vision. If Arsen were Micky, he'd read Popov religiously. *If* Micky could read, that is, but Arsen bets he can't. He's right.

Micky assures him that Joan's not on drugs and that Art Popov is like a brother to him. "He dates Crystal Belle," he says, "who's like a sister to me. And he gets tips from Sister Sabrina, who's like my own mother. If I didn't have to escort this gorgeous diabolic lady back to her apartment so she could get her insulin shot fast, I'd take you over to the Reading Room myself and introduce you to the whole family."

"Diabolic, huh?" says Arsen.

"Here. Take this card. Any time you have a communication problem—you know, with the beyond—just bring it over and tell Sabrina that Micky sent you. She'd be glad to help. She's really super. And you and Art would get along great, no question. He loves everybody who reads him, especially people who read him religiously, because that's what he writes for, to be read like that. He's always talking about how all reporters are preachers at heart, and how they're at the mercy of their conflagerations."

"You mean congregations," says Joan, her eyelids fluttering open as she raises herself upright in her seat.

"If you say so," says Micky. "Hey but it's great to have you back among the living."

"Is this guy gonna drive?"

"Yes ma'am," says Arsen.

Because they are friends of Art Popov, the cabbie not only gives them (along with the dog) a free ride to St. Mark's Place, he also offers to carry the TV upstairs. But Joan, who by this time has her strength back, declines the offer. She's focused on the first pitch, and she isn't particularly thrilled with the prospect of sharing the experience with her pint-sized admirer. So as he opens the front door for her, she says, "You know, I'm not the greatest company while the game's being played. In fact, I'm lousy company, and you might be better off going."

"Say no more," says Micky, raising his palm like a traffic cop as his dog scoots past him and up to the third floor. "But why don't you give us a break and let us stick around. You won't even know we're here."

When they enter the apartment, Micky sees that something's wrong. His dog sniffs and growls menacingly at the closet door. The boy asks Joan if she'd mind if he investigated, but she just plugs in her new television and sets it down in front of the old and fiddles with the antenna until she hears the announcer say, "This is it! It all starts now!"

Micky tugs at the closet door without any luck. "Hey lady," he says, "this door is jammed."

Joan, rapt with the screen, doesn't answer him.

A man in a black beret and green fatigues crawls out from under the bed, dusts himself off and says, "She wants you to go away."

Joan cheers at a called strike one.

"Hey lady," says Micky, "do you know this guy?"

"Her name's Joan," says Raoul.

The dog is still sniffing and growling at the closet. Raoul pets him on the back. "She don't hear you," he says, "because she don't want to. She has the gift of tuning things out."

"Sounds like you know her."

"Not firsthand. But I will. I came here to kill her."

"Duke!" says Micky. But the dog pays no attention, still preoccupied with the closet. "Duke! Get over here!"

"He tunes you out too," says Raoul.

"He never does that."

"So sad. Your best friend in the world gives you up." He flips Micky a small gun. "Try this."

"You want me to . . ."

"Sí. Shoot me."

"But . . ."

"You don't have the courage?"

"Sure, I do."

"Never mind. You watch while I do her in; learn something valuable. My wife right now is with this woman's lover. Her lover's my best friend and he's my wife's lover too. Is this fair, I ask you?"

"It's a free country."

"Sí. So I'm free to ruin Joan. She's free to resist, but I'm stronger, and I'll win."

He squats behind Joan and puts his hands on her neck as Angel Guerrero—the Yanks' slugging right fielder, a notorious bad ball chaser—knocks the home team's first run in with a double he tries to stretch into a triple, only to get cut down.

"That's all right," says Joan. "You done good. We're ahead. And you've got to take chances, test those outfielders' arms."

Raoul slides a hand down the front of her peasant blouse, puts his lips to her ear, and says, "I'd like to test you, chiquita. If you don't mind, or even if you do."

"Huh? Who the Christ..." Joan grabs his arm with both her hands, tries to flip him over, doesn't budge him, gives an elbow to his massive chest, gets a laugh in return.

"Choice sends you his love," says Raoul. "And so does Satan. I'm the postman who's come to deliver."

"Raoul?" She twists around to face him. "Listen . . ."

"Already did. It's why I'm here. I listen to your secret thoughts."

"But be reasonable, man. I mean I hardly . . ."

"Know me? Don't you remember our nights in Salem? I was first on the stake. Now it's your turn." He grabs her by the shoulders and kisses her fiercely on the lips. When she tries to break away, he looks astonished. "Hey chiquita, you promised favors," he says, flashing a snaky grin. "Do me a favor and let me set you on fire. Just like the Doors sing. They're one of your favorites, right?" His yellow teeth sink into her neck.

"Oh please, you're hurting me," she says.

"Fire will purge you of all bourgeois fears. Only then can you love with abandon. Comprende? The Swan don't take no ordinary lovers. He wants a woman who'll die for him. How'd you like to do it?" He rips the cord off the TV. "If I strangle you with this, you'll be in hell before you know it. I'll show you the place, so you feel right at home."

Micky shatters the window with the blast of his gun. "That'll be enough, mister," he says.

"Go ahead and shoot, little boy. See what happens," he says, leaning forward over Joan, whom he now has pinned to the floor, TV cord tightly wrapped around her neck.

"Go away!" Joan screams. "Both of you. This can't be happening."

Ramming the gun up against Raoul's temple, Micky fires. The bullet makes such a clean hole through the man's head that for a moment the boy, who's on eye level with it, sees as if through a peephole in a ballpark fence a picture of Nick Spillage congratulated by teammates after breaking the all-time single-season strikeout record. Then the blood gushes out as though shot from a fire hose, catching Micky full in the face before he can step aside.

Joan pushes Raoul's knee off her and squirms out from underneath him as his body falls backward. The bleeding continues, to Micky's surprise. Wiping blood off his face with the emerald-green sleeve of his oversize sweatshirt, he says, "I didn't think he would bleed at all, you know? I thought he was a ghost."

"I've got to get out of here," says Joan. "Like I've really got to get out of here and never come back."

"You want to burn your britches?"

"My bridges. I should leave Eliot some kind of note, but what am I going to tell him?"

"Who's Eliot?"

"None of your business."

"Just thought I could help."

"I don't want your friggin' help. Just leave me alone." She walks through the door and into the hall. "Don't follow me, you hear?"

"Joan, wait." He starts after her. "Please let me help you. I know where you should go. I know where you *have* to go."

Choice waves as they drive past but Joan doesn't notice.

. . .

It is possible (and Joan knows it) that even if the four-foot high Dalmatian with the black left eye whose neck she has her arms around and whose side she has her turbaned head against did not look exactly like the Dalmatian pictured on her wall in ten different places, she might think he did because she wants him to so much.

"You could be a bulldog," she has already said to him. "You could be a horse, a cow, a goat. But if you are, I'm in big trouble, because I'll never believe it. My senses tell me you're a very special dog, and I'm committed to my senses, right down through the sixth. My boyfriend Eliot thinks I'm afraid of making a commitment and if he saw me like this, he'd probably have me committed, but what does he know? Not half as much as you do. You know how much I love you, don't you?"

She didn't find the dog, the dog found her, and she takes this as further proof that he belongs to the Swan. She'd had her nose pressed against the display window of the Sound and Sense radio and TV store for a solid ten minutes before he arrived and was debating whether to watch the game where she stood or go inside when he put his front paws on her back and almost knocked her through the glass.

Now, while she hugs and strokes him, telling him how beautiful he is and that it's only fitting that he should be, but also scolding him for wandering so far from home, she debates whether to take him back to her place and wait for the official news that he is missing or whether to bring him inside the store and ask if she could use the telephone to call the stadium.

"What if your master finds out you're gone when he's in the middle of a tight situation?" she says to him. "Nick's rhythm could get all upset and speaking of upsets, my stomach feels like it's been through a carnival. I've been having these dizzy spells too."

7

SIGN THIS

Mirlanda Wo, a compact Haitian woman with cornrowed beaded braids, high cheekbones, and piercing brown eyes who recently learned from the gypsy down the block that her endlessly scheming, ever-abusive husband Raoul has made her a widow, is in no mood for playing games.

She is on her front stoop with Choice, his pink Bentley double-parked across the street, a Baby Ruth candy bar in his hand, proffered with a typically extravagant bow. He claims that Raoul isn't really dead, he only thinks he's dead because he's gone through hell.

"Fact is," says Choice, "he's responsible for that car, which I happen to know is your favorite color; he's responsible for this candy bar, which I found on the front seat, and he may even be responsible in an indirect way for the outfit I'm wearing," he says, motioning to his Savile Row suit, "which I hope you like, because I bought it with only you in mind."

"Too flashy," says Mirlanda, her hands at hip level on her ornate floral pink-and-lilac halter dress. "And I don't buy a word of it. Man never did have no sense of responsibility. He's an evil human being."

"Got a strange sense of honor, that's for sure. Here, take this candy. See he wrote your name on it with a little heart around it and an arrow too. Never took him for sentimental."

"He's got no cause to haunt me." She has rings on all her fingers, but her wedding ring is upstairs.

"Of course not," says Choice. "But he feels betrayed. Won't believe me when I say it's not true that we're lovers, wants to impress us with how crushed he is, but at the same time (and this is what I mean by honor), he bends over backward to show how, in his heart, he doesn't blame either of us. He just won't come home."

"I don't want him home, dead *or* alive, not after what he's done to me. But to me, he's dead as can be, so I don't want to talk about him."

Choice grins broadly. "You want this candy? My back's starting to hurt. Even for you, I can only bow for so long."

"Huh. Let's see how long." With her right thumb, Mirlanda twirls a loose jade ring around her index finger. She intentionally keeps it loose because it relaxes her to twirl it.

Choice stands up straight, tugs his pin-striped vest. "Suit yourself," he says, unwrapping the Baby Ruth and popping it in his mouth.

"I will," says Mirlanda. She taps her platform shoe on the concrete as she watches him chew, and when a pockmarked young Korean man in a monk's robe approaches, carrying a wooden clipboard and drawing heads out of windows with his cries of support for the Satanic Vanguard, she motions him over by crooking her finger. "What you want me to do?" she says.

"Sign this and you're beautiful," says the young man. It's a petition stating that the Vanguard has the right and the duty to execute Mayor Lightly, who manifests all that is rotten with this stinking metropolis. The Creator has abused his power in letting this capitalist mess fester, says the petition, and we must overthrow his oppressive rule for the sake of all mankind.

One thing Choice hates and that's sanctimoniousness. He also doesn't like the young man's arm on Mirlanda's exposed shoulder, so he lifts it off and says, "She's beautiful without signing. You blind as well as dumb?"

"Don't feel beautiful," says Mirlanda as she writes. "Feel fat from sitting around while my men screw me over."

"You're a woman of substance," says Choice, "but that's all right because it proves you're mature, which signing this doesn't. Didn't anybody ever tell you that a name's a precious thing? You shouldn't just give it away to any weirdo who comes along."

"Gave away my baby, can give away my name," says Mirlanda. "I'm in the mood to shed some old fur."

"You gave away what?" says Choice.

"You heard me. There." She dots the *i* on Prince St. and hands the clipboard back to the young man, who promptly shoves it under the actor's nose.

"Sign this and you're beautiful."

"*Am* beautiful, weirdo."

Choice clacks the clipboard over the young man's head and flips it into the street where a "Save the Cities" campaign truck runs over it before the young man can say "Sodomite!" and chase after it.

"Who'd you give your baby to?" asks Choice, pointing a finger at Mirlanda's nose.

She knocks it away. "Don't point at me," she says with a piercing stare. "And watch your tone. Now I don't feel like telling you."

"Hold on. I'm the God-daddy. Don't I have a right to know?"

"Don't care if you're the daddy. You're standing in my space."

Choice takes a step back, holding his hands up as though under arrest.

"I gave him to Sister Sabrina for safekeeping," says Mirlanda, nodding to neighbors as they exit their buildings. "Best move I made since the day I gave birth."

"Well," says Choice, "if you gave him to a nun that's not so bad. Not a Catholic myself but I respect their discipline."

"Sabrina's not a Catholic. She's the gypsy down the block."

"But she's not a stranger."

"Lord no, she's a seer."

"What I mean is you can get Junior back when you want to."

"If I want to. When I'm famous I might not."

"How do you think you're going to get famous?"

"Don't know. But Sister Sabrina said I would."

"She's talking through her hat."

"She's talking Yiddish with the dead, including my no-good skunk of an ex-husband."

"I told you he's not dead. But on the other hand, he told me . . ." Sirens in the distance make Choice nervous, as he thinks of the mayor he left bound in a closet. "Come on," he says, grabbing Mirlanda by the hand. "I'll take you to see your Yankees lose."

"You got tickets?"

"From Raoul."

"I don't believe it. And all this time you've been yak-yak-yakking?"

8

NEVER SURRENDER

In the top of the fifth inning, with Nick "The Swan" Spillage nursing a 1–0 lead in the Series opener, Eliot regains consciousness, loosens the knot in the rag with which Raoul tied his hands behind his back, slips free, and bursts out of the closet.

The apartment has changed since Eliot last saw it. Spillage pictures still cover the walls and the sink is still full of Great Moments in World Series Play dishes; books, records, comics, and art magazines are still scattered everywhere; but the window has been shattered, a new TV sits in front of the old, and in front of the new one Raoul lies on his back with a hole the size of a subway token through his head. The beret is at his side. There's a gun on his green-fatigued lap and an electrical cord wrapped around his wrists. There's no blood anywhere.

Eliot removes the red-and-black checkered handkerchief from the gagged mayor's mouth, unties his hands and feet, and receives an embrace and a kiss on both cheeks.

"My boy, you're a hero," says Mayor Lightly. He has spindly arms and legs, a concave chest, and a lean, sad face, along with the kind of belly that Eliot would love to help Joan have, provided she can move beyond her present kick.

During his forty years in politics, the mayor has developed the habit of looking just to the right of whomever he is addressing. "You've done a great service," he says, "and this country will soon know it."

"Thank you, sir," says Eliot, thinking of his father, a professor of logic, who always looked a little above whomever he addressed. His father, George (whom Eliot jokingly referred to as King George when the old Philosopher King would get on his high horse during arguments), never thought much of the mayor, calling him a clown, but Eliot never thought much of his father's politics, so he's happy to accept Hizzoner's praise. After all, he's running for president against the idiot who told New York to drop dead; who's continuing to wage an insane, losing war with the Vietnamese; who burgled his opponent's headquarters and stole his reelection, among other scandals; who crashed the economy, cratered the currency, egged on the race rioters, divided the country like no time since the Civil War, and managed through it all to stay in power. Who could be a bigger clown than Tricky Dick?

Eliot's always been a Nixon hater. The first vote he ever cast, in 1968, was against Nixon, whom he saw as a tool of the military-industrial complex even before he came under the influence of his Marxist-leaning New School history professors. The political issue that has always infuriated Eliot the most is the Vietnam War, which Nixon didn't start but vastly expanded and continues to wage. In his first presidential campaign, Nixon boasted he would achieve "Peace with Honor," which Eliot never believed for a minute. In his second, the stolen election, he proclaimed "Peace Is at Hand," another obvious canard. And now, thoroughly disgraced but still on the throne, he's flouting term limits to run for a third time under the banner of "Never Surrender."

It amazes Eliot that anyone could still buy this crap, given all the problems the abominable, unsuccessful war has created at home, though he knows King George would if he were still around. Joan's father too, who according to her brother, masterminded Nixon's first two presidential election campaigns, before he got caught up as a fringe player in one of the scandals that almost caused Nixon's downfall. Funny how the academic purist and supreme agent of commerce had this one stupid thing in common. But then, as Joan has cautioned, just because her father sold Nixon to the public doesn't mean he believed in him. All Big Daddy believed in, according to Joan, was self-gratification, deception, and the almighty dollar. Man, does she hate that guy, Eliot thinks. She hates him with the kind of passion only Joan can muster, the kind of passion you love when directed at other things, yourself once included. She's down on her mother too, on that whole generation, angry they've made such a mess of the world, and she doesn't understand why you don't share that same level of disdain.

On the war, though, there's no disagreement. Eliot opposes it with even more intensity, given the continued though diminished risk that he'll be called on to fight it. From the time he entered college, Eliot protested the war vehemently, and he was determined to avoid it at all costs, even if it meant leaving the country to escape being drafted. His protests included joining the occupation of the administration building at his New School campus during his freshman year, when students across the city were manning the barricades, including at Brooklyn College, where his parents taught.

He fought bitterly with his World War II vet father over that, almost coming to blows, on the night when he introduced his parents to Joan. Definitely a low point in their relationship, which he regrets in light of the Philosopher King's untimely death.

Professor George Howe fell, or was pushed, or intentionally jumped in front of an arriving Q train at the Avenue H stop near his home in Flatbush, Brooklyn. Unlike the Fleeting Life insurance company, which refused to pay the inflation-eroded claim, Eliot doesn't believe the act was intentional, though King George was clearly depressed at the time, still mourning his wife's death from ovarian cancer a few months before. His parents bickered all the time, with Eliot often the mediator, but without his wife his father was lost. He could have just slipped, Eliot thinks, having ventured to the edge of the platform to see if he could catch sight of the long-delayed train (the trains are always delayed these days). Still, Eliot is more inclined to attribute the death to random violence, given the declining neighborhood's soaring crime rate.

It happened around the start of spring training, just about the time Spillage burst on the scene, and thinking back on it now, Eliot marks it as the start of the current cycle of weirdness that's engulfed his life. It triggered a rare blowup with Joan, who didn't want to attend the funeral, never having warmed to the Philosopher King after their big fight over the war on the night they first met. They fought over art too, Eliot recalls, with stern King George, a staunch realist, bluntly saying she was just too far "out there" to make any sense. He was diametrically opposed to the dadaism, surrealism, pop and graffiti art embraced by Joan. And music? Forget about it. For King George, there was nothing worth listening to past 1791, when Mozart died, and rock and roll was a symbol of the moral decadence of America's youth. Joan had other ideas, which she wasn't shy about expressing.

It's nothing personal, Joan insisted, when she refused to go to the ceremony, though Eliot suspected it was. She said she just thought she had compromised enough in attending Eliot's mom's funeral. But Eliot felt obliged to show respect for his father. He was grateful to his aunt for making the arrangements and felt bad he wasn't closer to his parents since he'd moved out of the house. Even though he rarely ventured into Brooklyn to see them, he had to admit that without them he felt a bit lost himself.

Losing his mother was difficult, but he had some time to adjust to her condition, to make his peace before she passed. A professor of mathematics who specialized in game theory and loved to gamble, deploying her quantitative skills to great success in her many trips to Las Vegas, his mother, Helene, was sanguine about her illness, saying she just drew an unlucky number. And Eliot drew comfort in that, telling himself he was lucky to have had her as long as he did. But the suddenness of his father's death, combined with the uncertainty of how it happened and the cumulative impact of one rapidly following the other, was another story altogether. He felt alone, adrift, despite having Joan at his side. His favorite superhero, Spider-Man, found his mission in life as a crime fighter after his Uncle Ben was shot down, another victim of random violence. But Eliot, at twenty-six, felt far removed from any mission. He was an adult now, no excuses, almost past the age where he could have been drafted if the draft had continued, but he had no real idea of what he wanted to be in the world.

He didn't believe in afterlives or reincarnation, though he knew that millions did from his New School studies, which he continued for three years beyond his undergraduate degree to keep his draft deferment. He didn't believe in heaven, hell, God or the Devil, angels, eternal spirits, or any of that stuff, though he didn't discount the possibility altogether. His father, a confirmed atheist, and his mother, a semi-committed one, never encouraged such beliefs, but nevertheless held to the idea that there was a divine order to the universe, embodied in their fields of study.

To the end, Helene Howe, ever the optimist, liked to say, "Every equation has a solution, if you know what you're searching for." And she paraphrased Albert Einstein when she talked about her faith. "God may exist, but I wouldn't bet on it," she told him once. "Then again, Einstein believed in God, and I wouldn't bet against him either. Only Einstein said his God doesn't play poker, and you know how I love poker. I could never worship a God who doesn't play."

She claimed to have some gypsy blood from her own mother's side, which contributed to her luck and intuition at the card table. Meanwhile, King George, whose ancestors hailed from the same Lincolnshire town in England where Sir Isaac Newton was born and lived, never gave up on the power of logic. But with both of them gone and the world careening out of control, Eliot felt for a time that his last bastions against the mindless chaos of it all went with them.

That's when he started dreaming about Adlai Stevenson, a politician he knew little about, except that he lost the presidency twice to the war hero General Ike and young Tricky Dick. Running and losing, running and losing. He couldn't get the phrase out of his mind. He'd lost so much. He was doomed to be a loser. The only thing he had in life was Joan, and why should she stick with such a sad sack, anyway?

His funk lasted about a month. Baseball started to pull him out of it, as he embraced Joan's newfound passion for the Yankees after introducing her to the Swan. While he curses himself for it now, initially he was totally supportive—they both needed a change. And then he got going on his marriage, family, and job thing.

His mother always used to say he would make a great diplomat after he brokered peace between her and King George. Of course, it was her willingness to compromise that usually sealed the deal, he thinks, but she saw in him a special ability to navigate disputes, to see the merits of all arguments and a path in between. That, she said, was his superpower. Joan just saw the trait as conflict avoidance. But maybe he could put this power to good use now, working for his new best friend, Mayor Lightly. Maybe that's what his political dreams were about, a harbinger of what's to come.

"No time for thanks," says the mayor, dusting himself off. "Thank me when I make you attorney general, or secretary of state. Which do you prefer?"

Which would Joan prefer? "Well, sir, both sound great."

"Both!"

"I mean I'm awfully . . ."

"Power hungry, but that's all right. You're young, you think power will make you attractive. You imagine three women for every day of the week, and you'll have them, of course, but what about the one you left behind? Oh, she may not seem like much to you now, but believe me she will."

"She does." Was she here? Too bad she doesn't wear perfume; would leave behind a telltale scent. A dog was here, he's sure of that.

"She'll grow in importance with each botched affair, be it international or domestic. The cards are stacked against you. No winning in this game, my boy, I want you to know that before I shove you into it.

The Communists on the one hand, Fascists like Nixon on the other—
the decent politician tries to steer a middle course, but the road gets
narrower every time it curves. See your friends drive off into ditches.
Animals in those ditches, they're known as the press. Be on your guard
against the press: that's your first rule of thumb."

Raoul's smiling from the floor. He wasn't before. And there's a roll
of bills sticking out of the pocket of his green fatigues. "I don't like the
press," says Eliot. At least one member of the press, he thinks.

"Bully for you," says the mayor. "You've seen through the myth. Do
you like me?"

"Of course, sir."

"Just testing, just testing. I've been so vilified I almost don't like
myself. Would you mind if I asked you a personal question?"

Inching toward Raoul as Mayor Lightly discovers Joan's wall collage, Eliot sees that the roll of bills has his name on it. "Not at all, sir,"
he says, stooping to take it.

"This isn't you, is it?"

"Pictured, no."

"Take me for a fool and you'll lose my trust, find yourself without
an important friend. I know who's pictured, I only wish I didn't. What
I'm asking is whether you hung the pictures up."

"No, sir, my girlfriend did."

"Explains things. I empathize. You view him as a threat then."

Too late for that. He's already broken through the village gates,
ransacked the temple, carried off the slaves. The most willing slaves in
history; they'd sooner die than return to their families. Or at least one
would. "I don't love Nick Spillage, sir, if that's what you mean."

"Can you fake it?" The mayor tears a picture off the wall of the
pitcher being doused with champagne by Sheila Dugan after a Yankee
victory. Joan has drawn an X over the heiress's face, and the mayor
kisses it where the lines cross.

"The mark of a good politician," he says, "is to be able to hide your
true feelings when they get in the way. The Swan threatens me too, but

I'll never let on. The public must think I love him as though he were my own son. They must think I love you because you remind me of him. Actually, you remind me of myself when I was your age, but don't let it go to your head. Do you think I'm joking?"

"I don't know what to say, sir."

"A diplomat, wonderful. However, I'm not joking. I'm incapable of joking, of laughing without thinking. I can cry though. My opponent can't."

"I've heard."

"You're a spy too? Just what my team needs. This room isn't bugged, is it?"

Raoul winks at Eliot. His left leg now appears to have been amputated at the hip, the green fatigues folded neatly on that side and safety-pinned to the top. Will he disappear altogether before the mayor can notice? Or is he altogether invisible to the mayor already?

"No, sir," says Eliot, "the room isn't bugged."

"Then tell me what you really think of Sheila Dugan. At my side, if you catch my drift."

"Frankly, sir, I don't know much about her."

"This . . ." The mayor turns abruptly from the window, his finger on the heiress's pictured, black-lipsticked lips, ". . . is Sheila Dugan. Need you know any more? Who's the wounded soldier and where's his wheelchair?"

"Better yet, where's his blood, see that hole in his head? He's the man who abducted you. I think his name's Raoul."

"You shot him."

"No, sir. He was already shot."

"Out to crucify me, a Communist devil. Of course, he's bloodless; he's also spineless. No moral supports. Call the boys with the notebooks, I've got my angle now. And be careful not to contradict a word of my speech. I'll tell you what you did to him. Did he just lose an arm?"

"Yes, sir." Eliot picks up the phone. "He got back a leg though."

"They're all unstable."

9

CROSS THAT BRIDGE?

From the second inning to the sixth, Nick "The Swan" Spillage strikes out thirteen straight Phillies, matching the number on his pin-striped back and setting a World Series record.

During this stretch, Joan covers a lot of ground. She zigzags over to the mammoth black cube that sits on an edge at Astor Place and that has on each side freshly painted white pitchforks, then angles on to the Bottom Line, a bar where the Satanic Vanguard, featuring Raoul Wo on bass guitar, appears to be playing nightly.

She doesn't buy tickets, not the least bit tempted. She doesn't buy any loose joints in Washington Square either, doesn't buy any acid, doesn't buy any cocaine, doesn't bet on the red card at the three-card monte stand, doesn't bet on the baseball game (though she does hear that the score is 1–0 Yankees and that comforts her), doesn't play Frisbee, doesn't play chess, and doesn't make love in the playground area.

All of these things she's invited to do, but instead she walks so fast through NoHo, SoHo, and Little Italy that Micky has to steal a moped to keep up with her.

The boy knows he could stop her at any time by just instructing his dog to sink his teeth into her long, flowing dress, but he doesn't want to get her mad. She knows that he's behind her without looking back and isn't trying to get rid of him so much as she's trying to rid herself of all thoughts.

She'd like to imagine that they appear in cartoon clouds, three or four feet over her turbaned head, and that if she moves fast enough, she can get out from under them before they register. It's a lost cause.

She doesn't want to be homeless. She wants a bigger, stronger Eliot to carry her to the north country and build her a log cabin where they can cuddle in peace on a bear rug by a fireplace. No, she doesn't. She doesn't want Eliot to change one bit. Well, maybe a little bit. But nothing that radical.

He took her for granted, that's what started it. To think he could get away with that marriage proposal. And she'll never leave New York, never. It's too much a part of her. The diamonds on Canal Street, the diamond in the Bronx.

Raoul told her she could be the Swan's lover if she dies, just as she dreamed it—remember him now? He must have been there, how else could he have known. Is your soul already signed, sealed, and delivered? Maybe its absence is what accounts for the nausea. You'd think a conscious decision would be required, though, and that hasn't been made yet, has it?

She decides not to cross the bridge into Brooklyn. She says aloud, "I could cross that bridge if I wanted to, but I feel like walking down the Bowery instead. This is an honest-to-God spur-of-the-moment decision I'm making all by myself right now. And to prove that it's not Satan making it for me, I'm going to change my mind and walk over the bridge after all."

She turns around, walks back toward it. "Just because that kid put into my head that I'm burning my bridges behind me is no reason for me to be afraid that the thing will catch fire while I'm walking across. I mean think how many cars are crossing that bridge, think how many people would be killed if it really did burn. Crazy notions that pop into my head and pop right out can't be responsible for the death of all those innocent people. I just can't believe I have that kind of power.

Can I believe anyone else does, that there really is a Devil? Signs sure pointing in that direction."

But there's something about going into Brooklyn now that seems wrong. Brooklyn is Eliot's borough. He grew up there and the only times she's ever gone have been with him. He loved taking her there, exploring all the nooks and crannies, and she loved being taken, loved it when he led the way. What was the name of that pizza place just under the Brooklyn Bridge? Ray's? Sal's? Best pizza in New York, he'd said. And Junior's—best cheesecake. And Brighton Beach—best corned beef on rye. There was that tiny little bar in Red Hook that served the best draft beer, which they let you take outside in plastic glasses, at a site so close to the Statue of Liberty you could practically reach out and grab the torch. And how about that spot on the Brooklyn Heights Promenade where you watched the fireworks light up the Manhattan skyline? That was the neighborhood where one of Eliot's favorite authors, Thomas Wolfe, wrote *Only the Dead Know Brooklyn*, one of many stories he read to her in bed, a favorite pastime. "Dere's no guy livin' dat knows Brooklyn troo an' troo," the narrator said. But Eliot came close, and Joan loved that about him.

He knew Brooklyn's underground too, the intricate maze of subway lines that crisscrossed the borough. In their "Subterranean Homesick Blues" period, as he called it, when they sang for their supper on the trains, they'd gone all the way to the far end, emerging at Coney Island, where they rode the Wonder Wheel and visited the aquarium, fantasizing about learning to scuba dive so they could really get to know the world beneath the sea. That night, Eliot read Jules Verne to her before they made love, and it was sweet. But maybe the best place Eliot took her to in Brooklyn was the train yard near Gravesend Bay, where the subways went home to sleep. That's where she worked magic decorating the trains with graffiti. It was, she recalls, some of the best art she ever created.

No, she thinks now. Going into Brooklyn means going back to Eliot, and she's not ready to cross that bridge yet. So she turns around and walks north on the Bowery again, past the Salvation Army place where she and Eliot bought their dishes, past bars with color TVs tuned to the game but serving clientele she wouldn't want to mess with, past hardware stores with alarms going off, past welfare hotels where old men loiter, holding bottles camouflaged by paper bags, and past the "Save the Cities" campaign headquarters.

You'll feel right at home in hell, Raoul had said to her. It's not hard to figure out why. *So how do you want to do yourself in? Heroin? That's what Janis chose.*

For a time, Joan was as devoted to Janis Joplin as she now is to Nick Spillage, though her love for the singer never came between her and Eliot. They went to see her at Woodstock, at the Fillmore East, at Forest Hills. When Joplin died in 1970 at the age of twenty-seven that Joan is fast approaching, they fasted for a week together, then made a nighttime pilgrimage to the graveyard at Trinity Church. There, in a sleeping bag borrowed from their neighbor Art Popov, they made the most exquisite love they ever made. Eliot was on fire—that was his night to be possessed!

As Joan decides whether to turn west and head toward Trinity Church, which she hasn't visited since, the Phillies tie the Yankees 1–1 because right fielder Angel Guerrero, fleet of foot but with notorious butterfingers, plays a routine pop fly too casually, drops the ball, trips over it, then makes a wild throw home.

The capacity crowd, according to announcer Al Deep, takes it as hard as he'd take it if his wife of forty years up and told him she was leaving him. With the exception of one lunatic, Deep says—a bald, Black man in a dapper pin-striped suit—they look like they've been put under by a master magician. The lunatic is standing on his seat near the Yankee dugout, slapping his wide-brimmed hat against his thigh while with two fingers in his mouth he whistles the funereal *t*aps louder than Lucrecia Vendetta, the opera singer, sang "The Star-Span-gled Banner" before the game. And Vendetta sang into a loudspeaker.

"Well," says Joan, "I wouldn't have to cross any bridges to get there."

The church graveyard is in the Wall Street area, south and to the west. She turns around. Raoul will be waiting for her there, she'd bet on it.

"Don't go that way," says Micky, catching up to her. "Just listen to me, would ya? I saved your life, but I don't need any thanks for that. Who knows, maybe you'd be better off dead, like the ghost said. You make a deal with the Devil, you win the Swan. Maybe Swannie's made a deal with the Devil himself. It's not preposthumous."

"Preposterous."

"It's not that. But on the other hand, you're dealing with some pretty shady customers here. They could have something planned for you that I wouldn't wish on my worst enemy. So take my advice, all right? Be on the safe side. Come with me to Sabrina's. She'll be able to help you."

Joan gives a long look at the boy, considers that nothing could be lost from following him, and nothing would be gained from going in the direction she was headed. And off to Sabrina's they go.

Part
TWO

10

TIME FOR SOME NEW STUFF

There's no one in the Reading Room when Joan and Micky arrive, looking for Sister Sabrina.

"Where do we go from here, squirt?" asks Joan.

"We wait," says Micky, fiddling with the TV. "This should work," he explains, though it doesn't appear to. "At least the picture should be good. Been soundless for as long as I can remember, basically because Sabrina wants it that way. Strange that she'd want picture and no sound instead of visa versa, since she can't see worth a hoot on account of her cataracts but can hear like a demon—I mean things you only dream of saying sometimes—but then again, maybe it's not so strange, since she usually falls asleep within five minutes after she turns it on."

He gives the box a knock, and the picture comes on. It's a Burger Boat commercial that makes Joan cringe, even though she can only see and not hear it, because she knows the infernal jingle by heart. It's the one Big Daddy created years ago, when she was still a little girl, the one that sent his career into high gear. She can't believe they're still airing it. "Time for some new stuff!" she wants to shout, but doesn't because she knows it won't do any good. There will probably be some old TV playing that friggin' jingle long after the inevitable nuclear holocaust has destroyed the world. Big Daddy lives on, she has to admit, even though he's disappeared from her life, and maybe from the planet. It's not enough, she thinks. She wants him, and his work product, nullified. Make it so he never existed at all. Except then, she realizes, there would be no you.

No, she thinks, you can't go that far. Can't blot out his existence, just the space he takes up in your head. But even that's hard, since he created so many things that live beyond him, things you bump into wherever you turn. On the tube, on the newsstand, on the big Times Square billboards. He was an artist, she has to admit, who knew how to move people, if not how to love them. In his prime he had the magic touch.

She remembers the time it all took off, when the Wheel of Fortune clicked on their number. She was seven years old, and she had a huge crush on him, would crawl into bed between him and Dear Mother whenever she had trouble sleeping through the night. That was before things got creepy, when he started climbing into her bed. He was flying high, and he took her with him, delighted in showing her off. He'd bring her to the sets where they shot the ads, sit her in the director's chair, and ask if she approved of the takes. Dear Mother thought she should become a model, following in her own footsteps, but she dismissed the idea, just as she dismissed all her suggestions. At the time, she was very much Daddy's little girl. He took her to fancy events like the Clio Awards, where he won big, on cruises around the city with his ad agency colleagues, to high tea at the Plaza Hotel, carriage rides in Central Park, shopping adventures at Bergdorf Goodman, FAO Schwarz. Nothing but fake affection, as she later discovered.

Even then though, she knew something was wrong, something she couldn't quite put her finger on at the time. All that success, all those accolades, all that money coming in all at once changed him. Beneath the slick, smooth surface, there was always a dark side—a mean, controlling side—which would flare into violent outbursts when he didn't get his way. And the higher he rose in the business world, the more his sense of entitlement grew, the more impatient he became at home, the more intolerant if you dared to cross him. It went to his head, screwed him up big-time.

He was a narcissistic bully, Joan thinks. The world revolved around him, and only him. He never really understood you, and at a certain point he stopped trying. Too much bother, when there was business to be cultivated, ads to be created, junk to be sold. Sure, he wanted to show you off, pretend like he loved you, buy you expensive things. But he'd get angry when you didn't seem to show enough appreciation, because you couldn't work up the level of excitement he expected. Demanded. Thinking back, there was nothing of special meaning or lasting value you received from his spending spree, and that's sad. His frenetic gift-giving actually increased the distance between you. As the Beatles sang, "Can't Buy Me Love."

Nothing special at all, she thinks, except for one thing: the cute little Shetland pony he got you for your twelfth birthday, not much bigger than the Dalmatian sitting at your side. He didn't need to be a genius to know you loved horses. They were all over your bedroom walls, just like Spillage pictures are today. But it was still a big surprise when he brought you to Connecticut to give the gift, and you thanked him profusely with a huge hug and kiss. As it turned out, it was the last hug and kiss you'd ever give Big Daddy. It was sincere, she recalls, even though you already had pretty much written him off. It was your "I hate you for what you've become but you're still my father and I wish I could love you more" embrace, something you now regret.

Joan called the pony Eddy after the talking horse in the TV show, Mr. Ed, because she wanted so badly to communicate with him, make a spiritual connection. She's always had a thing for creating special bonds with creatures who spark her interest, dating back to when she had an imaginary friend, Yumi the unicorn, as a little girl. And she made some progress, she recalls, with Eddy the pony before everything fell apart. That gift could have been special, if you had more time to spend with him. But you sensed from the start that time was not on your side.

You knew. You knew Big Daddy was a fraud before his secret family got exposed. You can see these things in people; it's a power you have. What Eliot calls your Spidey-sense. So, you can't pretend you were shocked. Angry as all hell, but not shocked. Immediately, you broke all his pricey presents into little pieces and threw them in the garbage. Abandoned the pony, made Dear Mother sell it. Refused to see him for a final goodbye. And swore to yourself you were done with him forever, though that's been a hard pledge to keep.

Everything Joan knows about Big Daddy since he left her life she's gotten from her older brother, who migrated to California with him, then used his connections to break into the film business, where he now produces grade B horror flicks that she gets a kick out of seeing when they come to the neighborhood. They shared a love of spooky stuff when she was a kid, and she still has fond memories of him taking her trick-or-treating up and down Lexington Avenue in their vampire costumes. Though they were five years apart and never really that close, there were times when she benefited from his older sibling wisdom, and she doesn't mind maintaining the connection, if faint.

What he's told her is that after reaching the top of his profession selling products people don't need, Big Daddy turned to selling political hacks they need even less. And one in particular, Richard Nixon, whom he helped send to the White House twice. Admiral Dugan, his biggest client and Nixon's biggest financial backer, introduced them after Nixon lost his bid to become governor of California in 1962. "You won't have Nixon to kick around anymore," the politician famously said after that defeat. But soon after, he and Big Daddy were kicking around ideas for his eventual comeback.

While for the most part she studiously avoids politics—it's more Eliot's thing—the fact that Nixon is Big Daddy's Frankenstein monster is a big reason Joan is rooting for his defeat. If he wins a third term, he'll likely go for a fourth and a fifth, and she'll never be rid of her father's influence. Eliot can think of a dozen reasons Nixon should go down, most importantly the Vietnam War, but for Joan Nixon's war on free expression is right up there too. The museum closings, book banning, blacklistings—all that bullshit about subversive art. Art's supposed to be subversive, you stupid jerk! And then there's his war on the cities, his war on clean air, his wars on women, Blacks, and youth, all fought under the umbrella of his war against the Commies. Big Daddy didn't create all that's wrong with America, she thinks, but he made a big contribution. Time for some new stuff, she silently repeats.

Her father's successful partnership with Nixon spanned a decade, and along the way it opened up even greater business opportunities for the legendary Mad Man. But in the end, when scandals threatened to end Tricky Dick's presidency, Big Daddy became one of several advisors to be thrown overboard to save the ship from sinking. It had something to do with money laundering, her brother said, involving a Latin American dictator Nixon was propping up with arms. Big Daddy, the bag man, can you believe it? Though he was never charged with wrongdoing, his corporate clients deserted him in droves, beginning with Dugan. And that led him to take on more political work, particularly with corrupt politicians south of the border. For a time, this was lucrative enough for him to maintain his lavish lifestyle in L.A., while keeping up his alimony and child support payments to his first family. But then he lost a fortune speculating in foreign currency when the markets crashed. And a few months ago, around the time Nick Spillage burst on the scene, Big Daddy disappeared entirely, while on a business trip to Venezuela.

Joan never told Eliot about the disappearance. He was so caught up at the time in his own parents' demise, she didn't want to give him another death to think about. And anyway, she didn't really think he'd died. He'll pop up again like a bad penny to torment me, she'd thought. And here he is now, on the screen, through his work.

She turns the channel until she finds the game and tries to concentrate on her dreamboat, who's pitching a masterpiece.

The phone rings as Art Popov and Crystal Belle burst into the room, Mirlanda's baby in tow. Never seen anyone so made up, thinks Joan, stealing a glance at the teenage girl. And what could she possibly see in that fat old walrus? The child's adorable, though. Looks to be about one year old.

"It's for you," says Micky, handing the phone to Art, who doesn't recognize the voice on the other end.

"I feel sorry for you, Popov," says the caller. "You're missing all the action here at Joan and Eliot's."

"Who is this?" says Art.

"Never mind. Just come on over and say hi to Mayor Lightly. By the time you get here, he'll be finished with his speech."

"Lightly? He's been found? What happened to the Vanguard?"

"You're the Vanguard now."

"Me? You can't be serious."

"You're Russian, sí?"

"I escaped from Russia."

"No matter. You belong on our team."

"You're with the Vanguard, aren't you. Trying to set me up."

"Just trying to make sure you get your scoop."

"I'm on my way. But I'm calling the cops first."

"Cops are already here. Everybody's here. Especially Eliot. He can't wait to see you."

"Is that so? Ask if he wants me to bring his girlfriend."

"Let me speak to her."

"Here." He shoves the phone at Joan as Nick Spillage blows a third strike past Al Hamilton for the first out in the ninth. It's his twentieth strikeout of the game. "Friend of yours wants to chat with you, Joan. Guess you've really been getting around, eh?"

He runs out the door as Joan takes the phone, and Baby Wo crawls out after, while Crystal buries herself in a celebrity magazine, a black cat curled in her lap.

"I missed you at the graveyard," says the caller, and hangs up.

11

NO SNAKES ANYWHERE

"Swannie into his dance, his chant, and here comes the pitch to Madison," says Yankee announcer Al Deep. "Swing and a miss, strike two. Eight straight strikes for Swannie here in the ninth, his pitches darting this way and that past these Liberty Bell Creekers who were in this game all the way, but we're one strike away from wrapping it up as our wonder boy asks the ump for a new ball and Holy Hosanna what a Series debut for the young man who I hear may soon enter politics.

"The mayor's been found—we got it in on the wires—he's asked Nick to be his running mate and what a combo they'd make, assumin' the law can be changed. We'll try to reach the pitcher for comment when we go to the locker room, but in the meantime, he's got his sign from Dert and here we go again—the fans already busting through the police line—hope it's strike three because we'll never finish this game if it's not—and it is! Ball game over! Yanks win it 2–1 on the strength of Swannie obliteratin' the record book. Twenty K's for the southpaw, couple of timely hits by Angel, and look at this, would you just look at this?

"All hell breaking loose in The House That Ruth Built, fans swarming on the field from every direction, boys in blue trying to keep them back but they can't do miracles with the cutbacks and what-have-you. Lucky we have them out there at all and I'm not just saying that because my brother-in-law's a lieutenant. You looking at this, Gus? Imagine Gus is with the mayor, who he's been tracking ever since the Vanguard nabbed him, but right here we got a ballpark full of zanies, fifty thousand-plus after a piece of Swannie, and unless you take the clubs to them or let go the gas, no way you're gonna stop them. Would you look at this?

"Yanks win Game One of this Series in a squeaker, Nick Spillage with his first Fall Classic win, and the fans are tearing him to pieces. There goes his hat, all those golden curls revealed, and now someone's got his right sleeve, his left, his belt. They're tugging his pants and whoops! What a scene this is!

"But wait . . . oh my God! That loony in the fancy suit's got a knife and he's after—no! He got him in the arm, that strong left pitching arm, Swannie's face contorted in pain, his hand on the spot, blood gushing. I can't look! Some loony has tried to assassinate Nick Spillage, or cut his left arm off, which might even be worse. To have that pinned sleeve as a living reminder of what coulda been, no, I can't bear to think about it, and thank God I won't have to. It's all right, Swannie's saying to police on the mound, just a scratch, I could pitch another nine. Police have the madman in cuffs. Wonder what could've possessed this guy?"

. . .

A squeegee man who once served in the Navy with Admiral Dugan finds Baby Wo on the street at the corner of Bowery and Houston and teaches him to lift windshield wipers so he can spread his rag underneath. "Attaboy, mate," he says. "We're gonna make some real money now! Never mind those nanny state child labor laws. They don't apply to the likes of you and me."

The squeegee man considers himself an expert on the human condition, having traveled to the four corners of the globe and mingled with a host of cultures, including those of remote Pacific islands studied by Darwin. In the Navy, which he joined after Pearl Harbor as an under-age enlistee, he manned the periscopes of many a submarine, plumbing the depths of the deepest seas, weathering the fiercest storms. Then as a civilian, working in construction until the economy crashed, he scaled the heights of the tallest skyscrapers, welding the steel girders that kept them upright. So he believes he's seen the world from all possible angles and his big takeaway is that it's all about self-reliance.

That's why he is adamant about not taking any government hand-outs or taking up residence in any of the city's shelters, which Mayor Lightly has established at a record pace. A Nixon man, he doesn't think New York, or any other big city, should be bailed out either, despite all those unfinished buildings marring the skyline, the garbage on the streets, the boarded-up storefronts, and the rampant crime. Let the cit-ies fend for themselves, like he does. Make your own breaks, he thinks. When a cute little tot comes crawling to you out of nowhere, grabbing hold of your leg like it's a blooming life raft, you've got to take that opportunity straight to the bank, no matter if it means stretching the truth a bit. That's the way the game is played.

"Hundred bucks to help feed the baby!" he shouts to drivers who stop at the light. "Mother died on this very spot."

•   •   •

"Thank you, Mayor Lightly," says Eliot at the impromptu press confer-ence being held in his apartment, "on behalf of all of us."

"Let's plunge right into it, my boy," says the mayor. "Cannonball from the high board. Meet my new press secretary, ladies and gentle-men. He's the greenest of the green but you watch how fast he savvies. Now then . . ." He clears his throat.

"Question for the mayor," says Eliot. "Yes?"

Six reporters near the sink piled with Great Moments in World Series Play dishes say their names at once as Raoul disgruntles several near the refrigerator by pulling its door open. Empty, thinks Eliot. The only empty space in the entire apartment, aside from the space on the floor Raoul's body used to fill. Strange how they haven't moved into that one, despite the way they're all crammed around it. You'd think it was a snake pit.

"Let's see," he says, as Raoul extracts an apple from the fridge he somehow missed and hands it to a tall woman who looks vaguely like Joan, with thick red hair that runs well below her waist. He points to one of the reporters and says, "The frail-looking gentleman over there, with the kind of beard that I used to have."

"Hartline, *People's Voice*. In your speech, Mr. Mayor, you referred several times to a dead man. Do you mean to imply that the snakes in this pit devoured him? Or do you wish us to believe that since all Communists are devils, it was more than natural for him to metamorphize into snakes during the period when for most of us rigor mortis would set in—during your introductory remarks, in other words?"

"One moment," says the mayor. He cups his hand over his mouth, leans to his left, and whispers to Eliot, "You don't see any snakes, do you, my boy?"

Eliot does see a few in the red hair of the woman slicing her apple with the knife Raoul found for her, disgruntling several reporters by the silverware drawer in the process. These snakes don't seem to the new press secretary like the ones Hartline is talking about, though.

"No snakes, sir," he whispers back. "No snakes at all. Anywhere. I'd swear to it."

"Good," says the mayor. "The man's berserk. I had him picked for a nutcase the minute I laid eyes on him. The more years you serve, the more quickly you can judge these things. Now watch how a pro plays it."

He drops his hand from his mouth. "Mr. Hart," he says, "a word about snakes and then a question for you. This country's first political cartoon concerned a snake and it was a potent one, the cartoon I mean. Ben Franklin drew it. He cut the snake up and labeled the pieces with the initials of the colonies. They were divided, you see. And Ben's call, like mine, was to unite. Unite to save our cities! Only united can we clean up this mess, take the high moral ground."

"The war," whispers Eliot. "Talk about the war."

"Thank you, my boy. Quite right." The mayor coughs, as Eliot beams. Maybe I'm good at this, he thinks for a moment. Just for a moment, though.

"We'll never seize the high ground if we're bogged down in the rice paddies of Vietnam," Hizzoner continues. "We need to end this senseless war. All that blood and treasure, we need that at home! We can't just tell our great cities to drop dead. They'll take everyone down with them, and then where will we be? But that's not my question for you, sir. What I want to know is this: how did you manage to fly out of the cuckoo's nest?"

Eliot feels deflated. This is going off-track, he thinks, as he sees Raoul wink. Clearly distraught, fists clenched tightly around his notebook and pencil, his look-alike Hartline says, "I resent that, Mayor Lightly."

"Calm yourself," says the mayor. "I fully understand the stresses and strains of your profession, of all professions in these depressed times. You're not alone in your anxiety! But that doesn't entitle you to project your inner turmoil onto the rest of us when we're trying to discuss the affairs of the nation."

"You old windbag!" Hartline snaps. "How could you think you could see inside me? No one could possibly know the trouble I'm going through."

"Let me guess," says Raoul, fooling with the apple eater's red hair. "Your girlfriend left you."

"My girlfriend left me!" shouts Hartline, throwing his notebook and pencil into the air and grabbing his beard with both hands like he's trying to pull it off. "So what can I hold on to? There's nothing good anymore. The ground just crumbles wherever I stand. The snake pits are everywhere. The world's gone insane. And your nonstop babble is making it worse!"

"Rubbish," says the mayor. "Remove this man."

"All right, boys," says a little man by the window, dressed in the kind of tweed suit Eliot's father, the professor, used to wear, only more crumpled. Several patrolmen haul a fighting Hartline out the door.

"Question for the mayor," says Eliot, relieved his look-alike is gone. Not the kind of guy you'd like to spend time with, much less be, though you can kind of relate to his despair. He points again, to a reporter who could pass for Choice. "Green-eyed gentleman in the pin-striped suit," he says.

"Chance, *Free Soul*," says the reporter. "I've got something mean to ask you, Mr. Mayor, but I bow to the lady with the rich red hair. She had her hand up first."

Did she? Oh, yes. Raoul's supporting it, while she attacks that apple with the fervor of a rabid dog. Wish it wouldn't keep looking like she's only taken one bite no matter how many times she goes around it.

"Let's you and I split, Chance, and screw till Armageddon," she says with abandon. "Unless you want to do it here."

"I do love an audience," says Chance, smiling broadly.

Several reporters stomp their feet, several slap their knees, and several clap their hands, until the man in tweed says with authority, "That'll be enough."

Another ten seconds, thinks Eliot, and I would've joined in. "Big mistake," the mayor whispers to him. "It's your job to keep control, my boy. You've got to think twice before you yield the floor."

Smoke rises through the cracks between the floorboards where Raoul once lay. Let someone else shout fire, thinks Eliot. "I take it you have no questions, Miss," he says.

The woman with the red hair finishes her apple. "Jones," she says. "*Mother Jones*. I don't see where you get off thinking that the Swan's gonna come near your phony campaign, Mayor. And the closest thing I see to a dead man is your deadbeat press secretary."

Something in the smoke gets in Eliot's left eye, making it tear. The mayor says, "The young woman is quite stunning, but she doesn't seem to fathom what constitutes a question. Next!"

"Excuse me, Mayor Lightly," says Eliot, rubbing at his eyes. "I'd just like to respond to her."

"Let it pass and it will fade away," whispers the mayor. He clears his throat.

"I'd just like to respond," Eliot says again. He'd very much like to respond, can feel the harsh words welling up in his throat. His inner Hartline is about to burst.

"You sir, in the tweed suit," says the mayor.

"Not now," says the man in tweed, removing a stick of tobacco from his jacket pocket. "I'd like to see how things develop first. As a cop, that's always been my philosophy."

"The young woman's wrong," Eliot shouts over him. "I'm not a deadbeat. She's an arrogant bitch. She thinks she's the center of the universe, that she can get away with stomping all over people."

Did he really just say that? Not about Joan. About this Joan wannabe, whom Raoul has conjured up.

"My boy," says the mayor. "Remember your position."

"Sorry," says Eliot. What's gotten into me? "Next question."

"I believe I had the floor, my man. Chance, *Free Soul*. What you plan on doing, Mr. Mayor, about this paternity suit the Haitian Hell-Raiser's bringing against you?"

"Preposterous," says the mayor.

"Hear she's got pictures from her nightclub, all kinds of pictures, a whole lot juicier than what's filling these walls. Now people might understand if it happened last month, your wife being shot and all, but with the baby a year old that puts the affair way back before she got killed. Seems you've got quite an image problem, your campaign resting on this moral crisis jazz. Folks might begin to think you planned the assassination attempt to get the old hag out of the way."

"I didn't know you had a wife," whispers Eliot, his hand cupped over his mouth.

"I didn't, really," whispers the mayor. "It was only a marriage for appearance's sake. But what am I telling you for? You don't listen." He clears his throat. "Beware, Mr. Free Soul, of my opponent's propensity for dirty tricks. He's famous for them and this is clearly one. He's trying to distract from his own moral turpitude by projecting it on me, when every shred of evidence points to the contrary. The fact is that my dear, beloved wife had her brain pierced by a member of the Satanic Vanguard, who wanted to assassinate me because I am doing God's work trying to save this country, and who, come to think of it, rather looked like you. Officer? Is it conceivable?"

"Nah," says the man in tweed, biting off a chaw of tobacco. "Certain things are inconceivable, and that your man escaped is one of them. We've got him in a special place."

"Glad to hear it," says Eliot. "Makes me feel more secure. Even though I'm more than capable of taking care of myself."

"Really? Like you took care of the nonexistent Vanguard leader on the floor?" says the woman with the red hair, whose legs, Eliot thinks, aren't quite as long as Joan's, and whose eyes are neither as big nor as wide set. "Are you sure it wasn't your shadow you saved the mayor from, deadbeat?"

"I didn't recognize you," says Eliot, clearly agitated. "Didn't recognize you at all. And I'm not about to recognize you now. So would you just shut up?"

"Control," whispers the mayor. "You're walking on eggshells."

I don't know this woman, Eliot thinks. Don't know her or the real Joan. Eight long years and I don't know a thing. Don't know what moves her. Don't know what's moving me.

"I'm afraid," says the mayor, "that my interim press secretary is a bit disturbed."

"I am not!" shouts Eliot. "I'm completely unruffled, just like the Swan. I'm at my peak when the bases are loaded. Three balls and no strikes." He winds up, kicking his leg as high as he can and throwing an imaginary baseball in the direction of the open door.

Art Popov enters. "Well, well, well, well," he says. "Look who's on the mound. Nice pitch, kiddo. Too bad the game's lost. So when did you join up with Mayor Lightweight? When Joan started messing around with little kids and big dogs? Just left her at my girl's place. She waltzed in with her latest conquests while Crystal and I were going at it, and damned if she didn't try to push her way in. Glad she got wise and left you, no offense. Knew you could never hold on to her, buddy. But this is a new low, even for a jilted lover. You're not really in the mayor's camp now, are you?"

"Sí," says Raoul, "But not for long." He disgruntles several reporters between the refrigerator and the bed while clearing a path from Eliot to Art. As he pushes people aside, he says, "Mayor Lightly's much too smart to stay mixed up with the kind of campaign manager who lets old flames get in the way of crucial issues of the day. The mayor doesn't have time to teach the ropes to a guy who won't listen and can't keep his cool. He's a city-saver, not a babysitter."

The mayor tugs Eliot's elbow. "You're fired," he says, then points to Raoul. "You're hired."

Flashbulbs pop as the mayor embraces Raoul and they exit together, followed by the reporters with the exception of Art, whom Eliot lunges at, hitting him with a left to the breadbasket that sends him banging into the refrigerator, and then a left-right-left to the head as the *Mercury* reporter begins a slow descent.

"Here, use this," says Raoul, popping back in for a second to toss Eliot the TV cord. "Have fun, Señor Ensign."

Only the man in the tweed suit, chewing tobacco by the window, sees Eliot use the cord to finish off Art.

12

THINGS COULD CHANGE

Yankee right fielder Angel Guerrero spirits Mirlanda away from the angry mob at the stadium to his SoHo loft, directly above Sister Sabrina's Reading Room. "You're safe now," he says.

"I'm not," says Mirlanda. "You don't know my no-good skunk of an ex-husband."

"But I do," says Angel. "Sister Sabrina told me all about him."

"How do you know Sabrina?"

"We share a mission. And an elevator."

"So my baby's downstairs? I gave him to her for safekeeping."

"Sorry, afraid she dropped the ball on that one. Or her daughter did. But don't worry, we'll get him back, if you trust me."

She sizes him up with a hard stare. He has a reputation as a great humanitarian for his help getting food and water to victims of the storms in his native Puerto Rico. And she loves the way he flies across the field, ponytail flapping, to chase fly balls. Hits with power too. But he makes his share of unforced errors. "How I know I can trust you?" she says.

"I love you as only an Angel can."

"I don't believe you," she says, same as she said to Choice and Raoul the first times they told her they loved her. Choice shouted it out on a crowded boat to the Statue of Liberty. Raoul snuck up behind her on the street and whispered it. Of the three, she figures Choice loves her the most, but he loves her in streaks, and a fat lot of good his love is going to do her while he rots away in some cell for ninety-nine years. Man should've thought ahead, never should have abandoned her.

"I know you." The outfielder takes her hands in his. "You come from a family of great Haitian revolutionary leaders. Not afraid to raise hell to support a just cause. Proud people who fled the evil Papa Doc to come to the land of the free and the brave. Fell in with some bad characters here, though."

"You got that right," says Mirlanda.

"I'm your Angel," says the slugger. "And you're my Hell-Raiser."

. . .

Crystal sits depressed before her makeup mirror as she runs a bath. That nose, she thinks, that horrible, hooked gypsy nose, straight from her mother, ugh! She really needs to get that fixed. And what's this, another zit? The acne, she knows, will ultimately pass, but will it leave scars? She powders it up. Casting her sight lower, to her exquisite breasts, helps counteract her sour mood. The total package, she thinks, is still something to behold, attractive enough for Art, at least, though she wishes she could offer more. And she wishes he wasn't so totally dismissive of the idea of her having his child, even though she knew she wasn't ready. The whole abortion experience has definitely left a scar, she thinks, invisible though it may be.

"Why are you so sad, chiquita?" says Raoul from behind her.

"I lost my baby," says Crystal. "Art wouldn't let me keep it."

"You lost two babies, including mine."

"I don't care about *your* baby."

"I don't like him much either, to tell the truth. He belongs to Choice. But he was your responsibility. Your mother will be mad."

"Screw her. She can't control me."

"Come take a bath with me, Crystal." He puts his hands on her shoulders. "I'll make you rich, famous, beautiful—if only skin deep. You'll own the Yankees. You'll own New York. Your business empire will know no bounds. Forget about babies—you will be queen."

She eyes him through the mirror, stripped to the waist. He's the opposite of Art. So hot it's not funny. "What's the catch?" she asks.

"Just your soul."

To hell with Art, she'll show him, she thinks, as they step together into the tub, sloshing bubbles onto the floor.

* * *

"Well, son," says Lieutenant Gus Berkley, a wad of tobacco puffing his left cheek as he squats with Eliot beside Art Popov's body, which hasn't moved since Eliot stopped strangling it. "Looks like we've got a little unintentional homicide on our hands."

"Looks like it, doesn't it. Stick around, though. Things could change," says Eliot, wondering how in the world he could have gotten so enraged. Totally unlike you, he thinks. And not helping the cause at all, if the cause is winning Joan back. What if that really was her? No, it was just Raoul's trickery. He made you do it, the devil-dust he blew in your eye was the culprit. So much for your career in politics. How do you beat this guy?

The lieutenant spits in the direction of the spot where Raoul's body once lay and says, "Doubt it. But you never know for sure. Any particular change you have in mind?"

"Oh, I don't know," says Eliot, laughing silently at himself for folding Art's hands across his too-tight yellow shirt. "The body could disappear the way the last one did. Or you and I could disappear."

"You mean walk off and forget it?"

"I meant disappear." Eliot stands. "But we could do it your way, if you'd like."

"You're a plucky kid." Gus empties Art's pants pockets. "I like that."

"You take bribes?"

"How long were you in politics, son?"

"Couple of hours, more or less."

An alarm goes off not far away, capturing Gus's attention momentarily. "Deadly profession," he then says glumly. "Especially for bright young kids like you. If you're anxious to get ahead, as you evidently are, you're susceptible to all kinds of corrupting influences."

"You remind me of my father, you know."

Gus transfers cash from Art's wallet into his own, transfers tobacco from his left cheek to his right. "Would your father take a bribe?"

"Absolutely not. He was like the last of the late, great moralists. A professor of logic."

"Passed on, has he."

"Yeah. Pushed under a subway."

"Happens too often these days." The lieutenant plays with the little plastic bag of cocaine he finds in Art's pocket, squeezing it, flipping it from hand to hand, weighing it. "I've got five of the cutest, sweetest little girls in the world waiting back in Flatbush for their daddy to come home," he says.

"Hey, that's where I grew up!" says Eliot, taking a step back. He remembers feeling safe when he was a little kid, before New York hit the skids. Safe playing stickball on the street with his friends. Safe seeing the burly cops watching over him, munching donuts beside their squad car. Safe in the stands at the ballpark we used to have. There was the time his father, a Dodger fan, brought him to Ebbets Field, just walking distance from their apartment, and he caught a foul ball. No fear. Just stuck out his glove and hauled it in. He remembers feeling safe too under the covers with Joan. When did that feeling end? "Tough what's going on in the neighborhood," he says. "Been gone a long time?"

"Ever since this Satanic Vanguard thing broke. A month. Two months. You lose sense of time the more sleep you lose." He opens the plastic bag, pokes a finger inside, and gives his finger a lick. "Dogged persistence can be disorienting. But it can pay off too. Ever think about joining the force?"

"I've thought a lot about being a father," says Eliot, watching the detective pocket the bag. He thinks how much more comfortable he'd feel if the white powder was all that was left of the big body below it, which he feels inclined to cover with Spillage pictures and set fire to. If he finds himself engaged in this task, and the fatherly flatfoot tries to stop him, will he methodically kill him the way he killed Art? He doesn't feel even a flicker of animosity toward the detective, kind of likes him in fact, but still, having already done the deed once . . .

"Can you help me up, son?" asks Gus, still hunched over Art.

Eliot extends a hand, which Gus takes, creaking slowly up with a lengthy grunt.

"Used to be quite a defensive catcher," says the lieutenant, smiling a crooked little smile. "Couldn't tell you how many times I leapt out of that squat, gunned the man down at second. Never imagined I'd see the day when I'd have the kind of troubles with my back that I have now. Guess you never imagined your girlfriend would get tired of you."

"Nope," says Eliot. "Always suspected she would."

"Urban paranoia." Gus pulls at the lapels of his rumpled tweed jacket, which smells musky to Eliot, who smells musky to himself. "Care to turn around, put your hands against the fridge, and spread your legs so they're shoulder length apart?"

"You know I kind of suspected you'd get around to this sooner or later," says Eliot, turning.

"I'm a predictable guy." Gus starts at the armpits. "One of the reasons I never made it to the big leagues. The pitcher didn't have to be Swannie to make me look bush. If he threw it in the dirt I'd be right there after it, swinging and missing, swinging and missing."

"Running and losing," Eliot mumbles, Gus's inordinately large hands like hot compresses along his ribs. "Running and losing," he repeats, glancing toward the closet, where he half expects Raoul to step out with Joan or Ms. Jones. He wonders if the latter is a soulless version of the former, Joan as she appears to the world having already made her bargain with the Devil. Is it too late to save her? Then again, maybe there's a more plausible story behind the woman. Joan had a half-sister, didn't she? Her evil twin, as she called her, whom she never met. Belonged to her father's secret family. Does the old Mad Man have a part in this? Another master of illusion.

"Running and losing what, son? Your head? If you're trying to explain what moved you to violence, spit it out. Be good for your soul to confess. Whatever you say will be strictly between us—that's a promise, I swear, and I'm a man of my word. I'm not out to punish you, don't see what the point would be. You'll punish yourself plenty without the law's help, and I've got bigger fish to fry. All I want to do is gather information, and you seem like you're privy to things that I'm not. So clue me in. What's gone on here?"

"It was only a dream."

Gus spits tobacco at the TV cord on the floor beside Art. "Wish it were, son. Truly do, for all of our sakes." He takes a wad of bills out of Eliot's pocket. "Where'd you come by this?"

"I took it off Raoul," says Eliot. "He's the guy behind all this, the one that Mayor Lightly was talking about in his speech. You remember? He kept pointing to a nonexistent dead man on the floor."

"Member of the Vanguard."

"That's Raoul."

"Okay." He pockets the wad. "Tell me more. I'm all ears."

His ears are indeed huge, and combined with his dark-rimmed, bloodshot eyes, they give him the air of a beagle to Eliot, who, perhaps to test his loyalty, says, "It'd really be a relief to like tell you everything. But I mean everything, from the time I was in the box."

"You did time?" Gus asks.

"When I was a baby, see, my father was buddies with this Nobel-prize winning doctor, who had this theory about controlling behavior."

"Please," says Gus, "I don't need this, do I? Not for the Vanguard case."

Eliot shakes his head. "I guess you don't," he says. "But I kind of do, just to get my head straight."

The detective wanders to the cable-spool kitchen table, picks a record album off the pile alongside and peruses the cover as though it's a clue. It's *Sticky Fingers*, by the Rolling Stones. One of Eliot's favorites, though he decides not to volunteer that information.

"What you need is a job that gives you a sense of self-worth," Gus says, "a feeling you wake up with in the morning that you're doing some good, taking your lumps on behalf of your fellow man."

He smiles his crooked smile, which Eliot finds oddly ingratiating. His father loved detective novels—Sherlock Holmes, Agatha Christie—loved watching Perry Mason on TV. Took pride in using his deductive powers to figure out the ending before it was revealed. He'd agree with what Gus is saying, said the same kind of thing more than once. So is this the career for you? Would King George approve?

"I'd be willing to work for you," says Eliot. "You seem like you'd be a good boss, could teach me a lot, and I'm not just saying that to get on your good side. Whatever I say or do these days has very little to do with what gets done to me. I did one thing that has meaning. I loved Joan. Asked her to marry me. But marriage the way I envisioned it turned out to be impossible, and ever since then, impossible's been the norm."

"Joan's the redhead, I take it."

"No, that's Ms. Jones, a friend of Raoul's. I mean he brought her, I think. She's like Joan's demon image. Or maybe her sister, I don't know. Choice—her first lover beside me, unless you want to count the Swan, who's strictly fantasy, or was, since nothing seems to be strictly fantasy or strictly real anymore—his demon image was here too."

"Free Soul."

"Yeah. You're catching on."

"Got it. And the walls are covered with Swannie's demon images."

"No, those are real images, like from real newspapers and stuff. Joan put them there before she ran off. She loves making collages."

"I see," says Gus. He yawns, moves over to the bed, and lies down, clasping his hands behind his head. "I'm beginning to see things now about this case that I never saw before." His eyes look glazed, having difficulty staying open.

"You know I think that's my brother-in-law on the TV across the street," says Gus, staring dreamily out the window. "He announces the ball games. Does a heck of a job."

Eliot nods. The lieutenant, still gazing out the window, says, "What he does best, maybe best in the business, is fill the gaps in the action with chatter."

Then he snaps his fingers, sits up in the bed. "I've got a hunch," he says. "It's worth a try, at any rate. At the worst we wind up blowing our little bundle on a good time." He stands and dusts off his tweed trousers. "You ever hear the mayor talk about Sheila Dugan, son?"

"He mentioned her, yeah. I think he's in love with her," says Eliot.

"Are you?"

"No. Why should I be. You?"

"A little. When I was a kid, I went bananas over Dietrich, and Sheila's got some of her appeal."

"You know, Lieutenant, I'd be willing to bet that if we found my girlfriend, we could really get to the core of this whole Vanguard thing."

"Funny you should say that, son," says Gus, bending with some effort to tighten a loose knot on his right shoe, "because I was about to say the same thing about Sheila. She's involved with the mayor, she's involved with the Yankees, she's involved with the underworld, and we know just where to find her. We've got enough dough to zip right over, so what's stopping us?"

"Where is she?" asks Eliot.

"Gulliver's Island. The Dugans' offshore paradise, where they launder all the money. Nice little casino there, too." He smiles his crooked smile. "Let's go for it, son!"

13

THE GOOD WITCH

While waiting for Sister Sabrina to arrive at the Reading Room, Joan finds a sheet of pink, perfumed stationery, and stretched out on the carpet, she writes:

My beautiful, darling angel Swan, I'd feel so corny doing this kind of thing with anyone else, you know, writing a love letter and all when you probably get millions—you deserve millions—but I just want you to know that I love you. And even if like I don't ultimately die for you, it's not because you've let me down in any way.

You were wonderful to watch today in your first World Series game. I was lucky enough to catch bits and pieces, especially in the opening inning, before this guy Raoul tried to strangle me with a TV cord. I was so involved, it was like I was inside you, riding your heart like I was on a winged stallion, and what better thrill could a girl ever have? I just wanted to spur you on to faster and faster speeds, greater and greater heights. Places that only you could go.

If I do die for you (and I'm not saying I won't, just that it's hard to decide once and for all), and the Devil lets me come back and <u>really</u> love you, like in the flesh, for no matter how short a time, I'd want you to feel me holding fast to your heart like I felt myself to be in that first inning when you blew ten straight strikes past those flabbergasted Phillies.

I don't want to weigh you down, Nick. I don't want you to feel the slightest bit of pressure from me. But Nick, I do hope you find me beautiful, inside and out, in spite of the fact that there's some weird stuff going on inside me these days. Because that's the way I see you, and it's not just the way you pitch. I know your spirit is pure.

But who am I to think you can love me? You don't know me at all, do you. So let me introduce myself, as the Stones did in one of my favorite songs. Never mind that it's about the Devil, who may have power over me. Just look past that, to who I really am at heart. Who am I? I'm an artist.

I make art from found objects, in the great dada tradition. I make graffiti art on subway trains, murals on abandoned buildings, sculptures from trash, collages with newsprint. I've turned my apartment into a giant collage of you—my ultimate found object. My muse! I'd love for you to see it if you can break away between games.

I was brought up in Manhattan, on the Upper East Side. But I'm not an uptown girl, far from it. I've lived in the East Village for more than eight years and that's where my spirit is.

I've never sold any of my art, Nick. Never tried to sell any, never had the desire. My father was a super salesman, could sell snow to the Eskimos. He snowed everyone with his catchy slogans, and I saw it destroy his soul. My parents were both terrible, all surfaces, fakes. But I'm determined to find my true self, and that means being with you.

I'm nearly twenty-seven years old, Nick. That's not too old for you, is it? I'm almost at that age people swore in the '60s they never wanted to pass because it would mean they'd have to change in some dramatic way no matter how much they tried to resist. And here I am going through these changes, wondering whether it really is time for me to die, but not for any of the reasons I used to think it would be.

My boyfriend Eliot's father died suddenly a few months back, at the beginning of spring training, and I think that was the beginning of the end for us. I didn't want to go to the funeral because I hate that kind of rubbing your nose in it and I never liked the guy. He was a terrible father, maybe not as bad as mine but awful enough, and I can't pretend to feel sorrow when I don't. I'm just not a pretend person.

I <u>am</u> too old, Nick, aren't I? And maybe I am no longer beautiful, with my head shaved, even though I shaved it so that I'd be yours alone. I may even be pregnant, Nick, you should know that. And how can I hope you'd treat my child as your own when you're a child yourself? Nick, I'm afraid I'll be bad for you. If I've made a deal with the Devil to get you, then how can I be anything but bad for you?

Still, you seem so invincible, so I don't know, blessed maybe, that no matter how bad I am, it won't destroy us. I guess what you are for me is the freedom to be bad. I loved Eliot because I trusted him to bring out the good in me. It was some hidden part of me that he was responding to, or maybe some part he just made up off the top of his head, but I believed in what he made up. You know what I mean?

You probably don't know. I don't think I know myself, and I'm running out of room here. No time to go on a riff about Eliot. Why should you care about him? Trust me, he's no competition, not in your league. You'd probably like him if you knew him. Everyone likes Eliot! But that's because he tries too hard to please. At least he's tried too hard to please me. I'd erase all the stuff I said about him, just erase him from my life entirely like I want to do with my father and move on, but I can't. He's too much a part of me. And here I am with ink all over my fingers from this lousy, leaky pen, and I haven't said what I wanted to say.

Nick, my sweet invincible angel, I just want to say that if I don't die for you—like I know Eliot would die for me—it's not because I love someone else more. I still love Eliot, but in a different way. And this other guy I just did it with, Choice, I don't love at all. That was just for the hell of it, to help me break free. You're the only one who matters to me now. You're so pure, Nick, and I feel so stained, but I want you so much, I can't help myself!

XXXXXXXXXXXXXXXXX
Joan

As Choice rubs two sticks together to make a fire in the center of his graffiti-ridden jail cell, elsewhere in the city the squeegee man with the baby adds to his fortune at the Houston Street entrance to the FDR Drive and Admiral Dugan takes off for his Gulliver's Island compound in his private plane.

The admiral, flying high off his first Series win, is determined to confront his niece Sheila over her new paramour. Private detectives have informed him that she's gotten herself mixed up with an underworld figure who's hell-bent on stealing their fortune. Mayor Lightly expresses his hopes for America's bankrupt cities, declaring, "We will emerge stronger from this near-death experience. I'm sure of it!"

Meanwhile, Choice's rubbing produces a spark.

The admiral is disappointed to learn that his regular pilot, an anti-Castro Cuban, is sick, but he's glad that the fellow has found his own replacement.

. . .

As Joan inscribes her last kiss, she hears a click and the ringing of little bells. By the time she's given her love and signed off, Sister Sabrina has appeared on the TV screen beside Yankee announcer Al Deep in a postgame replay of their interview, while at the same time entering the Reading Room in her wheelchair preceded by her black cat.

"Look, my *kindern*!" says the gypsy seer. "That's me on TV!"

She puts her mottled hand to her heavily creased cheek, closes her cataracted eyes, and swings her head back and forth like a run-down pendulum. The cat skits across the petrified-wood coffee table, throwing a deck of tarot cards into disarray. They land on Joan's letter, which the cat tries to rip from her.

"Bubba!" says Sabrina, leveling a finger in the general direction of her pet, but then moving it about a foot to the left, a foot to the right, and back to the middle again (either because she has to focus, thinks Joan, or because she's casting a spell with some invisible wand). "*Gey veck!*"

The cat darts beneath the TV.

"Excuse my great-grandmother, Miss Jones," says Sabrina. "When it comes to affairs of such passion as yours, she always wants to horn in. She's had many hard lives."

"I believe it," says Micky, giving the tube another knock to get a better picture. "Life's hard all over. But listen, Ma. I want to formerly introduce you to someone who needs your help. Joan, this is Sister Sabrina, who can appear in two places at once, communicate with the dead, and do a hostess of other incredulous stuff. Sabrina, this is Joan, not Miss Jones, but Joan. I don't know her last name. We were intimated from the start."

Sabrina looks unsteady to Joan, as she rises from her wheelchair. In her black shawl and red sack dress, the gray-haired gypsy sways back and forth like she's about to topple.

"Would you like some help?" asks Joan, starting to her feet, but Sabrina motions her to stay where she is.

"How very thoughtful you are, my dear," says the gypsy. "Yet I am not so interested in movement at this moment." She tilts her head to smile. "I would rather look at you a second longer. Such lovely red hair. Hmm."

Joan thinks she feels it, as long as it ever was, tied tightly at the base of her neck and fanning out across her back, but when she reaches up to touch it, she finds only her blue turban.

"You shouldn't hide it," says Sabrina. "Any more than you should hide what you feel."

Joan hears a bark and turns toward the window, where the dog has his paws up on the sill, his master beside him, not much taller. What do they see out there?

"Alvin's such a nice boy," says Sabrina. "I know his mother. He comes from good stock. It's not wrong for you to feel sorry for what he's going through."

"You don't mean Eliot, do you?" says Joan, knowing she does, but how much does she know? Assume she knows everything. This is a good witch, right? The Good Witch of SoHo, at your service. Joan's never seen more lines on anyone's face, yet she finds her more attractive than her own mother, with her total absence of wrinkles, her artificially stretched skin. She's the opposite of your mother in every way, seeing nothing on the surface but so much that's underneath. The question is, can she help you?

She reminds Joan a little of her high school art teacher, Ms. Godunov, who first introduced her to dadaism, cubism, and surrealism, and whose life story was an inspiration. Born just before the dawn of the twentieth century, she escaped persecution as a child in czarist Russia by stowing away on an America-bound freighter. And then, as a young woman, she returned to help Lenin and the Bolsheviks seize power, acting as a battlefield nurse. That's where she met her lifelong lover, Gertrude, another nurse, and in the immediate aftermath of the Russian Revolution, when it seemed as though the arts would thrive there, she began to paint, while Gertrude wrote poems. An artist-poet combo, Joan recalls, just like you and Eliot. And one that lasted forever, defying conventions all the way. It can be done!

It didn't take long, though, for the pair to sour on Russia's prospects, deciding that Paris was the better place to be. And what a place Paris of the 1920s was! The creative center of the world, Joan thinks, a place of unparalleled artistic innovation, before or since, and her teacher was right there in the epicenter, Montparnasse, about the same age you are now. That alone would be an experience worth selling your soul for, but there was more, years later, after fighting underground against the Nazi puppets, when she came back to America and became part of the New York school of abstract expressionists, just as the city was coming into its own as a creative mecca.

She achieved only modest success as a painter, but she was an awesome teacher and spiritual advisor to Joan after her parents' divorce, at a time when she desperately needed the advice, as she feels she does now. Ms. Godunov lived with Gertrude in SoHo not too far from here in a loft filled with her works. Joan can still remember the time she took her there, regaled her with stories, walked her through her gallery, enticed her to smoke her first joint. She and Gertrude seemed so loving. She wonders now what kind of bumps their relationship had along the way. Did they ever break up, have affairs with others? She never thought to ask at the time, keeping their conversations focused on art. It was a blow when she retired after Joan's junior year and moved down to Georgia O'Keefe's New Mexico to work with better light. Another good witch. What light can this one shed?

"Mit the beard. That's Eliot?" says Sabrina, yawning.

"He had a beard," says Joan. "But he shaved it."

"And for this you left him? Tch. Tch." The gypsy shakes her head. On the wall behind her, Joan sees a print she recognizes as Chagall's *I and the Village*, which he painted in Montparnasse during that magic period. Or maybe a little before; she can't remember the date. There's a Russian landscape with symbols from Russian folklore, images from his hometown—a church, houses, villagers, with some of the houses as upside down as she feels. Below are faces of a man, believed to be Chagall himself, and a lamb, which meet in the middle, their pupils connected by a faint white line—as though they are seeing into one another's souls, it seems to Joan. She's always liked Chagall, his grounding in peasant tales, his bold, bright colors, his childlike playfulness. And this is a painting Ms. Godunov introduced her to. A good sign.

"Well," says Joan, "it's not that simple."

"It's never simple," says Sabrina. "And yet I never left a husband. Not a one."

"How many have you had?"

"Nine."

"Wow. A whole lineup."

"I've lived a long time. But of course, the husbands were all the same man. Different names, different guises, but always the same. He's very clever, but in the end, he gives in and comes back home to his *liebchen*. I see him in the car right now, on his way."

Looking out the window facing west toward the sunset, Micky sees a Dalmatian not unlike his own lift his leg to a fire hydrant, while a tall blond guy with an untucked Yankee shirt and cap stands by his side with the leash.

Could it be?

They walk across the street toward a woman with red hair, who's pushing an old woman in a wheelchair across from the other direction. A pink Bentley cruises down the block with a guy who looks like Raoul at the wheel, and a plump, white bald man in a business suit laughing in the back seat. From the other direction, a Burger Boat delivery van approaches, which also seems like it has Raoul at the wheel. It looks like the vehicles are going to crash head-on, smashing the pedestrians in between, but then the dog breaks his leash and races toward the women, his master close behind, and they push the women out of harm's way while the vehicles swerve, and disaster is averted.

"I don't believe it," says Micky, turning from the window. "You know what I just saw?"

"Yes," says Sabrina. "A big crash. The first of many. Followed by a wave of cockamamie mergers. That's the way America works."

"Not quite," says Micky, "but a couple who looked like you two were almost creamed. I think Raoul was behind the wheel, both wheels, a fancy car and a big delivery truck."

"Raoul Wo," says Sabrina. "The noted underworld figure. Gambling, drugs, guns, prostitution. Be on guard with that man, he's nothing but trouble." She points her finger at Joan, then moves it toward Micky. "Accompanied by his boss, perhaps?" she asks. "Bald, round-faced, a mole on his nose. A touch of the peasant though he dresses as a businessman?"

"Don't know about baldy, except that he looked like he was having fun," says Micky. "But I know Raoul. He's the guy I killed at Joan's place. Of course, there were mythigating circumstances, his being in all possibility dead before and all."

"I forgive you," says Sabrina. "More than I forgive myself." She purses her lips and closes her eyes. "Oy, what to do, what to do about that girl," she says.

"Who, me?" asks Joan.

"Such a daughter I raised! She gets rid of babies like they're going out of style. First her own, then Mirlanda's, and now see how my baby loses her very self, leaping right into the Devil's cauldron. Is it too much to ask that she think twice, or even think at all, before taking such an awful leap?"

"Don't worry about Crystal, Ma," says Micky. "Me and Joan are the ones who the Devil has it in for."

"I am rich in worries," Sabrina rests a palm on Micky's cracked leather newsboy cap. "And most of all where you are concerned. I fear all your fears a thousand times over, Mickala."

"I'm not all that afraid," says Micky, stepping out from under her touch.

"All your guilt, Joan, weighs more heavily on my stooped shoulders than fifty sacks of gold."

"I can't help feeling guilty," says Joan. "I feel like I started all this when I rejected Eliot. And the chaos I brought to our relationship, I brought to the rest of the world, you know? Was it me who laid out the red carpet for the Devil? Did I invite him into my dreams?"

Sister Sabrina is slow in replying. In fact, she's asleep on her feet, and no amount of shaking will wake her either, according to Micky, who's seen her go like this before. Micky looks out the window to see the approaching Bentley on the street, though now it has Mayor Lightly's "Save the Cities" banner draped over its passenger side. In the middle of the intersection where the near crash occurred, the Bentley stops and a voice blasts over the loudspeaker, "I'm mad at you, Joan, so mad I tore the Swan's pictures from your walls. You don't think about me enough no more. You have too many second thoughts. I'm lonely, and Swan's lonely too. He's ready as ever to take you in his arms, but you're not ready to be taken, why not? You'd rather go home to your boyfriend who's not home. He's off chasing Sheila Dugan. He doesn't care about you at all. Just look out the window."

Joan can't look out the window. She's bent on waking Sabrina, for fear she'll fall on her face. Even if the old gypsy hasn't been much help, even if you feel like despite the show of concern she really disapproves of you, or would if she knew everything, which she supposedly does but just can't keep it all straight, passing all that she should find negative about you onto her daughter (and isn't that weird, the gypsy scapegoating), you'd rather not see her glasses cracked, her long hooked nose busted, lips split open.

"Señor Ensign, he's changed," says the voice over the loudspeaker. "He killed Art, and that changed him."

"Don't listen to him, Joan," says Micky from the window, not liking what he sees. The delivery van is approaching again.

"Eliot killed Art Popov?" says Joan.

"Sí," says Raoul over the loudspeaker. "And soon you'll kill the good Sister."

"You killed Art," says Joan. "Eliot couldn't."

"Maybe I helped in my own little way," says Raoul.

Sabrina stops in the middle of a light snore to say, "Everything centers around you, my dear. I just met your father. Charming man, so handsome, mit the red hair! Says he loves you, but I'm not so sure."

Tell me something I don't know, Joan thinks. "I'm sure. He doesn't. I heard he disappeared. Where'd you track him down?"

"Actually, he came to me," says Sabrina.

"Don't tell me he's here!" Joan gasps.

"Here." She points to the middle of her forehead, like she has a third eye. "He's looking for something, or someone he lost. He's lost so much."

"Well, if he's looking for me, tell him to forget it," says Joan. "I've got too much going on to deal with his problems. He deserved to lose everything for all the harm he did to his family, much less the world. Just tell him to go back where he came from and stay disappeared. Can you do that for me, please? Can you make him go away?"

"Only you can do that," says Sabrina. "Fathers can be strange. In gypsy lore, there was Abraham, a good man, but a terrible father. Ready to sacrifice at the drop of a hat his dutiful son Isaac, who reminds me of your Alvin."

"Trust me," says Joan. "My father was not a good man. And it's Eliot, not Alvin. Do you know where to find Eliot?"

"Already sacrificed," says Sabrina, "*in der kopf...*" She taps her temple. "But at the last moment spared . . ." Her voice trails into another snore.

Joan shakes her. "Where's Eliot? Can I get to him? Please tell me. I want him back. I want him to protect me."

"Such a mess you've made of life, my daughter," says Sabrina.

"You're not helping me," says Joan. "I can see it's a mess. But what the hell do you expect me to do about it?"

"Exactly what my husband used to say," says Sabrina. "Who said that?"

"Me, Joan French. I came to you for guidance. Guide me!"

It *is* him, thinks Micky, looking out the window at the pitcher walking his dog across the intersection. And here comes Joan again, pushing Sabrina in a wheelchair from the other direction. The car and the truck have circled back, headed right toward them. It's for real this time, he knows it. A certain collusion unless he stops it.

"Joan," he shouts, rushing out the door with his dog. "Nick Spillage is outside. And he's in danger!"

Joan lets go of the gypsy and rushes out after them.

The streetlights dim, and then go dark, as Lower Manhattan suffers a blackout.

14

GOING DOWN

Raoul tears down the Spillage pictures from Joan and Eliot's apartment, balls them up under Art, and sets them ablaze. Art goes up in flames like a Vietnamese monk protesting the war.

.   .   .

Admiral Dugan, circling the city in his private plane, senses it begin to descend and wonders what will happen to the Yankees if he dies. He wishes he'd changed his will when he had the chance, before his niece hooked up with that underworld character. She'll ruin them, he thinks, as surely as she'll ruin herself.

"Don't worry, Señor Admiral," says his pilot through the intercom. "The team is in good hands. Getting ready to take a big dive, just like you and the system that made you."

.   .   .

The last thing Micky remembers as he hops on his Dalmatian and flies into the collision, hoping to save Joan and Sabrina from being crushed in the middle, is seeing another guy on a Dalmatian flying straight toward him.

. . .

Walking around the block in search of the lieutenant's car with just the moon to guide them, Eliot remembers the last blackout he lived through, at the beginning of the summer. He and Joan were watching *2001: A Space Odyssey* at the movie theater on 12th Street in the West Village when everything went dark. It was right at the end, when the Star Child in its embryo was floating through the cosmos, a symbol of rebirth following the victory over Hal, the evil computer. What a mind-blowing scene, Eliot recalls, the kind that really makes you think about where you stand in the total scheme of things. The good news is that being a Stanley Kubrick fan, he had seen it a few times before, just as he'd gone to multiple showings of Kubrick's other masterpiece, *Dr. Strangelove*, so the experience wasn't completely ruined. This was a rare case, in his view, of the movie being better than the book. Joan loved it too, particularly the long opening sequence with the monolith that relied on images and music rather than words to set the scene. She loves Creation stories, he thinks. Also shares his love of great journeys filled with adventure, like the epic poems of Homer he used to read to her in bed. They intended to see the film again, though they hadn't gotten around to it.

In the blacked-out theater, after a few minutes of waiting for the movie to resume, a disembodied voice came over the loudspeaker, saying, "Don't panic. Stay in your seats. There's no place to go out there. Everything's dark." Of course, everyone in the packed theater took that as a signal to rush for the exit, and they almost got trampled in the stampede. Walking home to the sounds of store windows being shattered by looters and the occasional bursts of gunshots, almost brushed by shrapnel from an exploding garbage can, they held tightly to one another to avoid being separated. Just another night in the Big Rotting

Apple, he'd joked at the time. And he remembers her giving him a squeeze. We were so close!

He wonders if she's thinking about that moment now, too. Probably not, the way things are going.

When they find the car, the detective hands Eliot his keys. "You drive, son," he says. "I need a rest. You know the way to Kennedy, right?"

· · ·

In the burnt-out remains of an East Village tenement apartment, Raoul props an ancient Hermes typewriter, shrouded in soot, on the small, charred carcass of what was once a cable spool, later a loving couple's kitchen table, and gives a swift kick to Art.

"Up you go, comrade," he says. "You've got stories to write. Deadlines to meet."

Art types his first posthumous *Mercury* headline:

DUGAN DOWN!
YANKEE OWNER NOSE-DIVES INTO
CONEY ISLAND FUN HOUSE

15

WHITE RABBIT

A big, orange moon rises over Manhattan as Eliot, at the wheel of Lieutenant Gus's white Volkswagen Rabbit, strokes the stubble on his beardless chin, while the detective snores lightly at his side. He recalls that as a boy he once asked his parents if he could have a rabbit as a pet. Not a practical suggestion for their small apartment. But a natural one considering his love of rabbit stories, including his mother's favorite children's book, the one written by a mathematician, *Alice's Adventures in Wonderland*. The White Rabbit in that book leads Alice on her adventure, which Eliot's parents insisted had a certain logic to it. The Rabbit knew something, but he wasn't revealing. He was there, and then he wasn't. Alice needed to figure things out on her own, which she managed to do, more or less, as Eliot remembers.

Then there was Brer Rabbit, who always managed to outsmart Brer Fox. And of course, Bugs Bunny, who always managed to outsmart Elmer Fudd. Eliot remembers dressing as Bugs one Halloween, chomping on his carrot, spitting out wisecracks. He remembers using his rabbit speed to outrun the playground bullies. If only his current nemesis Raoul was as slow as they were, or as gullible as Brer Fox, or as dim-witted as Fudd.

Joan was not that into rabbits, Eliot thinks. Horses were more her thing. She had one in Connecticut, he recalls, but gave him up when she gave up on her father. Once she turns off, she really turns off. Is it your turn now for a complete disconnect?

That's hard for him to believe. The good times were just too good. And one of those times did involve a rabbit, Alice's White Rabbit, with Grace Slick, one of Joan's faves, soaring through Jefferson Airplane's surrealistic anthem in one of the best concerts they ever attended. It was during their "On the Road" phase, fall of '68, when they hitchhiked across the country to San Francisco, with a side trip south to the beach at Big Sur. They just woke up one morning and decided they had to go, had to experience the real Fillmore, the original Fillmore, as opposed to its pale East Coast imitation. Amazing, he thinks now, how they could pick up and go off on such great adventures together without a second thought, how natural it all seemed, their first year in love. A poster of that concert hung on their wall for years, until buried by Joan's Swan collage.

All the stars were aligned for that West Coast trip, and they were out in full force when you camped out on the Big Sur beach. Remember guiding her through all the constellations you knew from the time you studied astronomy as an early teen, inspired by Kennedy's race to beat the Russians to the moon? It was the most you've ever seen outside the planetarium, and she got off on your enthusiasm, really got off that night, making love on the sand. Just like you got off on her introducing you to Hieronymus Bosch at the San Francisco MOMA's special *Origins of Surrealism* exhibit. She was over-the-moon excited about Bosch's *The Garden of Earthly Delights* being on loan from the Prado in Madrid at precisely the time you visited, and lovingly took you down the path from this postmodern medieval artist to Miró, Dalí, and her other favorites. And then how about the good fortune of bumping into legendary Beat publisher Ferlinghetti himself at his City Lights bookstore, where you bought a signed copy of his poetry collection, *A Coney Island of the Mind*, that you read to her in bed that night. Incredible!

Where is she now? he asks himself. What's going through her head? Could she possibly be as down on him as the woman in the press conference, her evil twin? And could he possibly be as down on her as his inner Hartline proclaimed? No. It's all Raoul. He's manipulating both of us, but to what end? Whatever it is, it's not good. The probability is, it's colossally bad. Satanic. Total overthrow of the world as we know it.

The Satanic Vanguard, what's it really all about? He thinks of other radical groups bent on turning the world upside down. The Symbionese Liberation Army, which kidnapped heiress Patty Hearst, then converted her to their cause—like Joan? The Weather Underground, which blew up a building not too far from here, in the West Village, owned by a Mad Man buddy of Joan's father. "The sins of the fathers," she said at the time. She really hated her old man. But he fought with his own father over that one, arguing that their objectives were noble—ending U.S. imperialism, achieving racial justice—even as he agreed their tactics were abhorrent. King George called him naïve for thinking they were anything more than nihilists.

Rather than heading east for the FDR Drive to get to Kennedy airport, he considers taking a little detour west to another West Village landmark, the Bleecker Street home of another of his favorite superheroes, Dr. Strange. The Master of the Mystic Arts, Sorcerer Supreme, would no doubt be helpful if he truly existed, Eliot thinks, since Raoul is starting to feel a lot like Strange's archfoe Nightmare.

Nightmare, Lord of the Dream Dimension, has the power to infect your subconscious, play with your emotions, bring your worst fears to the surface. Is that where I am now, Eliot wonders, in Nightmare's Dream Dimension? As he fumbles with the car's stick shift, never having properly learned to use a manual transmission, it feels like he's at the blurry border of dream and reality. If he can just shift the gears in the right way he can shift over to the reality side, he thinks. But he screws up, the car stalls, and he has to start over again.

Horns are honking all over in the snarled-up traffic, sirens wailing in the distance, the streetlights flickering like strobes as the city struggles to emerge from the blackout. None of this rattles Gus, who looks content as he continues to snore away. He's the one who's dreaming, thinking he'll find answers on Gulliver's Island. Where will you find them? Don't have a clue.

You've been in this state before, he thinks, under the influence of LSD, but you swore off hallucinogens years ago, so that's not it, unless Raoul managed to spike your Burger Boat soda. Wouldn't put it past him, but no, it's not that. You would feel the drug surging through you if it were. You *know* that experience, there was a time you embraced it. But the days are long gone when you intentionally tried to get outside yourself, expand your consciousness, enter a new realm of being. What's going on now is different, against your will. The question is, do you bear any responsibility for setting all this in motion?

The answer, Eliot thinks as the car lurches forward, is yes. Something concrete happened to bring Raoul into the world, some astral door opened that enabled him to bring his mischief here. It wasn't the hazards of capitalism or the collapse of New York City that opened the door, though they may have unlocked it, and set the stage. It was something you did, or something Joan did, or something you both did, that blew it open. It started in your dreams. Sure, it would be helpful to have Dr. Strange at your side to cast a counteracting spell, but you don't. You just have to ride it out, let the Rabbit lead you.

He takes his hands off the steering wheel, looks for a sign. Like a Ouija board, it moves ever so slightly, counterclockwise. Going with the flow, he turns the Rabbit east, toward the FDR.

· · ·

The squeegee man at the entrance of the FDR drive puts his diapered baby on the hood of the Rabbit as the lights all over the city come back on and taps on the passenger side window while coughing blood into the rag he's been using to wipe windshields. As the roused lieutenant rolls his window down, the baby crawls across the hood to Eliot's side and peers in, his pudgy little palms and inkling of a nose pressed against the glass.

Much as he once thought he wanted a baby, Eliot's in no mood for one now. Not with Joan feeling ever more distant. "Please don't look at me like you want me to take you home," he says. "I've left home—yes I have—and I'm traveling far, far away. All the way to Gulliver's Island."

"Aye, lad. And it's a sad, sad tale of misfortune I could spin out for you if you're so inclined to hear," says the squeegee man to Gus.

"I'm all ears," says Gus.

"Sure, and you look like a man of compassion, too. Most uncommon, mate." The squeegee man coughs into his sleeve, then smiles a toothless smile. "Look at the way your son takes to that tot, like he had his share in bringing it to God's earth. Maybe he's made you a granddad yourself, eh? You and old Pops, here, we can relate, can't we."

Cars honk behind them as Gus says to Eliot, "Take the baby off the hood, son, and bring it inside, while the gentleman explains how it came to be with him. Seems to me I've seen it before, or seen someone it resembles."

"It's me own little grandson," says the squeegee man, "me one and only, I might add, born to me one and only daughter, who died on this spot. Fell in with some unsavory characters, Mexican drug cartel. Shot her dead right here."

Gingerly taking the infant, Eliot imagines himself with Joan in a hospital, learning how to hold a baby for the first time. Do you really want this responsibility? Are you really up for it? Not if she isn't. How could you possibly want to bring a child into a world like this? The first thing you're going to say to Joan when you see her again is, "You're right. We're not ready for a family. We're so far from being ready. And I'm totally fine if we're never ready, as long as we have each other. Are you with me?"

"Sí," says the baby, tugging at the windshield wiper, refusing to let go.

As the squeegee man tells his tale of woe to the detective, Gus buys a *Mercury* off a red-haired newsboy. That's right, thinks Eliot, tip the boy handsomely from that fat wad of bills you took from my pocket. Deserves it for looking like he could be Joan's son, which means your son. There you go again! Get off of this kick!

He sees the baby smile, a snaky little grin like Raoul's. He's got Raoul's coloring too, and his eyes. No, wait . . . they're too big, too green. Weren't they small, dark, and narrow a moment ago? Babies' eyes change, any prospective papa should know that. And the smile's gotten bigger, too. It's foolish to think he's Raoul's, tempting though that is. Speaking of fools, though, there's our mayor on the front page, with his new campaign manager in green fatigues at his side.

The squeegee man points at Raoul. "That's him," he says. "My daughter's no-good boyfriend. The one I just told you about, perfessor, who got her killed!"

"So it's professor, is it now," says the gleeful detective. "What do you think of that, son? A fast education."

"I swear on me mother's grave that's the devil who done my daughter in. Just like Sister Sabrina forewarned." He takes the SoHo seer's card out of his pocket and offers it to the lieutenant.

Eliot finally manages to wrench the baby from the windshield wiper, brings him into the Rabbit, and offers him to Gus, so the lieutenant can have a closer look. "Sounds like the man we're looking for," he says. "I'd be willing to bet this little monster is Raoul's son." And how much would you bet the detective will buy that? How much would Mom bet? She always knew the odds.

The baby's eyes widen and look off to the right and above Eliot in the manner of a certain politician he once worked for, while the detective, perusing the *Mercury*, pays no attention. The headline on Page 3 reads:

NEAR MISS FOR MAYOR: VANGUARD LAIR UP IN SMOKE

"Hate to contradict you, son," says Gus. "But I don't think it looks at all like him. My guess is that the baby's the subject of this paternity suit." He points to the page one headline:

HELL-RAISER TO MAYOR: WHY YOU SO HEARTLESS, DADDY?

"The Haitian Hell-Raiser," says the detective. "That's who the mother is. Just look at this face." He folds the paper so the picture is apparent.

"I say we turn around and head over to this Sister Sabrina's to see what she knows about the Vanguard," says Eliot. "Seems to me all roads are leading back there."

"Nope," says Gus. "They still lead to Gulliver's Island."

"But Art came from Sabrina's," says Eliot. "He was hooked up with her daughter. He said Joan was there and she's hooked up with Raoul. This baby's got to be Raoul's. How many clues do you need? And what do you expect to find on Gulliver's Island, anyway? I mean besides Sheila Dugan, who has nothing to do with anything."

"Slot machines, roulette wheels, card tables, craps. Gala entertainment, first-rate meals . . ." Gus smiles his crooked smile. ". . . and the Haitian Hell-Raiser, as you'd know if you read that article closely. Can't dwell on personal tragedies, son, if you want to crack a case. Got to force yourself to concentrate on finding leads. That's the life of a cop."

"Cops!" says the squeegee man. "Give me that baby back! You've got no right to take him from me . . ." He lunges for the tot, but Gus pushes him aside.

"How about I give you a thousand for the kid?" says Gus, flashing his wad of bills.

"This whole story's suspect, if you want to know what I think," says Eliot. He shows Gus the Art Popov byline. "I killed this man, remember?"

"Yes I do," says the detective. "And won't forget. Why are you so afraid of going to Gulliver's Island? Think you'll be drowned in a sea of corruption?"

"Aye," says the squeegee man. "Sailed that sea before, yes I did." He passes up the thousand-dollar bill that Gus offers. "It'll cost you ten."

"Stop trying to analyze me," says Eliot, as he said to his father many times. "I mean I'm allowed to have a different view of the situation, aren't I? It's like justified under the circumstances, and I'd rather not be maligned for it. There are good, solid reasons for our going to Sister Sabrina's."

"Stop being so stubborn," says Gus to Eliot, while handing the squeegee man his ransom. "Seems to me you've got some psychological problems. I wish I could get to the root of them but I'm not your shrink."

"You're a gentleman and a scholar," says the squeegee man, fanning his bills. "And you've got quite a family there, too. Should be proud. But I'd watch out for that lad if I were you. He's a titch on the uppity side."

"Don't I know," says Gus, taking the baby boy from Eliot and bouncing him in his lap, clearly enjoying himself. "Never had one of these before. Drive, son."

16

REAL PUZZLE

Raoul steps out of the fire that Choice made in the center of his cell.

"Hot damn," says the actor. "That's some entrance! Been a long time, Raoul. What've you been up to?"

"No good," says Raoul. "It's not so much fun. Would rather be a papa, like you."

"You're a puzzle," says Choice, sitting cross-legged before the fire in the center of his graffiti-ridden cell. "You're a real puzzle, my man. Know that?"

"Sí," says Raoul, sitting down next to him. He extracts a long, bent twig from his green fatigues.

"How long have you known, or think you've known, that Raoul Junior was misnamed?"

"Long enough."

"Since I left you at my bald momma's place?"

"She's not bald no more." Raoul scrapes bark off the end of the twig with his fingernails.

"You see her lately?"

"See her right now."

"Where? In the fire?"

"No. I see a no-good witch in the fire, going to town with her latest flame. Take a look, see for yourself." He makes a sharp point of the greenish-white pulp.

Choice fingers beads of sweat atop his smooth skull, ringed now at the temples and around the back of his neck by sparse stubble. No razors for jailbirds. Only hours have passed since he went into solitary, but the thought that it might last has wreaked havoc on him. He hasn't played a prisoner since Caliban in *The Tempest*, and never thought much of that part. Prospero was much more to his liking, more in keeping with his sense of self, but that sense is fading as he wastes away.

He's as famished as if he's been on a hunger strike, sporadically chilly despite the fire. Its lemon scent, gaining power as it burns, is making him nauseated, too. He's reluctant to look into its center. Rather, he focuses on the tip of Raoul's twig. "Say, what you plan on doing with that thing?" he asks with a smile to lighten the mood. "It's a bit on the flimsy side for whacking baseballs."

"Fetch me a mushroom from that heap of bones there," says Raoul, looking serious, pointing to a corner of the cell with his twig.

"Whoa. Ain't your slave, man," says Choice.

"Sí. You're my buddy. But you're better off if you do like I say."

Choice climbs to his feet, feeling weak. "Noticed those bones," he says, walking to the corner, "while I read the writing on the walls. Didn't see this big old mushroom though."

It's heavier than it looks. He lugs it back to Raoul, who pokes the green point of his twig into the stem and lifts it as though it were no heavier than a marshmallow, while Choice, sweating profusely, collapses into his former position. Raoul twirls the mushroom over the dancing flames, chuckles. "You've got to see this," he says. "They're really going at it."

"Who?" says Choice.

"Mirlanda and her Angel, the outfielder she dumped you for. You've got to see this crazy peep show!"

"No way," says Choice. "I'm not looking at no damned peep show."

With a slow movement of his right hand, he sweeps enough sweat off his glistening forehead into the conflagration to douse it momentarily, but it comes back with greater vigor. "That's a low kind of activity which has never been my thing. I'm no Peeping Tom and it'd take more than you to make me one."

"Maybe so. But Mirlanda could. She's some kind of witch."

"Hey, don't like to hear that. Especially from you, my man. You're still her lawful wedded spouse, and duty bound to respect her, whether you're the father of her child or not. If she was unfaithful, she had good reason, the way you treated her."

"She don't know what's good for her. Or who's good for her."

"I know this woman, and she's no witch."

"You don't see her like I see her." The mushroom drips, distorts as Raoul twirls it. "She's in league with that know-it-all gypsy, and you know about these gypsies, right? They're all bloodsucking witches, think they're the chosen ones. Pull all the strings for their Free Market God—a curse on mankind. We need to wipe them off this planet, end this oppression."

"Damn, Sam. Where'd you build up this ire?"

"I told you, Mirlanda put me through hell. And now you. Don't it make you mad what she's doing with that Yankee?"

"How about I get mad at you? That work? Got a notion you planted this feeling in me. Never had it until you came, until I caught a whiff of those lemons."

"It's her scent, lemons."

"Never did me wrong before."

"Neither did she. But she's doing you wrong now." Bubbles form on the mushroom's head, pop. Sections char. "While you suffer, she's having a ball. Go on, see for yourself."

"Told you before, I'm not gonna play Peeping Tom. Part don't jive with who I am." In the old days, he thinks, when times were better, he could be more selective about the parts he took. He's played all manner of human beings, complex characters, conflicted souls—and he's played them well, digging deep inside to make them come alive. He *lives* his characters, that's his method. And he's got great range. But he prefers heroes—even antiheroes—to outright villains, though he's played some memorable ones. And that's because he gets so into them, it's difficult to get out when he goes off stage. The villainy shows up here and there, like it did at the ballpark, when his inner Iago lashed out at the pitcher. The impulse took over. That's just who he is.

Raoul withdraws the mushroom from the fire, blows on it to cool it off. "I've got a new part for you," he says. "Yankee right fielder. You take the place of Angel." He sniffs the mushroom as though it were a rose. "Want a bite?"

Famished as he is, Choice resists. "Me? Play for the Yankees? You're out of your mind!"

"Eat this mushroom. It will make you more powerful than you've ever dreamed. Hit the longest homers ever."

"I don't need any more power. I'm comfortable in my own skin. I just need to escape. This jail's making me sick."

"You're an actor, you need a big stage. I'll give you the biggest stage ever."

"All the world's a stage," says Choice, remembering an old line. "And all the men and women merely players."

"I'll make you the player who matters the most. Put you in position to throw the Series. Turn the Yankees into big losers. How's that sound?"

Choice flicks more sweat into the fire. "Hmm," he grunts. "Maybe."

"No maybe. Take the deal."

"I'm thinking."

"No more thinking. Take a bite." He shoves the mushroom under Choice's nose.

"What's in this for you, Raoul? What do I need to give you to make this deal happen?"

"Just your soul."

"Just???" Choice pushes the mushroom away. "My soul's important, man."

"I'm not asking, compadre."

. . .

Mayor Lightly, absorbed in his *Mercury* in the JFK waiting area for his flight to Gulliver's Island, where he hopes to raise campaign funds and perhaps something more from Yankee heiress Sheila Dugan, doesn't notice Eliot, his police escort, and Baby Wo enter. The *Mercury* headline reads:

MAYOR LIGHTLY EXPOSED!
HAITIAN HELL-RAISER RELEASES DAMNING PIX

The mayor has never met the Hell-Raiser, but you wouldn't know it from the spread, in which he appears to be having the time of his life. The pictures look so real, he thinks, and she looks so wonderful, he imagines what life would be like with Mirlanda at his side. Would the Political Gods tolerate such a relationship? Could he still win the race? It's already out there, how could it get worse?

Lightly knows he's in for a tough fight against Nixon, despite the desperate state the country has fallen into under the incumbent's watch. The master of dirty tricks has a talent for pinning the blame on others, on painting his opponents as devils who would only make things worse. He's already labeled the mayor a Communist. Now he's added Satanist to the line of attack. And polls show that the attacks are having an impact. He's defining you as a bad guy, the mayor thinks. You have to do something dramatic to change the narrative and win this contest.

Adding Spillage to the ticket as a replacement for that bland senator from Illinois is one possibility, if the Yankees win the Series. Nothing like a hero to jazz things up. Nixon would never have gotten anywhere if he hadn't attached himself to Eisenhower, the war hero. He's still basking in that glow all these years later. And keeping his own war going to energize the "rally around the flag" gang. Sure, the anti-war sentiment in the country is rising, but is it enough? Are any policy changes enough? Not if you lose on character.

This make-believe with the Hell-Raiser is just another attempt at character assassination. But if all you do is deny it, you're still on your back foot and you won't get anywhere. Soon he'll find another indiscretion to throw at you, maybe even a real one. They're out there of course. Every politician has his share. No man is perfect; just look at JFK. But he had looks, charm, money galore, which reminds you of why you need Sheila, the purpose of this trip.

Sheila could help with cash, Spillage with charisma. And Mirlanda, could she help, too? If you just take that bull by the horns, own it, you come off as strong. You come off as having heart, the capacity to pursue love, wherever it takes you. And you give your young, multiracial coalition of Nixon-haters a fresh jolt of energy to take to the streets, the phone banks, the knocking on doors. Plus, you could have an amazing time campaigning with this captivating woman—the happy warrior!

Something to think about, that's for sure. You must ask your campaign manager what he thinks.

. . .

Settling down in his seat to wait for their flight, the lieutenant has so much fun bouncing Baby Wo on his knees that he doesn't notice the mayor and his entourage. Eliot notices, though. He also notices a wink from Raoul at the bar with Ms. Jones.

. . .

A dead reporter, under the gun, writes:

CHAOS CITY!
DUGAN BLAZE RAGES AS BIG APPLE
GOES DARK

The aftershocks of Admiral Dugan's Coney Island nosedive continued to multiply today, as volunteer workers from all over New York City united behind their shrunken corps of firefighters to try to extinguish the Fast-Food King's final flames.

Just as he exported his special brand of poison to hungry Third World people starved for real nourishment, the world's foremost Yankee imperialist seems dead set on exporting his private hell to all New Yorkers, with his raging fire threatening to extinguish one of the last remaining fun spots in this hellish metropolis.

And to top it off, with debris from his wrecked plane getting tangled in power lines, the Dugan dive triggered a massive blackout, sending all of the Big Apple into darkness and vehicles crashing headlong into each other from all directions. Among the worst of the calamities was a monster pileup in Lower Manhattan precipitated by—you guessed it—one of Dugan's Burger Boat delivery vans.

"Sorry," says his editor, ripping the article from the typewriter, balling it up, and throwing it into the burnt-out closet where he once held a presidential candidate captive.

"What do you mean, *sorry?*" asks the reporter. "I was just getting going. You're destroying my flow."

"I don't like your style." The editor paces in his green fatigues. "Don't like it at all. Doesn't click."

"You asshole. I made a name for myself in this town with my style. I've got millions of readers who can't wake up without their daily dose of my features." He stands, stretches.

"Better if you don't wake them. Be the last dream they have before they wake." He twirls his lit Havana between his fingers. "This will have more far-reaching impact."

"Sure. But how do you propose I do that?"

"Be more subtle."

"What?" Art paces. "And bombard them at the same time with this Communist claptrap?"

"Satanist."

"What's the difference?"

"There's a subtle difference."

Art thinks about how hungry he is. And horny. And dead. Three for three.

"Look," he says, "I'm trying here. But you've got the wrong guy. I'm a die-hard Nixon man. Law and order all the way."

"That's okay. I'm a Nixon man, too. For now. The payoff comes later."

"You're a walking contradiction."

"Sí," laughs Raoul. "You got that right." He puffs on his cigar. "Now get back to work. And remember, you're not writing just to sell papers like you used to. You're writing to mold consciousness. Mass consciousness. I'm giving you a great opportunity. This should make you happy."

17

GULLIVER-BOUND

"Who am I," thinks Eliot, in the wake of his beaning against the top of the Gulliver Island–bound plane's portal. The knock was caused by an unseen stiff-arm to his back as he started to turn in the direction of the gunshot he assumes was fired at Mayor Lightly, two behind him in line on the ladder. But the shot hit Lieutenant Gus Berkley instead. And as the cop went down, Ms. Jones sprang into action, snapping up the baby that Gus was holding and hustling the mayor off the ramp, while Raoul shoved Eliot inside and closed the door behind him.

Walking gingerly toward his seat on the empty plane, a hand to his throbbing head, Eliot dizzily ticks off the names of his father, mother, and all those with whom he's lately come into contact, their relationship to him and one another (certain, rumored, or merely imagined), in order to thoroughly establish his identity.

He's never flown on a plane before, though he did once take a magic carpet ride with Joan, zooming on acid in the good old days. At least that's what it felt like. They were testing out waterbeds at a showroom in Chelsea, not serious about buying, just out for the experience, and he can still remember the one they liked best. It had a pale blue base, the color of her eyes. Make a wish, he thinks. She's back. It's just like before. Only it's not. It can't be. Won't ever be again. You can't put the genie back in the bottle.

The problem is, he thinks, they flew too high, too close to the sun, like Icarus. Eight miles high, like the Byrds song. They were too much in love, two souls melded together, finding bliss in each other while the world crumbled around them. It wasn't sustainable, not in this world of planned obsolescence. Some deity got jealous—God or Satan, Zeus or Hades—and opened the door for Raoul to exact retribution.

Still, it's okay to be angry at Joan, he thinks, for doing the deed that caused the fall from grace. She ate the apple, after all, by making it with Choice. He saw her, or her evil twin, gnawing away at it ferociously back at their apartment! He has no doubt now that she cheated on him, no point imagining she didn't. The bump on the head has knocked some sense into him. Whatever devilish impulse possessed her, whatever you did to deserve it, she shouldn't have done it. Not without giving you even the slightest clue that she was ready to take such a dramatic step. Well, I suppose Spillage was a clue. And there were probably tons of others that you missed, Sherlock. Still, she owed it to you to be more direct, to give you a chance to change what was bothering her before taking the leap. Okay, you want me to change? I'll change big-time. You won't recognize me at all. I'll find someone else, get even. How's that?

He thinks of the superheroes from his youth who were changelings. Some, like the Human Torch, could control their changes, decide when they wanted to deploy their powers. Others, like the Hulk, didn't have that control. Dr. Bruce Banner became the big green monster when he got too angry. Your issue's the inverse. You can't get angry enough. Not anymore.

"Hey bozo. Want to buckle up? The plane's taking off," says a flight attendant who looks like Ms. Jones. But she couldn't be, Eliot thinks, because she ran off with the mayor and the baby when the cop got shot. He feels bad about the cop, who reminded him of his father, even more now that they met the same fate, succumbing to random violence. But it's liberating, too, removing an implicit threat, a witness to the crime.

He goes back through his relationships, like counting sheep, to take his mind off his throbbing skull. He remembers his mother putting ice on his forehead, the time he fell off his bike when learning to ride. His mother, the mathematically minded card shark, who always came out ahead on her Vegas excursions. Her spirit is with you now as you head to Gulliver's Island. Why should you be afraid of taking this trip? This was the cop's idea, not yours, but there's no going back. You're going to win lots of money, find a new woman. You're a free man, get into it.

But you're a lonely man, too, he thinks. Never felt so all alone. No mother, no father, no baby, no Joan. You still need to find her, he tells himself. Your one true love. Your soulmate. Give her the chance she should have given you. Rescue her from the underworld. Win her back. Your mother would want that. She loved Joan too, despite King George's opposition.

He's confused. He has a splitting headache. He doesn't know what to think. "Do I know you?" he says to the flight attendant, as she helps him with his seat belt.

"How could you?" she says. "You don't even know yourself."

He drifts off to sleep as the plane takes off.

* * *

Joan, semiconscious on the street outside Sister Sabrina's, feels embarrassed by the blood that has soaked through her peasant dress for all to see. Not that a crowd has gathered by the wreckage—yet—but she can see them in her mind's eye. She can hear them milling about. And she knows they're not going to do anything but gawk as the blood continues to flow. Like the famous do-nothing witnesses to the stabbing of that Kitty Genovese woman in Queens, they're not going to lift a finger to help her. They just don't care. She's nothing to them, just a spectacle, another victim of New York's decay. Lying here next to a pile of uncollected garbage. Nobody cares—except Eliot. Where is he?

She remembers the way he took care of her when her appendix ruptured and she had to have it removed, the only time she ever needed surgery. Took her to the emergency room at the closest hospital, filled out the paperwork, got her admitted. They wouldn't let him stay with her unless he could prove he was related—damned bureaucrats—but he managed to fool them, coming up with a fake ID. Big Brother! And there he was when she woke after they cut it out, handing her a little stuffed lion he found in the gift shop. A lion to keep her company at night when he had to go, a lion that made her think of him, a Leo. She named it Cabrini after the hospital and had it still, kept it on her pillow at home. It makes her sad to think how she tossed it to the floor after flopping down on the mattress to do her thing with Choice.

Eliot, my Leo, my lionhearted Eliot. Why aren't you with me now? Because I'm a Libra who needs to be free. Who needs to walk on the wild side, like the song we used to sing. A lot of good that's doing me, bleeding to death on the street. Can't you just come back and make this bad stuff go away? Wily Eliot, who beat the bureaucrats, you can beat the Devil too, I know.

He was her hero once, can be again, she thinks. She remembers thinking of him as wily Odysseus when he used to read Homer to her in bed. The cunning Greek who beat the Trojans, who beat the Cyclops, resisted Circe, and found his way home in the nick of time to rescue Penelope before she fell prey to her evil suitors. Well, maybe it's a little late for the perfectly timed rescue, but it's not too late, is it? I still have my soul. I've been tempted but not torched. A little dalliance with this one, a little fantasy with that one. But nothing truly bad. Nothing that can't be fixed.

Unless I really am dying here. She thinks of artists she likes who died in car crashes. Frank O'Hara of the New York school, an abstract expressionist painter and poet, run over by a jeep on a Fire Island beach. Ms. Godunov knew him. Eliot loved his poetry too. Jackson Pollock, who would drip, splatter, fling, and smear paint on his canvases in a norm-defying way she found incredibly appealing, died driving drunk. And then there was one of her favorites, who survived a horrific bus accident, Frida Kahlo.

Frida experienced phenomenal pain, in her body and in her love life, but she survived to create the most astounding art. Joan can see it now, her masterpiece, *The Broken Column*, a self-portrait in which she stands ramrod straight against a cracked and barren landscape, naked from the waist up save for the white straps of a corset that circle her body above and below her breasts, nails protruding from all parts of her and that broken column running straight up her cavernously gashed torso, ending at her chin. Under her unibrow, she stares straight ahead, unflinching, while tears run down her cheeks. Looking right at me, Joan thinks.

She was, without question, the best self-portraitist of all time, in Joan's view. The depths of self-knowledge she showed in her work were astounding. Joan remembers her own unsatisfying attempts at painting herself, at expressing the essence of who she is. She'd never measure up if she spent her whole life trying, even if she lived a long life, which she doubts more than ever she will. She can feel the blood oozing out of her. *Just how bad am I hurt?*

Frida was hurt too in love and survived that as well. Her stormy relationship with the great muralist Diego Rivera lasted more than twenty-five years, Joan recalls, despite constant cheating by both. Diego started it, but she did her share too, including a fling with Eliot's man Trotsky. What a scene it was down there in Mexico City in the 1930s. She's glad they visited the place to catch the creative vibes. Rising above it all, Frida and Diego's passion for each other never died. *So there's hope for us, dear Eliot,* she says to herself.

But do we have that kind of passion? *Sure, we care for one another deeply,* she thinks. She can't imagine anyone ever caring more deeply for her than Eliot. And there will always be a place in her heart for him. But passion? She's a woman who needs to feel great passion in her life.

And she's never felt passion the way she feels for her Swan. Passionate enough to die for him, to trade away her soul.

If I'm going to die here on this stinking garbage-filled street, she thinks, let's just get it over with now. The prospect of dying used to feel intimidating. She was scared when Eliot rushed her to the hospital with her burst appendix. But now it feels like death is going to be a gentle transition, like crossing the border to another country, the way they crossed into Mexico. If anything, she'll be more alive. She'll have Nick! Only the realization is setting in that she won't just have to trade a lock of her hair. She's going to need to sacrifice her relationship with Eliot. For good. That's what the Good Witch of SoHo was hinting at with her talk about Alvin.

The Janis Joplin song "Piece of My Heart" crosses her mind. Why can't you just parcel out the pieces, keep Eliot's piece whole and come back when you need it? And what about the baby he may or may not have given you? Do you have to let go of that, too?

That deed may be done already, she thinks. And it feels horrible, even though she's not sure the baby was ever there. She recalls reading of Frida's devastation when she miscarried and realized that she would never be able to have Diego's child. If she knew she was having Eliot's baby, if she really knew before starting on this journey, would she have changed course? She doesn't know. But she feels deprived that she didn't have that choice.

She wouldn't have had an abortion, that's for sure, she thinks. She believes she should have the right to make that decision, a right that Nixon wants to take away, but if a baby is there, and it's Eliot's, she will keep it, nurture it, love it with all the love she can give. All the love she never got from her own fake parents. The baby would change everything, be the center of your universe, give your life so much more purpose than it ever had before. You can have the baby and still do art, she thinks. No contradiction there. If anything, the experience of motherhood will enhance your art! But Nick, I'm sorry, I just can't die for you if I have this baby. I can't give up two lives. I'd never forgive myself.

Only looking down at her bloody dress, she feels sure the baby's gone, if there ever was one. Now someone's coming toward her in doctor scrubs. Lifting her dress to inspect the wounds. No, it's not doctor scrubs. It's green fatigues—Raoul. The border guard, the one who will guide you to the netherworld. But why should you have any faith he'll do it right? He's tried to kill you twice, she thinks, brutally both times. Said he's just the postman, delivering what you want, what you dreamed. Said he was in your dream with you, burning in Salem, but you don't remember that. He knows things about you, or seems to, but how deep does his knowledge go? Does he see things in you that you yourself don't see? Beware, said the Good Witch. Gambling, drugs, guns, prostitution. He's not a border guard, he's a smuggler. He'll turn you into a sex slave, a drug mule. There's got to be a better route to fulfillment. Nick, I love you so much, but is this really the only way?

The truth is, she's always been a little afraid of going too far with drugs. She saw what the painkillers did to her mother, and she suspected her father was hooked on something too, the speedy way he looked when he'd steal into her room late at night for a cuddle and kiss on her forehead. (Yes, mother. It was only the forehead. I'm not going to lie and say it was something else.) Sure, she smoked weed and did the occasional hallucinogen with Eliot, but tripping was more his thing. She went along for the ride but kept her doses small. And heroin, the drug that killed Janis? She never gave that a thought . . . until now.

Beware of Raoul, she thinks. Listen to the Good Witch. He's bad for you, so bad, bad news, a bandito. Don't let him touch you, don't let him drug you. Don't give him your soul, not for Nick, not for anything. No way. Nothing he promises will come true. He's a bully and a con artist, an Evil Genius, just like Big Daddy. Maybe he's already got his soul. There's something about the way he looked at you when he assaulted you in the apartment, something about that snaky grin, that reminds you of the Mad Man, who's looking for you, according to Sabrina, looking for something he's lost. Go away! But there's also something else about Raoul, some power he has over you, that's impossible to resist. You've gone too far. You're south of the border, in his world, where different rules apply.

She sees a face peeking over her dress, not Raoul. It's worse! It's her mother's boyfriend, the plastic surgeon. Go away, she screams silently. You've got no business down there! All you do is surfaces, just like her. The only place you can take me is backward, to that awful woman, who never understood what I was all about. I'd rather have Raoul. At least he sees inside me, she thinks, even if it's stuff I don't want to face. At least he offers the potential of having my darling Swan.

"Don't worry. It's only me," she hears Raoul say sweetly.

"Uh-huh." She feels relieved, more than she knows she should be. He lifts her head, presses a goblet to her lips and she drinks a fruit punch of sorts, not half bad. Come on, it's thoroughly bad, she tells herself, spiked to death with some ungodly shit, and yet she has a powerful thirst, and it feels warm going down.

As she drinks, she thinks she can make out two bald Russians who look like Khrushchev open the rear door of the Bentley that struck her and chivalrously help two Sabrinas out. They kiss on all four cheeks, engage in some heavy bear-hugging. Then double-talk, sheer double-talk. She can only make out names, and those vaguely, as her mind seems to slip through the seventh, eighth, and twelfth dimensions.

"How . . ." she asks Raoul, whose refreshment's now gone, but whose solicitous fingers linger at the nape of her neck, beneath her thick red hair, "how did Sabrina get into the back seat?"

"Through the windshield," says Raoul, lifting her up off the street. "It was very painful."

"But it doesn't make sense. Nothing makes any sense."

Nothing except that she's definitely been drugged.

"It's okay," says Raoul. "It will all make sense soon. Or maybe not. In the meantime, let's have fun." He carries her to the Bentley.

18

TIME WARP

Sheila Dugan, aka Crystal Belle, casts a series of spells, none of which have their intended effects. Instead of transporting herself to Hollywood, she winds up on Gulliver's Island. Instead of bringing Art to her side, his walrus frame transformed into the Swan's, she brings two Dalmatians and their riders together in a Lower Manhattan collision and blends them into one.

Raoul congratulates her on her first merger. More major consolidations will follow, he predicts. They are sure signs that the last days of the Capitalist God are at hand, hurried along by her subversion of punch-clock time.

"Surely you credit me with too much, darling," she says.

"Of course, I help a little," says Raoul. "So does your fat friend."

She marvels at the way she appears in the mirror behind the bar at her casino cocktail lounge. "Hooray for the home team," she giggles, raising a glass of champagne.

"You're with the visitors now," says Raoul, toasting her.

. . .

Nick "The Swan" Spillage, aka Micky O'Mann, is woken on the street outside Sister Sabrina's Reading Room by the licking of his Dalmatian

Gemini, aka Duke. Checking to make sure all his limbs are intact, he sees a Cuban-Chinese man in green fatigues place a redheaded woman in a bloodied peasant dress into a pink limousine with a smashed-in front hood, and then back away from the pileup. He jumps to his feet and hails a cab before they disappear from sight. "Follow that limerick!" he says to the cabbie—Okorie from Nigeria—determined not to lose his love.

"You mean that limousine?" says Okorie, pointing. "It's a Bentley."

"Whatever," says Nick, dusting off his too-small jeans, which only extend down to just below his knee, and his untucked Yankee shirt, which also feels shrunk. Cap still fits though. He hops into the cab, and his dog jumps in after. "I'm still woozy from the collusion. Step on it, okay?"

. . .

Daydreaming about the Haitian Hell-Raiser, whom he finds more and more appealing the more he thinks about her, Mayor Lightly loses his balance stepping into the Gracie Mansion hot tub his aide with the long red hair has prepared for him.

Falling, the mayor knocks his head against the tiled Tree of Knowledge that forms the left-hand border of the Garden of Eden bathroom mural and blacks out momentarily, but his aide saves him from further distress by propping him up over the water level with her free hand, the other holding a smiling baby. His? Who else's? And what a time he had having it with sweet Mirlanda! He can't marry her soon enough. What a jolt to his prospects for beating Tricky Dick, that coldhearted cretin. America, we've arrived—two for the price of one!

"Whoa there, big guy," says the aide as he stumbles. "Better watch what you're doing. We need you in the game."

. . .

In Lower Manhattan, near the Trinity Church, the cab carrying Nick Spillage pulls over an appropriate distance behind the parked pink Bentley it's been following. Nick rolls his window down to better hear a newsboy who's drumming up business by holding a paper high and shouting:

"*Mercury* Final! Read all about it! Admiral's last will and Old Testament! Gives everything to Sheila, who comments from Gulliver! Special exclusive interview with Sheila! Art Popov on the heiress, on Yanks' defeat in Game Two. Swannie, Angel no-show as Yanks go down to Phillies in 10–0 laugher. Get your up-to-date World Series roundup right here!"

The newsboy vaguely resembles someone Spillage knows, but he can't recall whom. Sounds familiar too.

"Coney Island blaze still raging!" shouts the newsboy. "Fresh off the press, your *Mercury* Final! The return from Katmandu of hot rocker Frenchie Jones! Says she'd love to get it on with Nick 'The Swan' Spillage! Lightly says he'll settle for Vice, if Nick wants the top spot, but where'd the Swan get to?"

"Here," says Nick. "I'm right here."

But the newsboy ignores him, plows right ahead. "Art Popov has conspiracy theories," he shouts. "Let him clue you in! World Series box scores, action pix! Starless Yanks go down 12–zip in Game Three, stomped in second straight Philly masochist!"

"Wait a minute," says Nick. "Just hold your hoses for a second. They just finished Game Two. What's going on here?"

The newsboy continues with his rapid-fire headlines. "Frenchie tells Popov she dreamed of Swannie, says she'll squat in Nick's pad until he comes home! Get the scoop on Frenchie's long trek through lands unknown to the Western World! Frenchie on the Vanguard's latest hijinks! Her fabulous red hair! On what she plans to do to Swan by way of Art! Full color pix! Her baby blues, right here! Get your *Mercury* Final, hotter than hot!"

"Who's this Frenchie Jones?" Nick asks the newsboy. "I never heard of her."

"She's before your time, kid," says the newsboy. "*Mercury* here! Escape from the Tombs!"

"You say you have pictures?"

"See the latest on the mayor and the Hell-Raiser! All the pictures right here!"

"Let me have a quick look."

"Ten bucks and she's yours."

"But I just want to see if . . ."

"Can't touch without paying. I don't have time to play Good Sumerian. Time is money and you're wasting mine. Inflation soars! Get the latest right here!"

"Don't you know who I am?" says Nick, rummaging through his pockets to see if he has cash. "I'm Nick Spillage!"

The newsboy ignores him. "Frenchie whistles, Swan's dog comes! Will Spillage follow? Art has theories. Popov on Gemini, Nick's Dalmatian!"

"This is my Dalmatian, right here," says Nick. "Tell him, Gem." The dog barks and jumps out the window, racing toward the limousine as the pitcher fishes out from his pocket a wad of bills with the name Eliot Howe on it. How did that get here, he thinks. And who's Howe? Is that Howie, the pitching coach?

"Meet Sheila's new boyfriend! Got it right here!"

"Here," says Spillage, forking over a twenty. "Keep the change."

He recognizes Frenchie right away. It's the woman of his dreams.

*   *   *

"Time marches on, but in a *verkakte* way, crazy, thanks to the spells of my out-of-control daughter," Sister Sabrina complains to her black cat, as she straightens her kitchen and lays out a platter of gypsy delicacies in anticipation of receiving a dinner guest. "More instability. The last thing we need. What to do about that girl, Bubba?" she asks the cat. "She's like a toddler who just learned to walk and now wants to touch and experience everything in her new line of sight. She doesn't care what she breaks, not one bit."

The seer settles back in her wheelchair, strokes the cat on her lap and glances at her soundless TV, where she thinks she can make out the two teams on their respective sidelines lowering their caps to their hearts as they await the national anthem. What game is it now, Game Four? It's all a blur, but she knows the key players, her players, are still missing from the Yankee lineup. She's been a fan for what seems like forever, since she first set foot on America's shore at New York Harbor's Ellis Island those many years ago.

"Let's see what happens when they return," she tells Bubba. "Our team is in a hole, and the hole will get deeper, but it's not too deep to climb back, so long as the right people are there to lead the way. God in his infinite wisdom chose these people, just as we were chosen, and who am I to argue? How it plays out with them, will it play out for the world. So we must give them courage, help them see the light, no matter the depths to which they sink. They need us, Bubba! We know from big struggles. We know how the game is played. We've been at the brink before, persecuted by the worst, and we've lived to tell the story. I've got to believe we can do it again!"

"But you don't know for sure," her cat's eyes seem to say. And that's true. There are limits to her knowledge, limits to her power. She can see into the future, but she has her blind spots. She can nudge things along, but she can't control events. People still need to act on their own, face down temptations, make decisions. And seemingly random individual actions can change the course of history, she's aware, just like the butterfly flapping its wings in Brazil can create a tornado that whips through Kansas and sends little Dorothy to the Land of Oz. (It's a joke, Bubba! You remember when we saw the film?)

This she knows. Her husband is determined to make a revolution, to overthrow the existing order. And to pave the way for this revolution, the Yankees must fall. Not just lose, but lose in the worst possible way, on purpose. Through Wo, he's enlisted his daughter in this *verstunkene* scheme.

"It should come as no surprise that she's jumped at the chance," she tells Bubba. "My late-life baby, always keen to catch up, act older, test her powers. I laughed when she was born, remember? And her father laughed too, a wonderful moment. But then he left to fight the next battle, leaving me to raise her on my own. Such a handful, from the start! He never cared for her until he needed her. Still, she yearned for him always, if only as a way to escape her mother. Is this why she fell in love with a man twice her age? She would have grown into a beauty, had she waited, instead of being transformed in an artificial way, with strings attached that she will come to regret. But she was impatient, like always. She had to have it now. She loved her Art, and her Art was enamored with shimmering surfaces, so poof, there you have it. Hello, Sheila. Let's see who you can win over now with your evil charms.

"Really, it was too easy, Bubba. I blame myself for that. But it won't be as easy for the others, I assure you. I know them, I know their souls. Spirited Joan, with her great passions; the persevering Alvin, her super-loyal beau; the unpredictable Choice, who can take on many roles; the marvelous Mirlanda, so brave, who of all of them knows hell best. She made it out intact, she has such strength. What an inspiration she could be if she becomes our First Lady!

"Who am I forgetting? My Mickala, of course, who's become the Swan. My gifted little pitcher, who I knew was special from the moment I found him, wasting away in that awful orphanage. Talk about revolution. He's revolutionized baseball in a way I haven't seen since I watched Babe Ruth become the Sultan of Swat, back in the days when the '20s roared. I saw the Babe's potential early, at *his* orphanage, well before he started hitting homers, just as I saw the Swan's before he threw even one pitch. Don't worry, our Swan will be back to start Game Seven, and he will give it everything he has. This I know.

"I can see him right now, standing on the sideline with his team-mates, Yankee cap over his heart, listening to his lovely, red-haired damsel in distress sing 'The Star-Spangled Banner' in that haunting voice, as she tries to break free of the Devil's grip. Not on the TV, Bubba, don't look there. In my mind's eye. We're at the stadium, both of us, cheering him on. He's committed to winning. He has a big heart. This I know.

"What I don't know is how much he will have left, and whether it will be enough, once Wo has done his work. What I don't know is how far Wo can get with the others on our team. Of their own free will, I know they would never do the Devil's bidding. But could they be forced, tricked, drugged, or hypnotized into doing it? Wo has his ways. Left unchecked, he can cause great damage. We have Angel, of course, but has the playing field become too uneven? Wo is all over the place, controlling the game's flow. I need to convince Nicki when he comes to dinner to stand back just a bit to balance things out. Let us truly see what even a smidgen of free will brings. His revolution will mean nothing if forced by Wo."

A disturbing image comes to her of Wo triumphant, his arms raised high in a victory salute. "Be careful, Joan," she says. "This Wo can be seductive." She strokes her cat. "You see, I'm warning her, Bubba. What? You think it's too late?"

Part
THREE

19

SAINT JOAN IN THE GRAVEYARD

Naked, Joan sleepwalks through the Trinity Church graveyard with Raoul. A Dalmatian follows along. The earth is damp, warm. Through a mist that swirls around her, Joan thinks she makes out a purple-hued forest rimming the graveyard, like stadium seating rims baseball fields.

They're walking in from the bullpen, from the open area—where a vista of Manhattan can be seen in miniature, the skyscrapers brutally jammed to fit—toward the pitcher's mound, home, at the edge of the forest. There are several mounds, actually, where graves have been dug up, coffins sawed through, mangled bodies set loose. The zombies pass in the opposite direction, do-si-doing, their sawed-off heads cradled in their arms like babies.

It's like a scene from one of her brother's horror flicks, Joan thinks. Maybe he can help her find her way through it. She looks around, doesn't see him. Instead, Raoul is urging her to wave to the crowd.

"You're their queen," Raoul says. "Their saint. Their redeemer."

"All that?" asks Joan, incredulous. "You think I can live up to it?"

"Sí. You rule."

So be it, thinks Joan. As their ruler, she longs to be closer to her people. She feels one step removed, perhaps because she still has her head. And all of her hair plus: it trails like a regal train, kept off the ground by the dog.

"Are they so happy because I've come?" she asks Raoul, who has an arm crooked through hers.

"Of course. Embarrassed?"

"Yeah, if you want to know the truth. Why am I the only one undressed?" However, she feels perfectly natural without any clothes. Center stage is the only place to be, she thinks—the big stage, Woodstock. You lock them in like Janis did by singing the blues so harsh yet so very sweet. That's her now. She can hear her in the distance, though she can't make out her form. And accompanying her is a shepherd boy, blowing a ram's horn with all his might. The call to his people—your people, he has your red hair. She sees them gathering, their heads intact.

A funeral? Art's? No, Art is presiding. And that's Eliot's father shoveling in the first dirt. She can feel the tears running down her cheeks. "Is it Eliot?" she asks.

"It's you."

"Then where's he?"

Joan's furious she can't find him, but not for long. For Raoul is stripping, and he's mesmerizing. She touches a hand to his massive chest. At first, lightly with her fingers, then pressing with her palm. Does he have a heart? To the left, yes he does, an alarmingly thumping heart. He possesses a tail too—long, curled, forked. Bunched up in his briefs it must've been so uncomfortable! Unless it just sprang, like his little horns. His tail has wrapped around her legs as a TV cord once wrapped around her neck, but she doesn't mind. It's lifting her, twirling her, making her giddy.

"This is so damned awesome" she giggles, overjoyed to find her hair supports her in the air once his tail has unwound. "It feels so good to be floating above it all."

The Dalmatian is feverishly digging up fresh bones. The funeral is breaking up. The shepherd boy is playing jazz. She turns her head toward him.

"Don't look back," says Raoul. "Look only at me."

Still levitated, Joan looks down at Raoul, expecting an erection, but instead she sees a long syringe she wants no part of. "Hey, what is this," she says, trying to keep above the needle.

Raoul doesn't force her down but spreads her legs open so she's doing a midair split. "Same stuff Janis used," he says with a snaky grin. "It gave her great pleasure."

"It killed her."

"It'll kill you. That's why we're here, right?"

"No," she says, in a moment of clarity. "We're here because you dragged me. Drugged and dragged me, against my will. I mean I consciously made the decision not to come, right?"

"You changed your mind. It's okay."

"No, it's not okay. You changed me. I don't know who I am anymore! But I guess it doesn't matter, 'cause I'm already dead. I died in that car crash. They just had my funeral."

"The car crash only knocked you unconscious. They jumped the gun with the funeral."

"Nice of them."

"They've got what they think is your best interest at heart. They know how much you want to OD."

"Me? I don't want to OD." But you do, he's right, you said you did back on the Bowery. And before, in Salem, only that was a dream. Is this? When you wake up, will you be in Eliot's arms? No, he's working nights, for the baby he wants. For the baby you maybe had but lost. What's the sequence here? Insane: you get so future-oriented that the present is like looking back, which you know you can't risk because you'll turn to salt. You're showing Eliot, right? By creating catastrophe. Setting yourself up to be saved this instant. I'm tied to the tracks, love, can't you see? That big horny choo choo's bearing down hot and heavy.

"Eliot!" she cries. "Help! I'm about to get creamed! Where are you? Move your ass over here!"

Eliot, in the distance, *is* moving his ass, but not in the direction Joan has called for. He's doing it with a fake blonde. Sheila Dugan! How on earth did he hook up with her?

"Stay away from that witch!" she shouts. "She'll destroy you, I swear. She's making you destroy me, and you'll never handle that. I know you, Eliot. I've lived with you, man. And I'm giving you this last chance to show you love me."

"You're such a fickle woman," says Raoul. "I can't keep up with you." Balancing her with his left hand, Raoul pulls a black garter strap out of thin air and reaches up the length of her leg to loop it over her thigh. It's a long stretch but he completes it with panache, going up on his toes to make the last few inches.

"I can't keep up with *you*," says Joan. It's going to be tight, she thinks, tourniquet tight.

"We're a perfect match, no? We both want to keep them guessing."

Joan looks surprised. "No," she says. "This is NOT what I want."

"Don't play naïve with me, chiquita. Or I won't be gentle. And I want to be gentle, with you of all people." He tightens the strap midway up her thigh by pulling one end as an archer pulls a bowstring and letting it snap back with stinging force.

Veins Joan never knew she had expose themselves shamelessly. "I'm sorry," she says, grimacing. "But the garter hurts."

"Sí," says Raoul. "But they're the rage all over. And you started it all, Frenchie."

"Who?"

"Frenchie Jones, great American hot rocker. Some say she's got the spirit of Janis inside her."

"People in the know, I suppose."

"Reporters."

A group of them have congregated nearby and are scribbling on pads the size of artists' sketchbooks. Contrary to her expectations, Joan recognizes none of them.

"What happened to Art?" she says. "This seems like his kind of place."

"Art's making news back at your place," says Raoul.

"What kind of news?"

"Sensational. He's uncovered all kinds of juicy scandal."

"I wouldn't happen to be involved, would I?"

"Don't you want to be smack in the middle?" He lets go of Joan completely. "Stealing the show with your soulmate?"

"My soulmate?"

"Me."

"You don't have any soul."

"It hurts me to hear you say that. You know better, chiquita. Do I look as though I've got no soul?"

He looks positively mortified, but she suspects it's just an act. He has her just where he wants her, she thinks, and it's not a good place to be.

"If you back down now you punish me more than it's humanly possible to imagine," he says. "Señor Satan will dish it out like there's no tomorrow, and with good reason. You're the key to everything."

"I don't want to be the friggin' key."

"Then why did you open the door?"

"What door?"

"The door out."

"Out of *what?*"

"Your relationship with God and Señor Ensign."

"I had no relationship with God."

"Sí. God of Free Marketplace."

"No God, man. I'm a total agnostic."

"You're the all-American girl. America runs on advertisements, and your daddy made the best. He can't get enough credit, if you ask me. Belongs in the Mad Men Hall of Fame."

"He was a fake. I hated him. He abused me!"

She shudders. Did you just say that? All those years of denial in the face of Dear Mother and her lawyers' pressure, and now you just blurt it out? Doesn't make it any more real, but it does make you question whether it was in fact possible, some deep buried secret you've kept from yourself that Raoul has the power to bring to light. For what purpose? Do you need to confront your dark side to achieve the greatest heights? Or is he just trying to make you more vulnerable to his temptations? It never happened, she says to herself. You would never have let that happen. That belief is core to how you see yourself, and you're not going to abandon it, not for Raoul, not for anyone.

He's trying to get you to doubt yourself, she thinks. He wants to destroy your self-esteem to make you an easier prey. Then he'll swoop in to make the new you, which will have to seem better, even though he's molded you in the Devil's image. He's a bully, just like Big Daddy. And he creates evil things.

"Your father never meant to hurt you," says Raoul. "He loved you more than you know. Don't you remember when you were a little girl, when the water got too deep and he saved you from drowning? Don't you remember him breathing life back into you?"

"That was a long, long time ago. And it doesn't make up for anything," she says. "Who wouldn't save a drowning child? Even the most heartless bastard would do that, and he qualifies, believe me. Anyway, what are you defending him for? What's your connection to him?"

For sure he has Big Daddy's soul, she thinks. Does that mean Big Daddy's dead? No, he could have gotten that soul years ago, made a deal that propelled the Mad Man to the top of his profession. But that deal didn't end too well. In the end, the guy lost everything. And yours is not shaping up too nicely either. Guess it runs in the family.

"We were both burned, me by my wife and him by his bosses. Same thing. True love and true success can't exist in God's free market. We've got to bring it all down to find our true selves. Your father knows this now and wants to help you. I'm helping him help you. Comprende?"

"Bullshit." Joan laughs—hideously, it seems to her—the guffaws skidding out of her as though greased by Southern Comfort. Janis's drink; Frenchie's laugh. "What a ludicrous thought, Big Daddy trying to help me find myself," she says. "If you think bringing him into this is going to make me more inclined to do business with you, you're out of your mind. You've got the wrong woman."

"I've got the perfect woman," says Raoul. "The perfect Miss American Dream. Red hair, white skin, blue eyes, thinks all Commies are devils."

"The Devil *is* a Communist: Nikita Khrushchev. Said we will bury you, fitting thing for him to say, right? Saw him with my own eyes banging that shoe at the U.N. Scared the crap out of me. And he was in the car that hit me, too."

"Don't jump to conclusions. Satan's not so scary. He just don't conform to bourgeois norms."

"Tell me this—why Khrushchev? Why not Marx, Lenin, Stalin? I mean they're the Communists of stature, aren't they? Compared to them, old Nikita's a cartoon."

"They were before your time. And you grew up on cartoons."

"It all goes back to my childhood, huh?"

"The all-American girl."

"Stop that! I shaved my lousy red hair off, didn't I?"

"You opened the door."

"Not to die. To live! You're taking me round in circles."

"Your Swan loves circles. He circles the mound with every pitch. And you love the Swan, don't you? You want to die to make him yours."

"Maybe. What if I'm having second thoughts? I want to keep my soul. I'm afraid to lose it."

"Who says you lose it? You're just not going to *own* it anymore. It will be something you share with me, with Señor Satan. The whole concept of private property don't fly in this neck of the woods. When I inject my love potion in your thigh, what I really inject is a mix of many souls. I extract your lonely, confused, separate soul, but I hold it inside me and from time to time, I give some back. That's why we're soulmates: we've got some of each other's souls. It's a communal thing. True, there are times when you'll miss yours something fierce, but when you get a dose from me, you don't know how you'll love it."

"But if there's no private property, how can I have the Swan all to myself? That's the way I want him, you know. That's the way I've always wanted it."

"So long as you get him to throw Series, we'll make an exception that he's yours alone."

"You're a flexible bunch. And what if he wins?"

"You and me will take shellacking. But it won't happen. I know you'll come through in a big way for our side, especially after you taste the greatest pleasure. It suits you much more than the greatest pain."

Joan's hair still supports her in midair, but her body feels too heavy for her to raise herself from Raoul's needle without some major act of will that simply isn't forthcoming. In the distance, the shepherd boy is blowing "Charge!" on his ram's horn, as he runs at the wolves threatening his sheep. And as he runs, he grows, becoming her Swan, pitching stones at the predators and knocking them down, one after the other. Hey Nick, toss one over here, she calls out to him silently. Knock my wolf down before he bites. It's become clear to her that she's never going to have the pitcher, not the way she imagined it. If she gives in to Raoul, she becomes his slave, she does his bidding against her will. She sees now why he's targeted her, but it's too late to stop him. She's gone too far.

Eliot's still making it with that witch Sheila, oblivious to your fate, she thinks. She's not jealous. She drove him to it, after all. She'd take him back in a heartbeat now. And of course, she'd take his baby back too, if she could. Give him time and he'll find his way home, she thinks, just like Odysseus. But that took ten years, and she doesn't have that kind of time. She feels herself sinking, the needle coming close to pricking her skin, finding the vein. It's okay, she thinks. Maybe you'll have Nick's baby instead. Or maybe you'll just sing amazing songs that will live forever, like Janis. Raoul's giving you a gift. Take it. No reason to be upset. It may not be what you longed for, may not be who you are, but what comes will come, you can't control it. Time to just relax, be laid-back. Accept the gift.

But no. Your Spidey-sense is tingling all over, like it did when Big Daddy climbed into your bed way back when. It's all lies! The gift is worthless. It's worse than worthless—it will fuck you over. You can't let him sell you this, can't let him remake you. You still have the power to resist this monster, stay true to yourself. "No!" she shouts.

"No?" says Raoul, looking hurt. "You really mean that?"

"No! No! No!" she shouts. "What don't you understand about no?"

She's still sinking though.

"I understand you better than you understand yourself. I've always understood you, since you were born. You'll see, once you're born again. You'll love it so much."

"No," she says, more weakly, a tear running down her cheek, as she sinks down further onto the needle. No one is coming to her rescue. Not here.

"There." Raoul's in her blood. "Better now, right? Like you're in heaven."

"Mmmmmmmmmm."

"It's heaven for me too, Frenchie."

He smiles his snaky grin.

20

GIVE HER A KISS?

Finding the Bentley empty, Spillage follows the Dalmatian through the Trinity Church graveyard as dawn breaks, searching for his true love, the woman of his dreams. Passing the grave of Alexander Hamilton, he pauses to reflect on his first World Series win. Hamilton, he thinks, plays third for the Phils. A money player, clutch, has good power. But a sucker for that sweeping curve if you set him up right, high and tight. Struck him out three times and you'll get him next time too, whenever that is. Do we travel to Philly today? Can't remember. First things first: find Frenchie Jones.

His dog finds her first, barks for Nick to come. She's naked, save a garter belt on her right thigh, on the ground beside an open grave, a big syringe stuck into her groin just above the belt. He's never seen a naked woman in the flesh before, at least not that he can remember, though he's had vivid dreams of this one. And she lives up to everything he imagined—and more—except she's so white, almost chalky white, and he's shocked by the needle tracks along her arms.

As the dog licks her face to try and revive her, he sees that her lips have turned pale blue just like her eyes, rolled back in their sockets and fluttering. He kneels over her, lifts her head. She's barely alive, he thinks, though touching her neck he can feel her pulse. He reaches down to take out the syringe, but it's more deeply embedded than he assumes on his first try. Too delicate, he fails to move it at all, and wonders whether he even should. What happens when you get it out? Will she deflate and skitz off like a punctured helium balloon?

Maybe it's better to give her a kiss, breathe life back into her. Her lips are parted slightly, inviting him. But something tells him it's not the right move. His dog is trying to get the syringe out with his teeth, with no luck. "Okay, Gem, here goes," he says, pushing the Dalmatian aside, and with a mighty tug he pulls out the syringe, leaving a red mark the size of a pinhead. Joan moans as he throws the needle as far away as he can, and her eyes begin to come back into focus.

"Nice throw, kid," says a man in green fatigues, stepping out of the open grave. "You can go ahead and kiss her now."

"Who are you?" asks the pitcher, not liking what he sees. He reminds him of an umpire he once had with a strike zone that kept shifting.

"Me?" says the man, with a snaky grin. "I'm her manager. Her backup band. Her all-purpose body man."

Nick doesn't like the guy, doesn't trust him. His dog growls at him, too. There's someplace else he's tangled with him before, but he can't remember exactly where.

"Nick?" says Joan, weakly.

"Frenchie?" says Nick. "Are you okay? Is this guy giving you trouble?"

"No," she says. "No trouble." She touches his cheek lightly, fingers his golden curls. "Nick, is it really you?"

"It's me," says Nick. "But I'm worried about you. Maybe we should get you to a hospitable."

"Hospital?" The man laughs. "She don't need no hospital, kid. She's going on tour. You're going with her. We're going to have some real fun while you rest between starts."

.   .   .

The high is so beyond her wildest dreams, Joan has to wonder whether it is a dream, as she tries to steady herself on the stage at CBGB, an

East Village club that she and Eliot liked to hang out at, back in the good old days before things got weird.

The whole graveyard scene, that was a dream, she thinks. So over-the-top it had to be. But when did you wake, how did you get here, and what kind of shape has it left you in? Still floating above it all, as you look out at the crowd. And it looks so real, this place, just like you left it the last time you saw a show. When was that, six weeks ago, seven? A great night, a night you might even have gotten pregnant, but don't think about that now, that was in another life.

It's a raw space, totally cluttered like your old apartment, with exposed rafters, pipes, and wires draping down from the ceiling. Stickers, flyers, and graffiti (some of which you made yourself) fill the walls and cover the tables and chairs where your fans are whooping it up, clapping and stomping their feet. They can't get enough of you. What do you give them next?

You know these people. They're your people, folks you used to hang with in clubs all over the Village. You know that bartender; he's been here for years. Those servers, those bouncers, that couple in the corner. That's you and Eliot, nursing your beers, clinking your glasses, totally content. The old you and Eliot, B.S. (Before Spillage). Contentment is not a feeling you can hope to recapture any time soon.

What you're feeling now is way beyond that, in a totally different sphere. It's so powerful, this high, surging through every part of your being as you fly across the stage. You're supreme, an enchantress, a wondrous spirit loosed upon this planet to free it from all constraints, usher in a New Dawn. Mere mortals will never understand. You've been to unearthly places they could never dream of going. And what you've brought back is this voice, this haunting voice, that can put them in a trance, that can change them forever.

Not that you care. You're beyond caring. That's a human emotion, and strictly speaking, you're not human anymore. You're nothing but the voice, the song that flows through you, the song that drives them crazy. They want another song. Can you give them what they want?

You're beyond caring that it's not you in the corner with Eliot anymore. He's clinking glasses with Sheila now, who will eat him up for breakfast. So long, buddy. Go do your thing with her and see where it gets you. I don't care one little bit. Not in this moment, not while I'm peaking. I'm wicked, man, a truly wicked spirit now. I've totally become my evil twin.

There, at the table closest to the stage, Raoul nods approvingly, puffing away at his cigar, his arm draped over his young companion's shoulder. Your doting Swan, your shepherd boy, sheepishly grinning like the lovesick kid he is. He wants so much to save you. And you don't care if you destroy him. Not now, not when you're feeling like this. Can you stretch this moment out for eternity?

No. You know it won't last. Just one more song, that's all you have in you, before you come crashing back to earth. And then you'll need your next fix from Raoul. That's all Frenchie cares about.

. . .

A plan is starting to come into place for Spillage as he club-hops through an endless night of Frenchie's performances, sitting always in the front row, hanging on her every note, totally enthralled by the way she belts them out, throwing everything she's got into each song like he does each pitch, then fainting into his arms at the end of each act. And it starts with getting her away from her handler, though how he can do that he doesn't know. Carrying her back to the limerick to drive to the next gig is so sad, he thinks, because he knows the guy is going to stick her with another needle, the only way to keep her going.

Some things are starting to come back to him. Like he shot this guy in the head once. Where was that, a dream? And there's a gypsy who has the answers, the gypsy who raised him after his mother drank and pilled herself to death when he was one. Father unknown, he was sent to an orphanage, and that's where the gypsy found him, put him under her protective spell. Then he found his own powers chucking newspapers onto front porches. Skipped the minors, straight on to the Yankees, where he blossomed under pitching coach Howie Love, who helped him perfect his whirling motion. Talk to the baseball. Find the spirit within. Spin it with all your might.

"We've got to find an antonym to this poison he's hooked you on," he whispers to her as Raoul does a sound check. She nods, her eyes vacant, then climbs onto the stage and goes right into a freestyle version of "Ball and Chain."

And as he listens, in a trance, he tries hard not to nod off. It's been such a long night. Need some rest before you pitch again, but can't let your guard down. Can't take the mound unless you save Frenchie. You won't have any control. Howie's money is burning a hole in your pocket but what good will that do? It's not about the money—it's the spirit in the baseball. The spirit, your spirit, Frenchie's, in trouble.

"Baby, baby, baby, baby," he hears her riff.

We can beat this Devil, he thinks. We can win. I always win.

"You gotta free me, baby," she wails, going down to her knees.

Don't want to take your eyes off her for even one second, don't take your eyes off *him*, because he'll screw you. Got to find a way. Make the perfect pitch.

"Try, baby, try. You gotta try real hard," she cries.

The gypsy has the antonym. Need to get to the gypsy.

"Free, free, free me, baby." She's on the floor, writhing in pain. "Free me of this monstrous ball and chain."

Sister Sabrina. He can see her now, in her Reading Room. Right by where the collusion happened. Got to go back. Pick up where you left off. So damned tired . . .

.   .   .

"What if like I don't want Nick Spillage anymore," says Joan, smoking a Camel and sipping Southern Comfort with Raoul at a table beside the stage at Whisky a Go Go on Hollywood's Sunset Strip, the latest stop on their whirlwind tour. "I mean this stuff you have me on is so friggin' amazing I don't know how he could take me any higher."

"Fake it," says Raoul. "We got him just where we want him."

She's faking it with Raoul. She really doesn't feel that great. As the tour drags on for God knows how much time, the highs have gotten less intense, the lows more intense, and the in-between, where she is now, just a nauseating bleh. "I dunno," she says. "I mean I still love him to death, you know. But it's different now that I have him, more like a mother's love. I mean he's just a kid, right?"

"He's yours, Frenchie. I gave him to you. You can make him into whatever you like. So long as it's something I like in the end."

"Yeah. But I just don't know what he expects."

"He expects to save you. Expects to win the Series. But it won't go down the way he expects."

She nods. Her great love looks so peaceful in dreamland on the table. Does she really have to ruin him? Through her drug-induced haze, she sees him as she first saw him, on the mound, triumphant. As she saw him on her apartment wall, throwing strikes from all angles, celebrated by teammates, by screaming fans. As she saw him when she rode his heavenly heart, pure of spirit, a Superman for our times. And she does care what happens to him, after all. She can't be the kryptonite that brings him down. She'd do anything to avoid that.

Except she can't. She has no soul. She's the Devil's slave. She sings the songs he wants her to sing. They may be captivating, but they're not hers. How did she get into this situation? She worshiped Janis, but she never wanted to *be* Janis. She craved the Swan, but it was just a fantasy, a crush like the Beatles. She never expected to really have him in her arms, to have real power over how he pitched. She wanted a change, new heights to explore, but not these heights, and not these lows. As good as Raoul's potion feels when she peaks, there's something depressing about it. It's artificial. Not her. Like Big Daddy, he's sold her something she didn't need, gotten her hooked. The bastard.

Who is this person you've become? Is it anyone you ever remotely wished to be? No, but here you are. Why can't you be more into it? You've got a voice that millions adore, a voice that can whip them into a frenzy when you sing. You've got the best damned pitcher on the planet wrapped around your little finger. Fame, fortune, adulation— what more could a girl ask for? You're going to pack stadiums, Raoul says, just like the Beatles, starting with Yankee Stadium in the seventh game, and the fans are going to love you to death. You're a star, the brightest star in the night sky. Your records will sell millions, people will play them for the next fifty years, far beyond the life span of Big Daddy's commercials. Isn't that what you always secretly wanted, to be more successful than him? Not really.

You wanted to love with abandon, pursue your passions. It was all about giving love, not getting it in return. That's the difference between you and Big Daddy. He needed to be paid for his creations, and he had no love to give. You were a giver; he was a taker, despite all of his attempted bribes. Of course, it was great to have Eliot's love, and it would be great to have it back, but you didn't set out to get it. Your love was unconditional. Unadulterated. Same with your love for Nick.

What Raoul's done, stealing your soul, is to steal away the child in you in more ways than one. Like Big Daddy crushed your childhood affection for him with his arrogance and deception. To be a great artist, she thinks, you have to be in touch with your inner child. Eliot brought out that child in you, that sense of wonder, delight in little things. Remember the time you found that ancient edition of *Grimms' Fairy Tales* at the Strand bookstore, took it home, and feasted on the stories for weeks in bed? Rapunzel, Rumpelstiltskin, Hansel and Gretel, and more. You talked about creating a children's book together. He'd write it, you'd illustrate. Another fantasy that will never come to pass. Would be so much more gratifying than this, even if it never made it into print.

You made art. You found art. You were a much better artist than you are now, even though you never sold a thing, never made one fan swoon. What's the point of selling art? Recognition? Validation? Cash?

Certainly, money was never your goal. You were rich once, for five years when Big Daddy first made it big, and it was the most miserable time of your life. You had Eliot's $50,000, you lost the $50,000, but so what? Inflation aside, it had no value to you. Besides, it came from Raoul, so it was probably counterfeit.

Face it: you never had major-league artistic talent. But so what, you enjoyed doing it. No enjoyment here. You enjoyed teaching it, like Ms. Godunov, when you had that job in the after-school program in Spanish Harlem, working with elementary school kids before the funding dried up. You made them feel proud of themselves when they created their art. You liked kids, you were good with kids. Now you need to go in the other direction, tearing this kid pitcher's art apart.

She wants out. How can she get out? How can she get back to who she really is? Or get to a new place that's equally hers? Hansel, those breadcrumbs, can they lead us out of the forest? Rapunzel, your hair's down, will Eliot climb to the top of the tower? Rumpelstiltskin, I know your name, give me back my child!

"Come on," says Raoul. "You need a break. Let's go to the ballpark, catch a little action. Big at bat coming up for your old boyfriend Choice. Then we can take a trip down to Gulliver's Island, a really fun place, so you can blow a kiss to your other old boyfriend, Señor Ensign. Maybe torture him a little too, while you're at it, to help him move on. It's for the best."

"I guess. But one more fix first."

21

BOMBS AWAY

"All right everybody," says Yankee announcer Al Deep. "Game Five of this, the 1976 World Series, is about to begin here in Liberty Bell Creek and it's do or die for New York today. The Bombers of the Bronx who've come so far on the strength of Swannie's arm and Angel's big bat are knockin' at death's door as we watch the team warm up, down three games to one and you talk about miracles. Minus their big guns once again, the Yankees are gonna need whole bunches of God's little gifts if they want to get out of Philly alive and limp back home for Game Six.

"Yup. Home seems like an awful long way away to this ragamuffin squad, whose owner went a long way toward wiping home off the face of the earth the other night when he took his private plane down into the Coney Island fun house. And that fire, by the way, is still raging. But the Yankees, whose manager Miller Casey looks like he aged fifty years since he came to Phillytown (you see him there talking to the umps and rival skipper 'Poor Richie' Franklin), are convinced that if they can, Heaven help them, pull this one out of the fire, their rookie sensation and big-bopping right fielder will join them in the Bronx.

"And wouldn't that be something! Nick 'The Swan' Spillage, returned from the dead, where a good many pundits got him pegged even now, to carry his team to a Cinderella finish! But that scenario's little more than a dream now as we get set to go here, New York having a bunch of no-names as their last line of defense—Toomich, Noyz, Dert, Krouds, Notnuf, Innerpeece, Evert, and Amdeeprist, with Allatime the pitcher batting last.

"So Lieutenant Gus Berkley, my brother-in-law who got killed in the line of duty at Kennedy—just like the Kennedys did—if you're out there watching, put in the Good Word, our no-names need help. We need our big stars, need them back fast, as the Liberty Bell Creekers, who need just this one to take it all, go with . . ."

· · ·

Yankee slugger Angel Guerrero, standing at the wall of sky-high windows in his SoHo loft, sees Choice at the doorway before Mirlanda does. The actor, looking sharp in a new pin-striped suit but with a crazed look in his bright green eyes, is tossing from palm to palm a short-fused, spherical, softball-sized bomb.

"Get your hands off her, Yankee," says Choice to Angel, flipping the as yet unlit bomb back and forth between his palms.

Fleet of foot as always, the outfielder manages to yank a window open and take Mirlanda in his arms as he tries to shield her and face down the threat.

"Choice, what's got into you?" Mirlanda says. "Get rid of that thing."

"Get away from that Yankee. He's going down now!" barks Choice.

"You don't want to do that. He's a good man. Look around you at all the people he's saved, all the games he's won." The walls are adorned with pictures of Angel's off-season relief efforts in Puerto Rico, Panama, and Nicaragua, as well as highlights of his baseball exploits.

"I see he won you, witch, while I was doing time. Seen you two going at it something fierce from my cell."

"Nothing happened between Angel and me but talk," says Mirlanda.

"He's telling me things I need to hear. What'd that skunk Raoul tell you happened?"

"I saw you with my own eyes."

"Your eyes look strange. Think he put you on something."

"On *to* something—your witch's heart." He gestures with his bomb. "It's as dark as the footlights in an empty theater."

"Huh," says Mirlanda, stepping forward with her piercing stare. "Look who's talking. Rather watch this poor mother get mauled by the mob than look her in the eye to try and understand what moves her, after you been the big mover all these years. Up to now I've been faithful to you and that skunk, though Lord knows why, the way I've been treated."

"What way, witch? How did I treat you bad?"

"Don't want to talk about it," Mirlanda says, folding her arms across her chest. "You don't know, that's your problem."

"Damn," says Choice, tucking the bomb under his left armpit as he wipes his sweating hands on his pin-striped pants. "There she goes on her high horse. I'm trying to save you, woman. Can't you see? I've got to free you from that Yankee, free you from that gypsy, get you over to our side before it's too late."

"Choice," says Angel, taking a step forward to stay next to Mirlanda. "You're the one who should change sides. You've got to know you can't win with that Devil. I know you have it in you to do the right thing."

"Stand back, Yankee," says Choice. "And stay out of this. I'm talking here to the mother of my child." He digs into his pocket for a stick match, finds a piece of Raoul's magic mushroom instead. Right. You're supposed to get Mirlanda to take this, seal the deal. It's been a long time since you flubbed a part.

"Going to fetch my child right now," says Mirlanda, making a move to her right to step around Choice. "Seeing how he's worth more than all you grown men put together, except for Angel."

"Where you think you're going to find him?" asks Choice, moving to block her.

"With the mayor," says Mirlanda. "May be president soon too, with me as First Lady, if the Yankees win. Imagine that! Think of what it would mean for Junior."

"Not gonna happen," says Choice. "No way."

"Why? Cause you're going to blow the whole thing up? What good's that going to do, Choice? Except for Raoul and his underworld buddies."

"Trust me," says Choice. "We're better off if we do what Raoul says. I'm getting a big contract to play left field. Multimillions. Enough to take care of you and Junior forever and forever more."

"That's nuts," says Angel. "First off, I play right field. And if you throw the Series . . ."

"You're dead, Yankee. And we're switching things up. Here, Mirlanda." He tosses her a piece of mushroom. "Take a bite of this and you'll understand."

She lets the mushroom fall to the floor and stomps on it. "Tell Raoul that's what I think of his mind-candy. I don't need anything to screw up my thinking. I'm done with that man. Done with you too, if you stick with him. He's made you his puppet, stole your precious soul. Why'd you let him? I thought you were a strong man, a free thinker. That's what I loved about you."

"I'm stronger than ever. Just watch." He wipes his brow, which has begun to sweat, and retrieves the stick match from his pocket. To thine own self be true, he thinks, remembering an old line, as he fumbles with his match. True enough. But he's too far gone with his performance now.

"It's me all right!" Choice shouts. "More soulful than ever too, having suffered through those Tombs. Raoul helped me escape. He can help you too. You think this Yankee Doodle Dandy's got soul? He's just a machine for whacking little hardballs. Just a Yankee imperialist free market tool."

"He's on the right team. He has a big heart."

"Damn his team! Hate those damned Yankees!"

Choice lights the bomb and throws it hard at the outfielder, aiming at his head, but Angel pivots quickly, catches it, and in the same flowing motion hurls it out the window, high and far into the sky, while the actor lunges at him and the two go flying in the direction of the explosion.

. . .

Arriving at Gracie Mansion, Mirlanda finds Raoul holding her baby by the grandfather clock in the elegant entrance hall.

"Qué pasa, dollface," says Raoul.

"Don't dollface me," says Mirlanda, who hasn't seen him since he died. "Give him over."

"Not so fast. We need to straighten some things out first."

"Huh." She folds her arms across her chest, arches her back, looks him up and down. "Like what?"

"Like you've got to stop messing around with Angel."

"Not messing around with him. He saved me from the mob, that's all."

"I know what you're doing with him. And it's got to stop, or you'll screw everything up."

"You don't know shit. You're full of lies. Like the ones you're feeding Choice to poison his mind."

"Choice is okay. He's into his new role. Now we need to get you into yours." He google-eyes the baby, tickles him under the chin, while the hands on the clock behind him circle fast. "Comrade Mayor can't wait to see you. He'll be down in just a minute."

She glances at the grand staircase leading up to the mayor's bedroom, where his aide is primping him for his next appearance. Angel told her to play along, but she's so bitter, it's hard. "Hate that man," she says under her breath.

"Comrade Mayor? What's to hate? He'll do anything you say. The mayor is your ticket to fame and fortune."

"Hate *you*." She glares at him. "For what you're doing in this world. For who you are. You're more wicked than Papa Doc and that's saying a lot. Maybe you *are* Papa Doc, got his mean spirit in you."

"Maybe. So what if I do?"

"Just hate you, skunk, that's all. Hate what you've done to your best friend, your wife, your child."

"Not mine."

"You're my husband. So you're the lawful father."

"The marriage ended when death parted us."

"Wasn't death did that."

He flashes his snaky grin. "You don't believe I'm dead?"

"Believe you've been dead a thousand years. Now give me back Junior." She takes a step toward him, but he motions her to stop.

"Not so fast," he says. "I need you to promise. No Angel. No gypsies. You're back on my team now. I forgive you everything, but you must do like I say."

"*You* forgive *me*?" She rolls her eyes. "That's a scream."

"You're better off if you do like I say. Junior's better off."

"Don't see how that's possible."

"No? How about this then?" He fishes a knife from his fatigues. "Junior's worse off if you don't do what I tell you."

She glares at him. "You wouldn't hurt Junior."

"You sure about that?"

"You need Junior and me both for your little scheme. Angel told me."

"Angel don't know me. And he don't know my scheme. You know me better, dollface. And you know what I can do if I make my mind up." He moves the knife closer to the baby's chin, grins. "I don't think you want to take that chance."

Play along, she thinks. Angel said play along. "Okay," she sighs. "You win."

"That's my girl!" he beams, moving toward her. "Just like old times." He hands her the baby, drawing so close she can smell a hint of sulfur, which she never smelled on him before. He slithers an arm around her waist, pulls her to him. "Don't worry," he whispers. "Daddy will take care of you. Now how about a kiss to seal the deal."

She breaks free with the baby, who she's happy to see doesn't seem any worse for wear, as the portly mayor steps down the staircase looking regal in his monogrammed robe. His red-haired aide follows, holding his train.

"Mirlanda, my sweet, where have you been?" says the mayor, holding out his hands to her. His cheeks are still flush from his hot bath and his ears are still ringing from when he slipped in the tub and knocked his head. "Reunited at last. And we're off to the races. What a wonderful tableau!" He gives her a squeeze, takes the baby from her arms, and tosses him lightly into the air. "I see it now. See the resemblance, clear as day. My Hell-Raiser, Mirlanda, look what we've made! The perfect family, multiracial, multicultural. Bridge the divide, save the cities, save America, we can do it all. A brave new world awaits! Tell the truth to the people, and the people will reward us. You're dead, Tricky Dick. Here we come!"

Fool believes it, thinks Mirlanda, taking back her child. He believes the whole story. She smiles. Play along.

"Jones," says Raoul, clapping his hands. "Get the drinks. Let's make a toast."

The aide wheels a liquor cart in from another room, places it in front of the fireplace, and pours four Manhattans, handing them around.

"To victory!" says Raoul. "The winning ticket!" He clinks glasses with the others, downs his drink.

Mirlanda takes the smallest sip possible, knowing it's spiked.

Raoul clinks her glass again. "Drink up. Seal the deal."

Against her better nature, she does as she's told.

22

ELIOT'S VOYAGE

Eliot dreamily disembarks from his boat on the shore of Gulliver's Island after a rough crossing that made him sick. Where his plane ride ended and boat trip began, he can't remember. But that's of no consequence now, as he hops into a pink limousine with his last name on a passenger window sign and barks at the driver. "Take me to the casino. I want to fall in love fast."

The driver, Jonathan from Trinidad, greets him with a hearty "Willkommen," which he explains is the traditional greeting of Gulliver, and says he's exactly in the right place. While Jonathan has visited just about all the Caribbean islands, he's never seen a place like this. It's an experience more than a land mass, an experience to remember, he says. Everything you could possibly desire is here. Bob Marley, whom he used to chauffeur around, introduced him to the place, and he never wanted to leave. It'll probably happen to you, too. The rich and famous all hide their money here. It literally grows on trees, as you can see. Titans of industry and finance—the Rockefellers and Rothschilds, Kennedys and Krupps, Tony Stark and Bruce Wayne—have all found their way to Gulliver. Movie stars, rock stars, sports stars, porn stars, they all make it their playground. Mickey Mantle was here, Willie Mays, "Shoeless Joe" Jackson, Joe Hardy—lots of baseball legends.

Hardy brought his girlfriend Lola. Remember the song "Whatever Lola Wants?" Nick "The Swan" Spillage is here right now, too, with his girlfriend Frenchie Jones, who's performing as we speak in our cabaret. Larger-than-life literary lions, musical icons, artistic luminaries, old masters and new, all come here to clear their minds, free their souls. If you're looking for inspiration, you'll find it right here.

Rulers of all kinds, says the driver, mostly disgraced, have come to Gulliver's Island to get away from it all—the Duke and Duchess of Windsor, the Shah of Iran, the Marcoses from the Philippines, Idi Amin from Uganda, the Duvaliers from Haiti, Richard Nixon of course. Nixon sat right there back in '72, just to your right, so close you could have stuck a pen knife in his ribs and saved America a ton of trauma, but your timing was a bit off. Came with his adman to plot campaign strategy. He was a guest of the admiral, his biggest supporter, may he rest in peace. It all belongs to Sheila now.

This is a place where you can wash your inner demons out and hang them to dry, the driver continues. They're not so imposing when you drape them outside like that. You'll see some on the phone lines along the road. The lines are just for show; we're totally off the grid. Don't worry, no matter what you do, your identity will be protected here. Anything goes. And everything that happens on Gulliver stays on Gulliver. Not like Vegas, which leaks like a sieve. There's no comparison. Just wait until you see our casino, Satan's Palace. Everyone wins. Everyone wins big.

Just keep your heart open until you meet Sheila. You'll fall under her spell for sure. Get close to Sheila, and she'll set you up for life. Close the door on the past and open the door to possibilities you could never imagine. I tell you, this is a special place. And only special people get to come here. So, you must be special. Who are you, anyway?

"Good question," says Eliot, echoing one of his father's favorite lines. "I came here to find out."

• • •

At the top of an endlessly long and winding road up the island's steep shoreline cliff, Eliot makes out the casino. It's a grand, unfinished, Art Deco–style building with neo-Gothic flourishes, standing high atop the mountain, with colossal marble pitchforks framing its angular, vaulted entrance, stricken-looking stone gargoyles staring down from just above, and above them a giant neon Satan's Palace sign billowing smoke that brings tears to Eliot's eyes.

Craning his neck to look up beyond the sign, Eliot blinks his tears away to see rows and rows of new stories being added to the structure, steel girders stretching to the clouds, with scores of construction workers welding away while some patrons, not waiting for the finished product, indulge their wildest fantasies on makeshift platforms for all to see.

The mishmash of architectural styles strikes Eliot as something Joan could get into. Is she here? Do you want her here? Of course you want her. You'll always want her, no matter the distance you travel from her, no matter who else you get mixed up with.

He's standing beside his limo, still holding on to his door, which detached as he stepped out, when he's approached by a greeter in green fatigues. "Willkommen, Señor Ensign," says the greeter in an all-too-familiar Spanish accent. "Pretty wild, eh? You're going to love this place."

"Raoul," says Eliot.

"Sí. Let me take that door from you. It's too much weight for you to carry."

He rips the door from Eliot's hand and cracks it over his head before tossing it aside. Shards of glass fly all over the place but miraculously, Eliot isn't hurt. "Jeez," he says, "what do you think you're doing? You could've taken my eyes out with that stunt."

"So what?" Raoul grins. "You don't need eyes in this place. Let me be your eyes. I'll show you everything."

He leads Eliot through the great revolving entrance door, ushers him past the myriad games of chance in the cavernous front lobby, which you have to walk through to get to the cabaret. There's row upon row of slot machines, roulette wheels, poker, craps, and blackjack tables, along with a World Series betting window, where a long line has formed.

Mom's kind of place, Eliot thinks. She loved casinos. Could use her luck, her intuition, her skill at playing games right now. But he doesn't see her anywhere. Instead, he catches sight of a tweedy gambler playing blackjack whom he recognizes as the detective he started this trip with, and one seat over, the mayor who employed him for a nanosecond. Makes total sense, he thinks. They were both drawn by the lure of Sheila Dugan, and sure enough, there she is, dealing cards, devastatingly gorgeous in her low-cut sequin dress.

"Impressed?" asks Raoul. "You can have her, you know. Just follow me and give up your soul. I can make you rich and famous, strong and sexy. You can screw any woman in the world you want."

"I want Joan," says Eliot.

"Sure, you do. But Sheila's not bad, you've got to admit. Besides, Joan's busy right now with some serious business, getting the Yankees to blow the Series. How about you help her out, make sure she gets the job done, by calling the shots from the dugout steps? She'll love you for that. Comrade Mayor will love you too. Manage things right and you'll zoom right to the top. The mayor bet a fortune against the Bombers. You see, he's headed back to the betting window even as we speak. Thinks if New York goes down, he gets the sympathy vote. Plus, he can ditch the Swan as his running mate, so the pitcher won't be able to hog the limelight. No competition for you either. Isn't that what you want? Maybe you can run with him, might as well dream big. You did once, didn't you? Just imagine yourself a heartbeat away from being Numero Uno, the Supreme Leader of the American Empire. Trust me, it could happen. You can change the world, compadre. But first you have to let the world change you."

He lights a cigar with the snap of his fingers. "Just give up your soul," he says with a puff, "and I'll take care of the rest."

From the blackjack table, Sheila blows him a kiss as he grapples with what's been offered. It all seems so detached from anything remotely conceivable, he has a difficult time envisioning it, much less accepting it as a deal for his soul. What kind of imbecile does this guy take you for? It defies plausibility to think that the mayor's presidential ambitions would benefit from a New York defeat, especially if it comes attached to a scandal. And whatever your mother may have thought about your diplomatic skills, they're not enough to take you to the top of the heap, especially if you start off buried in that same scandal. It all has the feel of a Tricky Dick dirty trick. So why is it so hard to resist?

You have no desire to get back into politics, or to get into baseball. You have no desire for Sheila Dugan, as rich and beautiful as she may be. At best she's just a way to get even, and even that's questionable, now that you think about it. And you have no desire to change the world, not fundamentally, not in the way the Devil wants. He wants to make it an even bigger nightmare! No, you only desire Joan. More than ever. But then you opened the door to all of this nonsense, he remembers thinking. You opened the astral door. And then Raoul ripped it from your hand. Maybe, if you find it again and get it reattached, you can get back on track with the task of saving your one true love.

The door to the casino's cabaret is right in front of them. On a poster to their left, Frenchie Jones is pictured as its star attraction. Joan, thinks Eliot. She's here. It's your chance.

· · ·

"My pet," says Sheila Dugan, putting a spell on Eliot with a gesture of her gold-sparkled cigarette holder at the bar of the cabaret in her Gulliver's Island casino. "You're mine now. To possess and corrupt. Will you light me please?"

She swivels on the barstool in her low-cut sequin dress, slit up her left thigh almost to her waist, inserts the cigarette holder between her black-painted puckered lips, and leans so far forward that Eliot's first impulse is to steady her. His second impulse is to pull on the gold neck-lace dangling between her mostly exposed too-good-to-be-true breasts, which at first seems to have a star as pendant, but then as he turns it, the star becomes an Iron Cross, then a hammer and sickle, then . . .

"Moo," says Sheila, grabbing the hand that's tugging her chain.

"Moo?" says Eliot.

"You're tugging on me like you want to milk me."

Eliot winces, releases his hold. "Your nails," he says. "They're like piercing my skin at the wrists."

"Of course. I desire your attention, pet. I sense you're distracted."

"Nah. Just a little jet-lagged." He strokes his beard, which has grown back, then reaches for a finger bowl filled with stick matches. But a bald, Black bartender with a sparkling smile beats him to it. Choice, Eliot thinks. How'd he get here? And what's he doing tending bar? It's what actors do between gigs, of course.

Unless it's Chance, the demon image from that ill-fated press con-ference, which feels like it took place years ago, in a different universe. Chance would be a better fit for a casino like this. No matter, though. Joan screwed around with both. It's still painful for Eliot to think about, even as he tries to focus on saving her.

"You've recently been released from a dreadful prison," divines Sheila, gesturing with her cigarette holder.

"How'd you know?" say Eliot and the bartender at the same time.

Sheila winks at the bartender. "I'm the *real* witch," she says. "The *true* conspirator."

She props her elbow on the bar, which has a mirrored top, and when the bartender positions his elbow beside hers, as though accept-ing a challenge to arm-wrestle for her favor, Eliot's eyes are drawn to their lowest point of contact. Seeing her reflection in the mirror, he can see why the mayor and the cop were so attracted to her—she does look a lot like Marlene Dietrich, though there's something a bit off, the makeup too heavy, a bump in her nose. He has no interest. Well, maybe a little. Maybe even a lot.

Circe, he thinks, Circe the enchantress, remembering the Homer he studied at the New School and read from in bed to Joan in the good old days. He loved those bedtime story nights, all cozy and snuggled up, no nightmares then. She loved them too. So why did they stop? He always got a thrill when Joan twirled her fingers around his beard and called him my Odysseus, my wily Odysseus. It gave him a boost of confidence which he sorely needs now.

That was their Greek period, when they fantasized about sailing the Aegean, but settled for finding the best Greek restaurants in Astoria, Queens, and gazing at the Greek urns at the Met. Museums with Joan were a trip. She had such a great eye, would point things out that he'd never see himself. Look here, in this corner, can you believe this? Breaking things down and putting them back together with her dada perspective, which he never quite understood but always got off on hearing. She was on her own turf, like he was at bookstores. The Strand near Union Square. City Lights on their San Francisco adventure.

This is Sheila's turf, he thinks. Her island, where she keeps you off-balance and calls all the shots. Circe had her own island too, and in the beginning, she was Odysseus's foe, casting a spell that turned his men into pigs. But he resisted, with the help of Hermes the messenger god, who was sent by Athena, the goddess of wisdom, to deliver a magic flower that could ward her off. With help from the gods, Odysseus was able to turn Circe around, get her on his side. Any chance of doing that with Sheila?

The bartender strikes a match to light Sheila's cigarette. "Guess we don't stand a chance," he says. "You tight with Raoul?"

"Shhh," cautions Sheila, taking a drag. "We must keep the young skipper barefoot and ignorant."

"That dude with his head down on the counter? He's asleep."

"Yet he hears."

Eliot hears a voice from someplace nearby that sounds like Janis Joplin singing "Piece of My Heart."

"And he ain't no skipper, neither. Wasn't nothing but an ensign last we crossed swords."

"He comes up in the world, darling." She blows smoke at Eliot. "If I choose to promote him."

The bartender laughs heartily. "You're beyond me, momma. But I'll keep trying."

"No," says Sheila. "*He'll* keep trying. We have other plans for you. Fix a stiff one for me please, and a double for the professor there, who's an undercover cop. See him? He stands at the roulette wheel thumbing through his wad, deciding red or black, casting furtive glances this way. So shy, my little bookworm. He's simply dying to make it all happen with Sheila. Traveled all this way, leaving wife, leaving children. Do you still crave children, darling?"

"Still believe in family," says the bartender.

"Not you," says Sheila. "You." She raps a knuckle against Eliot's crown. "Blackbeard. Yoo-hoo. Are you there, skipper?"

Eliot raises his head. He still hears the music from somewhere nearby. But where's it coming from?

"Rip Van Winkle," says Sheila. "He lives! He's awake! Tell me, what's changed the most since you went elsewhere, pet?"

"Joan." He sees her, beguiling in a flapper outfit, all bedangled with long necklaces and bracelets like Janis Joplin used to wear, singing from a gilded cage suspended over the stage Brobdingnagian bouncers are guarding so no one can get too close, except for the golden-curled youth with the Yankee shirt and cap, sitting with a guy Eliot knows too well in green fatigues and black beret at a front row table, leaning in with mouth agape.

"She was your warden in the prison of unrequited love. Now, released, you find her unappealing?"

"More."

"You'll get over it. She's a junkie, you know."

"She needs me."

"You? What in Heaven's name could *you* do for her now? She's made her pact with the Devil. She's dead."

"Joan!" Eliot calls. "You've got to stop! I know it sounds great with the Swan and all—and you sound so great, riffing on Janis—but the Devil's using you, can't you see? Look at me—I'm resisting. You've got to resist too!"

A Lilliputian newsboy strides through the casino, shouting *Mercury* headlines. "No-name Yanks come back from the dead! Dizzy Allatime spins gem! Bombers headed back home for Game Six! Art's got the details! Full color pix!"

Eliot's fingers get singed by the stick match the bartender handed to him when he wasn't looking. "Crap," says Eliot, dropping the match to the floor.

"Know your limits, son," says the professor, coming over to their table. "That's the way you win at craps. I've got a foolproof system to beat the house. Learned it from your mother."

You're not my father, Eliot thinks. Stern King George wouldn't be caught dead in this place. He didn't even want to go to the Broadway musical *Cabaret* when Mom had a backstage pass because her cousin had a bit part. Too decadent for his taste. You went instead and had the time of your teenage life, seeing the actors and actresses after the show without their makeup, so normal, making the memory of their debauched performances all the more incredible. What you'd give for a bit of normal now! No, your father wouldn't be caught dead here, in a smoke-filled room that brings to mind the musical's Kit Kat club, with its 1930-ish pre-apocalypse Berlin vibe. But then, he *is* dead, remember?

Still, it's not quite him, Eliot thinks. While his tweed suit looks the part, his face looks more like Lieutenant Gus's. The beagle ears, bloodshot eyes. You'd prefer it be the detective, wouldn't you? You had a nice camaraderie going with the cop, even though he could have put you away for life. Better than with the man who gave you life. But it's not the cop either. Not totally. More like a professorial meld.

Eliot watches the professor kill the flame with a scrunch of his winged-tip shoe, spit tobacco juice on it for good measure, then down his double, slap his glass on the mirrored countertop, lift another stick match from the full finger bowl, and say to Sheila, who's awaiting another light, "Allow me, Ms. Dugan. My boy's a bum. Tried to teach him fundamentals, but he was born a bungler."

"You didn't teach me anything. I'm on my own here," barks Eliot, swiping at the match. It snaps like a wishbone, the longer half to the younger man, who wishes he could storm the stage, carry Joan away. But that privilege is reserved for the golden-curled youth, who reaches through the bars of the cage to catch her as she faints. The professor gives Eliot a vicious shove.

"See how they fight over me," Sheila cackles, as the bartender hands the professor another double.

"I'd like a drink too," says Eliot. "Straight up."

The bartender inspects Eliot's burnt fingers. "I'd give it to you," he says, a wink of his riveting green eye to Sheila, "if I thought you could hold it. But you're in some kind of miserable shape."

"He'll recover," says Sheila, "the moment he commits to me."

She undoes the buttons of Eliot's shirt, runs her fingers through his chest hair, as he watches the youth carry Joan away. It *is* Joan, he thinks; she doesn't have that Ms. Jones edge. But where'd she get that haunting voice? He can still hear the notes, though she's long since stopped.

They used to sing together, he recalls, on the subways. Made some incredible music together. He wrote songs for her, songs she loved. How can he recover the harmony they used to have?

The newsboy shouts more headlines. "Yankee no-names win Game Six! Angel survives bomb to blast walk-off home run! Swannie sighted with Frenchie at Sheila's casino! Mayor makes it official with Hell-Raiser! Art's got all the pix! See 'em right here!"

"Ms. Dugan. Seriously," says the professor, his hand reaching into the bowl for another match, but preempted by the bartender. "Do you think you could love me? Could you give me just a little clue?" he pleads. "I know it defies logic, which I never do, but I'm smitten, I can't help it, can't you see?"

Sheila ignores him, kissing Eliot's burned fingers and then twirling her own around his beard like Joan used to do. "Such a lovely beard," she says. "I simply adore it, pet. We must go up to my room now and do the naughty. Make love, not war. But make love like a warrior. And after, we'll plot our game plan."

She turns to the professor. "As for you, my beagle-eared friend, I suggest you try your luck elsewhere. Take that wad in your pocket and cash it for chips. Play every game we've got, and if you manage to beat the house, I'll give you a smooch."

"I'll do my darndest, Ms. Dugan," says the professor.

"Good boy," says Sheila, motioning the bartender to take him else-where. She focuses intensely on Eliot from a few inches away, blowing smoke out the side of her mouth. "And you, my pet? Will you do your darndest, give me your all?"

Eliot's tempted, can't deny it, staring deeply into Sheila's long-lashed eyes. Circe, he thinks, I can turn you around. But he can't get Joan's voice out of his head.

"Forget her," says Sheila. "You belong to me now. You're going to manage my team. She's seen you with me, seen you're better with me. And take my word, you're better off, my pet. The woman can't cope with the world without junk, and only Raoul can give it to her. You want to try to share her with Raoul? I assure you, he won't leave you with much, if anything. Leave her to the Swan. He deserves her. He's such an innocent, he believes he can save her—while you, you're mature, you're above such fantasizing. Let her disillusion him. Let him disillusion her. Save yourself while you can. For me."

She's turning you around, Eliot thinks. But you're not going to forget about Joan. Ever. Odysseus spent two years with Circe, bore a son with her, but never forgot about Penelope. In the end, he returned home to save her.

Forget about two years. It's all going down this week. You either win Joan back or not. The path to Joan may be through Sheila, but just remember it's a path to Joan. You can do it with her, you *need* to do it with her, but it's just sex, strictly mercenary, while all the time you're thinking of how to outwit her. Wily Eliot!

The professor returns, upset, having lost his wad playing poker. "Don't listen to her, son. This place is rigged. I can see it clearly now. And it's suicide for you if you skipper the Yanks. You can't win, not by any stretch of the imagination, not with the Swan mixed up with that redheaded dope fiend. Take it from the old man. She'll destroy his morale and the whole team's with it, unless you can keep her away, which you can't."

Your father never liked Joan, Eliot thinks. No getting around it, this is King George, no matter how much he resembles the detective. The professor was always a cop at heart, a staunch law-and-order man, a badge-carrying member of the thought police, and now these tendencies have just risen to the surface. If only the detective could have transferred over something other than his looks—like his patience, his humility, his openness to new experiences. Not happening though. Old George refuses to budge on the important stuff, as he always did.

Of course, he wants you to give up on Joan. And how about the way he wants to ditch your mom for Sheila? What kind of example is he setting with that? Whatever his faults, Eliot always thought his father was faithful to his wife. And it's disturbing to think he might have been wrong. Where is she now, anyway? This is more her territory. He misses her terribly. Mom, I need you here to have any chance of winning!

"Can't you see we're *engaged*, Pops?" Sheila asks the professor, annoyed. "Now go away and don't come back." She pushes him aside, and he disappears. "Come, my pet. We have pressing business to attend to."

"Casey croaks!" shouts the newsboy. "Yankee captain felled by stroke! Sheila gives job to pitching coach Howie Love!"

"Come Howie," says Sheila. "Show me how you make love."

23

BARRICADE THE DOOR

"Why are we barricading the door?" asks Eliot, as he enters Sheila's Satan's Palace suite. He's taken aback by its Deco-inspired opulence.

"We need to make it hard for your father to get in," says Sheila, finishing the job quickly and slipping out of her sequin dress. "Can't you hear him, pet, sniffing about the corridors? He so desperately wants me for himself, but you mustn't let him have me. I despise him no end."

"Why?"

"He instilled in you this mania for questioning. Stop with the third degree. Am I your prisoner? Make love to me now!"

She sits naked, legs splayed, in a lush, deep-seated mahogany chair, and holds out her arms to him. Okay, here goes, he thinks. Guess it was meant to be. Just keep it physical, hang tight to your soul. But as he takes a step toward her, he hears a woman next door moan.

"What's that?" he says, panicky.

"Never you mind. There are all sorts of lovers in Satan's Palace."

Eliot kicks at the wall karate-style, finds it tears like paper, revealing the unfinished section of the casino. A gust of hot air nearly knocks him off his feet, until he grabs hold of a steel girder and finds his balance. The girders extend upward indefinitely, and on an exposed wood platform, one set of girders away, he sees Joan reclining in a waterbed with a pale blue base like the one they once sampled back in the day.

She's propped up by pillows, her red hair flowing across a white sheet that only partially covers her naked body, nibbling from a bowl of popcorn that sits on her lap. Beside her, the golden-curled youth whom Eliot remembers from the cabaret downstairs is curled up in a fetal position, sucking on her right breast like a newborn child. Spillage, of course. Who else could it be? His too-short Yankee shirt, ripped halfway up the back and open in the front, flares out like a set of pinstriped wings, blowing in the stiff breeze that provides no relief from the stifling heat. He has nothing on beneath.

Lord, thinks Eliot, how I want to be in his position. But he knows it's not to be. Not here. On the other side of the waterbed, Raoul readies a syringe, prepared to fend off any challenge.

"You see, pet," says Sheila, who's moved her seat to the open wall. "There's nothing to be afraid of. No one's getting hurt. Come get a better view." She pats her thighs.

"I've seen enough," says Eliot, gingerly taking a step in Joan's direction. Past the steel girders, and far below them, he can make out the rugged cliffs of Gulliver's Island and the white-capped ocean beyond. We must be forty stories up, at least, he thinks. He tries not to look down. The wood platform ahead is already sagging. It can't take the bed's weight much longer. "You're not safe out here, Joan. Let me take you to a safe place."

"Don't come near me," says Joan. "Go back to your rich bitch. She's who you really want. Admit it, you fool."

"Sí," says Raoul. "You know you want Sheila more. And even if you don't, Frenchie's way past you. She's a superstar now. She has different needs."

He lifts her left arm, finds a vein and shoots her up.

"Not true." says Eliot, flinching at the sight of her eyes rolling back, a horrible sight he never imagined he would see. "I don't care what she says. You've flooded her mind with that junk and her brains are like all washed out, the same as her eyes. But I'm devoting myself to her rehabilitation."

Joan snaps back to life. "I don't need your friggin' rehabilitation," she sneers. "I'll fight it, and you'll get burnt. Believe me, man."

If he could just get her alone, Eliot thinks, talk things through without Raoul hovering and Spillage sucking away. For all her insults, he's glad she's here. Better than being worlds apart, which is where he thought he was headed when he boarded the plane. Her words hurt, but he can take the pain. "I've been burnt before," he says. "Doesn't faze me."

She wraps an arm around Raoul's neck and lowers his head to whisper in his ear. "Condescending bastard," she says. "He thinks he knows my deepest secrets, the ones I only share with you. Who's he kidding? He's just a big doofus."

"I know," says Eliot, taking another unsteady step toward her along the girder. "I know what's in your heart. And I know you still love me, despite the big act."

"Never!" screams Joan. "Never ever! You hear me?"

He's never heard her scream like that. What did he do to provoke such rage? It's so beyond the woman he knew, though apparently not the one she's become. A super tantrum, befitting a superstar, fueled by a superstrong dose of the Devil's dope. Still, it's better to be battered by all her negative energy than to have her feel nothing at all, he thinks. The makeup sex will be incredible, if you ever get there. And the fact that your dreams are still intersecting is a good thing, even if they've been infected by Dr. Strange's Nightmare. You're totally in Nightmare's Dream Dimension now. Gulliver's Island is its capital. Where's my Rabbit? I need to shift gears.

"Watch your step, pet," says Sheila, holding him back. "The footing where you're headed would pose problems for a mountain goat. Besides, we're wasting time. We need to get back to *our* game."

"Go on," says Joan, with a fiendish laugh. "Don't let me stop you. Put on a show. We're all watching to see what you can do." She pops a handful of popcorn into her mouth.

She's enjoying herself entirely too much, thinks Eliot. Are you sure this is her and not her evil twin? He was so confident a moment ago. But now, aside from the way she looks, there's really nothing in this woman he thinks resembles Joan. Nothing where it counts, on the inside. She's just masquerading, pretending, Ms. Jones all the way. Just a soulless ventriloquist's dummy, that's all. The words, the screams, the taunts are Raoul's, which is to say they're Nightmare's. You can't let them bring you down, he thinks. You can't fold, like that look-alike at the mayor's press conference in your apartment. You have to see through the ruse, find the real Joan. Hang tough, stay true, and wrest her from your nemesis.

And if, by some cruel chance, it turns out the real Joan is right here in front of you, inflicting torture, you can deal with that too. Because this is the worst Joan you could possibly imagine, and if you can deal with this and still love her, then you really will love her till the end of time. It's like Jonathan from Trinidad said. When you wash your inner demons out and hang them to dry, they don't seem so imposing. You should *learn* from experience, as the Philosopher King would instruct.

He sees his father break through the barricaded door, wishes he'd reinforced it better when he had the chance. After all, this is the father who put him in an experimental box when he was a baby to test his response to stimuli and shape his behavior. The staunch paragon of logic, so out of place here, Eliot thinks. He created you, and you love him despite all his rigidity, but he's not the help you need with Sheila, not the help you need to save Joan. You need Strange. You need Hermes. You need your mother, Helene. You need to think outside the box, boy.

"Come, Howie," says Sheila, pulling Eliot up a diagonal steel cross-beam toward the platform above. "You'll confront him where the air is more rarefied. That *should* favor youth."

The golden-haired youth curled up at Joan's side lifts his head from her breast. Finally, thinks Eliot, wishing it was his turn. Somehow, he thinks they never actually went all the way. He's not a threat. He's just a kid, an impressionable kid. His baseball glove, ball nestled in the web, bobs like a buoy at the foot of the bed.

"You're the love of my life and I'll do anything for you, Frenchie," the youth declares. "Say the word and I'll throw the Series."

"What the hell," says Joan. "Throw it."

That's it, thinks Eliot, disturbed by her nonchalance. That's the one true threat, the one thing you must prevent. You can't let Spillage throw the Series, can't let Joan seduce him into throwing the Series. That's the act that seals her fate. All the rest means nothing. The Yankees win, you win. It's as simple as that. And Sheila's putting you in a position where you can make that happen. She's giving you that power, even as she seeks to dominate you. Well, it's a theory anyway, he thinks. Makes him feel good to think of it, if just for a moment.

But then his father intervenes, making his way onto the girder, grabbing hold of the crossbeam that Eliot and Sheila are climbing and scrambling up himself. "You know my son, don't you, Miss?" he says to Joan as he ascends.

"Oh, Lord," sighs Joan. She gives Raoul a kiss, which makes Eliot wince. Just a peck on the cheek, but still . . .

"Excuse me, Miss," Eliot's father persists, while Sheila hauls Eliot higher and higher up the girder, further and further from Joan. "I asked if you knew my son. Could you do me the favor of a simple reply?"

"Yeah, man," says Joan. "I know him inside out, all right? He pretends to care about me, but he's really a total ass."

She points a finger at Eliot shimmying up the crossbeam, and his lower half becomes that of a loaded pack mule. "See what I mean?" she giggles.

"Absolutely," says the professor. "That's the answer I was looking for."

You're not helping, Dad, Eliot thinks, looking down from his girder. But his father keeps climbing and seems to be gaining ground. "Stay right where you are, son," he calls. "You too, Sheila. We have some important matters to discuss."

Eliot's never felt so burdened by anything as by his saddle. It has several attachments, looped together by chains, including batting helmets, chest protectors, shin guards, knee and elbow pads, gloves, and a face mask. He nuzzles Sheila's calf with his nose. "Please," he says.

"Please what, my pet? Speak your mind," says Sheila, mounting him. "She hasn't rendered you dumb yet, has she?"

"No." The burden seems lighter with Sheila on top. In fact, he never wants her off him, even for a moment. "Can't you ride me bareback?" he asks.

"Not now," she says. "I fear your father would disapprove." She urges him up with a dig of her heels, to which his lower half responds with surprising vigor.

His hooves clickety-clacking along the crossbeam, Eliot says, "I was just thinking about this other stuff."

"You mean this?" Sheila covers his face with a catcher's mask. "It's your protection, pet, for when you manage."

"All of it? I mean I'm carrying a whole team's worth." A baseball Joan hurls from the waterbed strikes the mask so hard it dents two bars, becoming lodged between them and impairing Eliot's vision. Just how much is she capable of throwing at him?

"You've never managed in my league," says Sheila, pulling Eliot's head back by the hair, plucking the ball from the mask with two black talons, and giving him the evil eye through the bars.

This stops Eliot dead in his tracks and his father, catching up, says, "I've managed to win every game there is in this place. I'm ready for you now, Sheila—ready and raring."

Eliot rears and sends his father flying.

24

KITCHEN SUMMIT

Sister Sabrina's dinner guest slurps his cabbage borscht like a peasant while she looks on appreciatively from across her checkered tablecloth. Blind to his faults (as well as most of his features), she fidgets with her stringy gray hair and matching sack dress like the teenage bride-to-be she once was, before a full-length mirror warped at its extremes in those cloistered moments leading up to the ceremony, when she saw her groom-to-be behold her as she imagined he soon would under the gypsy *chuppah*.

Nu? Nothing's so different from that day, she thinks, save that he's lost all his wavy dark hair. He eats the same, *kineinahorah*, always a *fresser*, a gobbler, he'll want more. More than his wife in the end could give him. Some end. A year? A whole life lived in that year, Bubba. And how many lives do you guess maybe he's lived? He always comes back, that's the main important.

The black cat she addresses as her great-grandmother tastes the borscht to the left of Sabrina's wheelchair and makes no comment. Sabrina sips her own and thinks, You're right, Bubba, yours was better. An extra setting for the always-welcome prophet is a traditional part of the gypsy springtime ritual supper celebrating the exodus from Pharaoh's Egypt, a place Sabrina's guest remembers all too well. Things ended rather badly for him there, but it was fun while it lasted, he supposes, extracting the latest edition of the *Mercury* from the mouth of a handsome Dalmatian.

His left hand never stops ladling borscht as his right unfolds the paper and his thoughts traverse centuries. In the course of human events, he thinks, he's never wanted for opportunities to make chaos. Pissed most of them away, it's true, but that's history. Once the dream becomes realizable, it loses meaning. You must hold fast to your original impulse, struggle, or it dies, and he's a lazy Devil. Doesn't care enough (or hasn't; he can always change) about end results.

What he loves most is screwing around in cities and cultures on the brink of collapse. The Rotting Apple, he thinks, has been a veritable Roman feast thus far. Best time he's had since Weimar Berlin. He guffaws at a headline on his *Mercury*'s front page:

LOVE TO THE RESCUE?
HOWIE TAKES YANKEE HELM IN LAST GASP FOR NY

"Comrade Raoul, you have a sure editorial touch," he says, aware that the masses may not understand but willing to lose them for the sake of a good laugh.

"Read out loud to me, Nicki," says Sabrina, "the way you used to in the old country."

She remembers when he ran off to fight the revolution, but which revolution? There were so many. In her mind's eye, she observes her daughter Crystal, with new airs beyond belief, do the Devil's work on that nice young Alvin, who's still in love with the turbaned girl her little Micky brought home. Joan, now Frenchie Jones. Beautiful soul, beautiful voice, but with the Devil's cold fire now running through her veins. She needs to be saved, to save us all.

"You don't listen, *matyushka*," chides her dinner guest. "You ask for a story and then fall asleep on me."

"You were reading?"

"With gusto, as the story was meant to be read. A classic. You should be shot for such behavior."

"Forgive me, Nicki. But tell me, please. Will Mirlanda ever get there?"

"Where? Who?" His blood pressure rises.

"My neighbor, Mirlanda, whose baby my daughter lost. Will she get where she needs to be with the mayor? Not that she wants the responsibility."

"She wants it, don't worry. And even more she wants the power. All these American women want power because they sense their oppressors are losing their grip. They've been denied so long they're going crazy."

"Shame on you! You shouldn't force her to take that drink."

He bangs his hand on the checkered tablecloth, causing the china to tremble in their places. "You don't let me finish!"

"You're not going to harm her baby, are you?"

"Of course not. I'm not that cruel, my little Yankee. How you've taken on the ways of the women of this country."

"I'm sorry," says Sabrina. "One falls into habits, some kosher, some not so kosher. What can you do? In my heart I can tell you're not cruel, Nicki. You're as sweet as a fig."

"Don't give me from figs. I'm cruel when I want to be. Just not now." He snaps his fingers. "Go, dog. Fetch the boy."

"I love you still, Nicki," says Sabrina. She reaches across the table to put her hand on his, almost knocks his remaining borscht into his lap before he catches her. "No matter what."

"Shush. Don't you hear him?" He boxes the Dalmatian's ear. "Dumb muttnik. You want I should send you into outer space? Go, I said. Get."

Nick Spillage opens the Reading Room front door as the dog scrambles to his feet, calls, "Yo! Anybody home? I need guidance and there's a stinkhole outside the size of a crater, tough to get around. Must've been some implosion! Did you see what happened? Hey, you

left the TV on. I don't want to wake anyone but what's this: we're playing? That's not Yankee Stadium, jeez, when did we leave home? And
who's that pitching? What game are we on?"

"Here we are," he hears a man say as his Dalmatian jumps up to lick
his face. "In the kitchen. Come join us, sonny."

• • •

By the time Spillage enters the kitchen, TV in hand, and finds a place
to plug it in, Sister Sabrina and her dinner guest are engaged in a great
debate in a language he doesn't understand. The pitcher sides with the
gypsy who raised him before he knows what they're talking about or
recalls where he saw this guy before, although he's sure he has. Collusion really took something out of me, he thinks, the action in the
Bronx catching his eye as the bald man raps his soup spoon against the
checkered tablecloth and bellows, "I will *not* give her a get-out-of-jail
free card. No way! She got where she is of her own free will. Started
the whole cycle with her great obsession. That you of all people should
have the gall to broach the subject, why it's . . ."

"Don't yell, Nicki," says Sabrina. "I only asked."

"Just face the fact that she's hooked. He hooked her. We see the
stuff she's made of now. She's her father's daughter, after all."

Is that Angel? thinks Nick, watching the outfielder drop to one knee
near the stands by the home team dugout to pick up a bouquet of pink
and yellow flowers. Seems his eyes were never so big or green before,
maybe the TV's deception though.

"We don't see anything of the sort, and you know it," says Sabrina
to the bald man. "We see only the crudest display of brute force. You
are rolling all over her, you and your Cuban agent, this Raoul whom I
might add you'd better keep an eye on."

"It will be a pleasure," says the man, breaking into an expansive grin.
"I learn a great deal from his maneuvers."

"Don't make light. You may find yet he'll outmaneuver you."

"Silly woman. Wo is nothing if not loyal. Less than nothing, even. And fully aware of this fact, as are you."

" 'Scuse me," says Spillage, as the score comes on the screen. Cripes! It's Game Six!

"Never mind," says Sabrina. "He's so many places he forgets his place. He has his little harem, and he assumes it's his right to lord over . . ."

"Holy Motown!" says Spillage, as a hand-held camera, none too steadily held, takes him outside Yankee Stadium, where a little panzer-tank of a man in green fatigues clears a path for a long-legged, bangled and jangled beauty with mesmerizing pale-blue eyes, a rosy confection, and luxurious red stresses. Frenchie! How'd she get there?

"Hubba-hubba, eh, sonny?" says the bald man in English, swiveling in his seat. He pours two shots of vodka, extending one toward the youth. "Here, take," he says to Spillage. "Hundred proof, direct from Russia. Put some hairs on your chest. Give Frenchie what to play with, get it?"

"Nah," says Nick, waving him off. "I can't. That is, I don't."

"My son, the athlete," says Sabrina. "Go eat some liver, Micky, some herring, whitefish. You must be starving."

She gestures toward a counter where a buffet of gypsy delicacies wasn't a minute ago. The fact that they are gypsy foods, however, serves Nick as sufficient explanation for their sudden appearance, since he knows that gypsies have surrealistic powers. The only unsettling thing is what she called him. Because something tells him it wasn't just an innocent mistake.

In their foreign language, which Nick takes to be Yibberish, Sabrina says to the bald man, "Don't corrupt the boy. This is for the girl to do, or not do, assuming your loyal Wo doesn't interfere. He wants her for himself, you know."

Nick thinks, Hey, you gotta believe in yourself. You're the Swan, THE Swan, not some punk ugly duckling who'll reverse back to normal once the Series ends. This is normal, understand?

"I don't want to hear from this," says the man, whose cigar is already smoking by the time he removes it from its wrapper. He bites off an end, spits it out, and takes a puff, blowing a ring of smoke in Nick's direction. "Wo has no need for private property. He finds total satisfaction in subservience to the common cause."

"Your cause," says Sabrina.

"And why not? It is, in the final analysis, the best for mankind."

"Your final analysis. I happen to think differently, *liebchen*."

"Do you?"

"And how. I think our best bet is for you to withdraw."

"Not one inch." The flat of his left hand thuds down upon the tablecloth, shaking Spillage, who feels it on the seat of his own, too-short jeans in either anticipation or memory of being taken over the man's knee and spanked. *What'd I do to provoke him?* thinks Nick. And what am I doing standing here like a department-store harlequin while the game goes on without me?

"I won't pull back for even one second," the man continues. "I will not have Wo pull back."

"But you've made your point already, Nicki," says Sabrina.

"*Nyet!*" The hand comes down once more, making Spillage jump. "I don't make points, old witch. I make revolutions—permanent revolutions."

"I do not see these revolutions taking place," says Sabrina, peacefully stroking the black cat that's leapt to her lap from under the table. "Not where you want them, at any rate."

"What's this? Do you read my mind maybe?"

"A *bissel*. But mostly do I judge your character."

"Always the critic."

"Constructive critic. And why the hostility? If you truly loved me, you would listen a tiny bit when I try to better you."

"Better, schmetter. And who says I love you?" he says in English, chortling and winking mock-furtively at Nick, who doesn't get it, but winks back anyway, basically to avoid getting whacked again.

The old woman's really hurt, thinks Nick, who wishes he could protect her. But she's the one who's supposed to protect you, remember?

"Sorry," says the man. "I didn't mean that."

"I'm sorry too," says Nick. "And I hate to interrupt, but see I'm kind of in a rush here, the Series going on without me and all, and I just need some guidance on how to save Frenchie. I mean there's got to be some kind of antonym for that stuff she's hooked on, right?"

"Here," says Sabrina, pounding her heart with her mottled fist. "Here is where your revolution should take place. Forced from the outside, it's not a revolution, believe me. You can lock them in cages, impose hard labor, but it will not get you where you want to go." She reverts to English, pounds her heart more forcefully. "Here, Nicki. Understand?

"Not really," says Nick, unsure whom she's addressing, but feeling his own heart thump every time she pounds hers.

"You need to win her here," she says, pounding once again.

"But what about the antonym?"

"There." She points at his thumping chest.

"Here, there. You're confusing the boy," says the bald man, placing his cigar in an ashtray and pouring himself another shot. "Tell me, sonny. Do you like Frenchie's act?"

"Sure," says Nick. "It's phenomenal, but . . ."

"Her voice. It's ungodly, from another world. You could listen to it forever, right?"

"Sure, but . . ."

"Why change a thing? She's perfect."

"She's not, though," says Nick. "She's on some bad stuff. And I've got to get her off it or she'll die, just like my mom."

"She wants to mother you. Let her have what she wants. Just be a good boy and listen to her when she sings to you."

"Don't listen to him," says Sabrina. "And don't listen to her siren songs. Just be yourself, Micky, and you can bring her around."

"But I'm not Micky," says the pitcher. "I'm Nicky. I mean Nick."

"I'm Nicki!" booms the grinning bald man, taking Nick's hand in his iron grip. "Pleased to meet you, sonny. Now just listen to me."

"Stop!" shouts Sabrina. "You must stop, Nicki. Step back from the brink like you did mit the missiles."

"The missiles," says the bald man, raising his arms in exasperation. "We're back to the missiles? I never intended to use the missiles. I was just having fun with the young prince of Kennedy, who stole his election from my good friend Tricky Dick with the help of his bootlegger father. I'm having fun now, with Dicky in charge. Conditions have never been so ripe, the chaos so great. America is on the brink of disaster. When the Trickster wins again, with a little help from my merry band, the whole empire will go tumbling down, crushed by the weight of its capitalist excess. What a joyous scene! I can't wait for the day! Why do you always want to spoil the party?"

Sabrina reverts to Yiddish. "What kind of revolutionary is it who is so afraid to have a change of heart? Who could hope to move people who can't be moved himself?"

"Me! I can move people any way I choose," he says in the foreign tongue.

"You can't let the Cuban blow up the world."

"He's not blowing up the world. Just the old corrupt capitalist order."

"You know what I mean. You must clip his wings, if only a little."

The bald man scratches his temple, takes a puff of his cigar, puts it back down, and exhales slowly. "Maybe," he says softly, "for you, *matyushka*. If it means so much." He reaches across the table to take her hands in his, confident it won't matter in the end.

Awww, thinks Nick as they gaze into each other's eyes, look at the two lovebirds. His own eyes are averted by the crack of Angel's bat on the momentarily working TV as he sends one high and deep. Wow, what a shot!

"And if I do this," says the old man. "Do you promise to clip your Angel's wings too?"

"Yes," says Sabrina, "I do."

"Done!" He releases her to pound the table once more. "A mutual noninterference pact. We'll see how it all plays out." Then he turns to the pitcher, who's butt is really smarting, and says in English, "How's that sound, sonny. You up for that?"

"Sure," says Nick, not at all sure what he's agreeing to. "I guess."

25

DO OR DIE

In the burnt-out remains of Joan and Eliot's East Village apartment, *Mercury* reporter Art Popov writes:

DO OR DIE! ANGEL'S BLAST
FORCES GAME SEVEN SHOWDOWN

Swannie's just a memory today as the no-name Bomber pitchers, with the help of a pinch-hit ninth-inning homer by Angel Guerrero, continued their back-from-the-dead comeback with a 1–0 win over the Phillies in Game Six of this wacko World Series.

Miraculously surviving an assassination attempt at his SoHo loft by the same crazed actor who tried to slice Spillage up after Game One, Angel arrived on the scene just in time to pinch-hit for Red DePill, the fourth Yankee pitcher to hold down the fort. Harking back to all-time Yankee great Babe Ruth, the slugger pointed to the spot in the right-field stands where his shot would go and drilled it right there for the win.

So where were you, Mr. Spillage, when we needed you? AWOL like the immature brat you are, boozing it up with hot-rocker Frenchie Jones at every club in town, not worthy of the faith New Yorkers put in you, much less the faith of all America you're seeking on the ticket with Mayor Lightweight.

Swannie may be back on the mound today for do-or-die Game Seven, he may be President or Ruler of a New Theocracy by next month, there's no telling. Anything—including the burning of all of Brooklyn if that Coney Island fire keeps raging—could come out of this World Series, but right now Nick Spillage is the forgotten man, and no amount of barnstorming can change that, Mr. Mayor. Your choice of running mates has come back to haunt you, another in your long list of bad judgments the public will not forgive.

Blanket the country all you like with your little family circus and your doomsday homilies. You're not going to convince anybody of anything. Nixon's going to win in a landslide, and what happens to the country then? It's like you're throwing the race on purpose, which I wouldn't put it past you to do. You're just as morally bankrupt as the city you represent!

I used to be a Nixon man, but I've had a change of heart. If only there were a better alternative than Lightweight. My friends, America is truly at the abyss. But that, evidently, is what you get when you rely on the free market. Corrupt and more corrupt. Inept and more inept. Deeper and deeper into the rabbit hole.

Mayor Lightweight and his entourage are getting hooted off every stage in the country. He could not have timed his hasty marriage to the Haitian Hell-Raiser and whirlwind tour any worse. To compound his floundering campaign's problems (and who does he really expect will identify them with the nation's?), my sources are telling me that the Hell-Raiser was forced to marry the presidential hopeful under duress, that the ceremony wasn't performed by a proper judge or clergyman but rather by a member of the Satanic Vanguard, and that the baby is not really his.

The mayor claims otherwise, of course, but who can believe anything this lightweight says? His promises get bigger and bigger, emptier and emptier, while the only thing propping up his crowds is Frenchie serving as his warm-up act. For all we know, the baby could be Angel's, since he admitted to having a relationship with the Hell-Raiser after she was spotted leaving his loft.

Frenchie came to the game today with flowers cradled in her soft, white, punctured arms—sweet-smelling pink blossoms presumed to be for Spillage, who for a fleeting moment fans thought might also appear, but it was just a tease. Her surprise appearance didn't last long, but it almost got Angel ejected before he could take his fateful cut. The slugger was never known to be connected with the singer, never known to be connected with the Hell-Raiser either, but all sorts of hitherto hidden connections came to light in this boisterous affair today in the Bronx.

Angel wanted to give Frenchie a kiss, but umpire Manny Wo wouldn't allow it. This game had seen too many disruptions already. Poor Manny. No sooner does he talk the bull out of running loose in the china shop than a red flag gets waved in front of the bull's blazing green eyes (and where'd you get those peepers, Angel?). No one's fault, it just happened—Frenchie went faint. But Angel saw red because (as he later claimed) he put the blame squarely on her escort and manager Raoul Wo (no relation), the noted underworld figure who rumor has it is pulling the strings of the Lightweight-Spillage campaign as well.

Angel buys that rumor, claims Wo is everywhere, that he hooked Frenchie on junk and given time will do the same to the Hell-Raiser and on down the line. Never mind that Manny Wo had to forcibly restrain him from gallivanting through the stands in search of Frenchie, quite possibly never to return for his at bat. Never mind that Manny had to lead him back to home plate to tell him the show had to go on. Never mind that

Manny bent over backwards, as backwards as I've ever seen an umpire bend, to keep the troubled slugger in the game. Angel made it clear that all Woes are his enemy, related or not, and if they didn't give him his momma back, he'd crack their skulls open like he was about to crack the ball.

You listen to Angel rant long enough and you get the impression that the crazy actor's bomb did shake some marbles loose, even if it left his strength intact. But we'll see how it all plays out in the deciding game today, with new manager Howie Love saying he's penciling in Nick Who as his starter (no discipline for the kid, despite his AWOL antics), Frenchie on tap to sing the national anthem, the mayor and his new missus set to join the festivities, and owner Sheila Dugan, my Sheila, back at her customary perch in her luxury owner's box cheering her squad on. Art still loves you, Sheila.

"Cut that last line," says his editor, burning his hand with a cigar. "In fact, cut the whole thing." He pulls the article from the typewriter, balls it up, sets it on fire. "Don't like where this is going. Who told you to trash Nixon?"

"No one," says Art. "It just came to me."

"Well send it back where it came from. We can't trash Nixon. Not now."

"But wait, listen. It's brilliant. When you do the plague on both houses thing, it makes the attacks on Lightweight so much more credible. Plus, I got in the dig at the free market you wanted. What could be wrong with that?"

Raoul doesn't like the fact that Art is pushing back. Does he really think he can win an argument? He has the sense that something's shifted in their dynamic, that he's lost a tiny bit of control. Have to snuff that out quick, he thinks, before the resistance grows. "We don't need credibility," he says. "We need discipline. Stop freestyling and stick to the party line. Or else."

He flicks cigar embers in Art's face to make his point.

While he has good reason to hate Nixon, being in possession of his aggrieved Mad Man's soul, he knows the revolution depends on a Nixon victory. Only Tricky Dick can get the masses so outraged, he thinks, that they rise up and tear down the whole oppressive system. Comrade Mayor offers hope, and that hope must be obliterated. The mayor must be exposed as a total hypocrite, preaching high-minded values in public while privately abusing his Hell-Raiser girlfriend in unspeakable ways, proclaiming his love for New York while betting against his home team and getting them to take a dive. Make *him* the Devil in the eyes of the public—a hot, stinking, scary mess, just like the city he represents. That's the plan. That's always been the plan. And now that the pieces are all in place, it's all about execution.

Unless someone moved the pieces when you weren't looking, he thinks. What just happened to Señor Satan in that gypsy witch's kitchen?

. . .

"What's next, Angel?" says Yankee announcer Al Deep on the Game Six postgame show. "Hard to top what you did today."

"I'm seeing the ball real good," says Angel. "Better than ever."

"That's saying something. Wouldn't have anything to do with your eyes, would it?" asks Deep. "They look a little different. You get new lenses?"

"I had my eyes opened."

"They do look bigger."

"See every spin. See the way I've been spun. No telling what I can do now. Just watch."

"Yessir we will," says Deep. "Here with Angel Guerrero, Yankee hero of the day, a great slugger and great humanitarian too. Love what you did for the people of Puerto Rico. But can you do it for New York, bring the no-names all the way back if Swannie ain't there to help? Can you put this team on your shoulders and carry them into the promised land?"

The actor turned outfielder remembers an old line. "Uneasy lies the head that wears the crown."

"How's that?" asks Deep.

"No telling. Just watch," says Angel, smiling his megawatt smile and adjusting his wig.

. . .

In the predawn hour, as the slightest hint of daylight makes its way to the huge loft windows of her SoHo Reading Room, early riser Sister Sabrina rummages cheerily about her kitchen, clearing the last remnants of the dinner she served to her now departed husband. She's happy with the agreement they reached. As happy as she can be, at any rate, given their history.

"You see," the seer says to her cat as she loads the plates Bubba has licked clean into her dishwasher. "I told you we'd come back. We're not out of the woods yet by any means, but we have now at least a fighting chance. It's even Steven. One game to go."

She wipes babka crumbs off the counter, removes the tablecloth from the table, shakes it out, folds it up, places it in its proper drawer, and then, winded, retreats to her wheelchair. Her kitchen work is done. Time for her next task.

"I have hope, Bubba," she says. "We have more power with Angel in the lineup. And our Swan will be there soon, one way or the other. He knows what he needs to do. He's a good boy, always listens to me. And I told him what's what, did I not?"

She shakes her head, looking about for her bag. "He wants so much to save his Frenchie, who reminds him of his mother, which is not a big stretch," she says. "I do too! Believe me! But he can't let her sap too much of his strength. She's still under Wo's influence, fading though it may be. She wants badly to break free, but it's so, so hard. Wo knows her too well, he has her father's soul, and like the snake he is, he's poisoned her with his venom. She doesn't want to hurt you, Mickala, but that doesn't mean she won't!"

The cat, finding the bag first, has jumped in. Sabrina wheels over, picks it up, and puts it in her lap.

"Then there's young Alvin, who's lived through a nightmare," she says. "Such a baseball manager I've never seen! He too carries a huge burden, working in what for him is foreign territory. How quickly will he catch on, figure out the game? We must trust that he will make the right decisions, if he could just get from my *meshugah* daughter some breathing space. A big if, I must admit. At some point, perhaps she'll grow disenchanted, but not yet, I'm afraid."

"So much is at stake," she sighs. "So much at stake. A presidential election, the fate of the free world. What my Nicki has unleashed will not be so easily contained, even if he keeps his part of the bargain. Is this what America needs, Bubba? Another revolution? You're right—perhaps, after two hundred years, the time has come. For all his bluster, Nicki could have a point. But please not the revolution Wo is cooking up! That would not do at all."

She wheels herself, with Bubba in the bag, toward the door. "I still worry about Wo. He's angry now. And he'll stop at nothing if it helps his cause, deal or no deal. *His* cause. *Verstehst?* What did I tell you, Nicki? Wo is not to be trusted! He wants only to rule. You think he serves you, but watch your back!

"It's going to be close. Very close," she says, pausing before turning off the lights as she tries to remember if there's anything she forgot. There's something she can't put her finger on. Lipstick, wallet, ticket, teeth? No, the teeth, so often missing, are in their right place, ready for the big smile when the moment comes. And the rest is in the bag with Bubba. What then? It comes to her. "Our ace in the hole," she recalls, "is Mirlanda. We need Mirlanda to work her magic. Knock her ex-husband down another peg, give the country fresh reason to believe. Brave Mirlanda. This I don't want to miss! Come, we must get to the ballpark early to root, root, root!"

Part
FOUR

26

COMMITMENT

"Say yes, pet, please," says Sheila Dugan to her lover on the final leg of their private flight back. "I'll throw in part ownership if you commit yourself now."

I ought to be committed, thinks Eliot, fiddling with his seat to get the right angle. It was insane, he believes now, to think he could do it with Sheila and keep it all transactional. Once he got rid of the protective gear, once he gave her permission to counteract Joan's spell, it was all over. She had him. And he has to admit, it felt phenomenal.

Of course, there were extenuating circumstances. It was Gulliver's Island after all, the capital of Nightmare's Dream Dimension. So it didn't *really* happen. But then it kinda did, he thinks. He can't deny it. And while he still loves Joan and feels terrible about the whole thing, even though she cheated on him first and all but gave him the green light, he's certainly enjoying the comforts of being Sheila's tool up here in the sky. Not a bad life, if he can avoid looking at what's outside the bubble. Only problem is he can't.

"What's the big deal? You're already compromised," says Sheila.

"True," says Eliot. "But I'm not committed yet." The only saving grace is that he can't remember giving an unequivocal yes to Raoul's deal for his soul. His blonde bombshell sidekick knows this. She's still trying to get him to yes before they complete the journey. Still possible to turn her, or at least cut a better deal? He senses that as they've flown what feels like a thousand miles away from her diabolical island, her power over him has ebbed. Just a little bit, but enough to make a difference? Emboldened, he asks, "If I commit to you now, would you promise me Joan will be taken care of?"

"I'll promise you anything, pet."

"And mean it?"

"Depends on how you mean 'taken care of.' She's being well taken care of even as we speak, independent of all promises."

"Give her back. As she was. Once the Series is over."

"Out of the question, I'm afraid. There's no going back."

"What becomes of her if the Yankees win?"

"Unspeakable punishment."

"I can't let that happen."

"Then manage! Manage your heart out for me! She'll be in a box right over the dugout. It's all arranged. Blow kisses if you like. The odds are imposingly stacked against you, but if you do as I say, you win everything, don't you see? You represent New York, the vanguard of cities. The cities are America, America the West. The West is teetering at the edge. If you can keep this World Series from going the wrong way . . ."

"What's the wrong way, though? You're with the Devil, right? Are you trying to tell me I should manage to lose?"

"I'll tell you when the time comes. Trust me, pet. You'll be better off if you do as I say. Your former girlfriend too. But you must commit now. The plane is about to land. I must know you're totally with me."

"But why me? Why do I have to be the one?"

"Call it a whim, call it love."

"You don't love me."

"No. But I *am* committed. Perhaps I just want you in the same Burger Boat. I can't know. Don't ask me to fathom myself. Just say you'll manage for me, let me own you until the Series ends."

Maybe, thinks Eliot, it's because you're such a loser. Like she needs your personal dark cloud to ensure New York's defeat. He looks out the window to collect his thoughts, sees the oncoming megapolis and imagines it sinking. The Devil has torn it from the continent like a piece of wedding cake and offered it to his bride. But the bride doesn't want any. She doesn't know what she wants. And so the piece has been dumped into the champagne's ice bucket—the city destined, like Atlantis, for the bottom of the sea. Lost.

As the plane circles, Eliot thinks he can make out the stadium. Zooming in, he can see himself on the super-green Yankee infield grass, trying to come up with a workable strategy. The truth is, he knows little about baseball. He's followed it off and on over the years, gone to some games, but never got deeply into it. As a Brooklynite, King George was a Dodger fan. But he gave up on them after they left town. He became a Mets fan when they started in 1962, suffering through their years of futility until they won the championship in 1969. Then, after they traded away their best pitcher in a money dispute, he gave up on them too. Such a perfectionist. And that extended to his son as well.

He gave up on you a long time ago, Eliot thinks, when you dropped out of graduate school before getting your master's. When Nixon ended the draft, opting to fight the endless war in Vietnam with a volunteer army instead, what was the point of another degree? The only reason you'd gone as far as you did was to keep your deferment. You could always go back to school, once you figured out what you really wanted to be. Mom was good with that decision; King George, not so much. Apparently, he'd already figured out your career path—you were to be a professor, just like them. Typical of him. He probably would have preferred you have an arranged marriage too, to a woman of his choosing, who met all his arbitrary criteria, fit neatly into his ordered worldview. Certainly not Joan. He blamed her for your dropping out, blamed her absentee father for the monthly checks that gave you the flexibility to drop out. That was just before the economy crashed and the checks stopped coming. It didn't matter. You were done with school.

"What do you want to be when you grow up?" he remembers his mother asking when he was a little kid. "I don't know," he recalls answering. "What do you think I should be?" "You could be anything you want to be," she said, and it did seem at the time that anything was possible. She made it seem that way, with her relentless optimism, her faith in his abilities. "How about an astronaut?" he recalls saying, enchanted by the Apollo space program, which had just begun. And she laughed, saying, "Sure, the sky's the limit for my little boy." She even bought him a telescope so he could study the stars. But the closest he ever came to outer space until now was in the science fiction he read and watched with great enthusiasm throughout his teens. Asimov, Herbert, Bradbury, Le Guin, *Star Trek*, *Twilight Zone*, *2001*. He lapped it up, and she encouraged him. Now Nightmare knows better than to let her into your Dream Dimension, he thinks. She'd help you escape, no doubt.

The truth is, though, he still doesn't know what he wants to be, other than back with Joan. And he wasn't getting much closer to finding out, even before the weirdness started. He was never going to make a living writing poetry and rock and roll songs, however much he fantasized. No more than she was going to make a living doing art. Even if the economy hadn't crashed, he knew that neither of them were destined for artistic greatness.

So what has his recent experience taught him? He's not too good at being a fast-food restaurant night manager. Can't prevent the place from being held up and besides, who wants to work nights? Forget about politics; it's just too mean and he finds it pointless. Detective work? Too dangerous. Logical next step? Managing the Yankees, of course. It may not be anything he ever thought about before, may not be the real Eliot doing it, but it's as good as any other option for the moment. At least there's a prize if he succeeds. Maybe.

Have faith, Eliot says to himself. You'll figure things out. Use your mother's intuition, be the optimist she was, rather than rely on your father's faulty logic. You've never heard of Howie Love, so no sense trying to impersonate him out there on the field. You're just Eliot Howe in a different uniform, dealing with a different, upside-down world. The baseball answers will come if you don't try too hard to find them. Relax. Take a deep breath. You've still got a fighting chance.

He can see himself approaching the mound, trying to keep his eyes off Sheila's luxury box because it makes him feel like such a hopeless ass to see Joan unable to keep her hands off Raoul, off the needles in the pockets of his green fatigues. He's looking right at you, gives a palsy-walsy wink and says, "Don't worry, Señor Skipper. It's all a big game."

The pressure's mounting like crazy, the fans on their feet. "Okay, Skip, I'll give them nothing but smoke," says Swannie, standing between you and the sun, your good buddy now, still innocent, golden curls extending down his long neck, glove tucked in his armpit and ball between his palms, spit on and rubbed up. He looks so much younger than he did on TV, in the papers.

"Give me the ball, Nick," you say.

"You're not taking me out, are you, Skip?"

He actually believes you could. "Nah, I just want to rub it some myself, give it luck." Precisely what you don't have to give. But here's the rub: it feels like maybe you do, for a change. Your mother's gypsy luck. "They're grooving on your smoke, Swannie. You've lost your zip."

"I'll reach back for something extra, Skip."

"No. Take something off. Give 'em junk."

And does it work? Could they possibly not know, through Raoul, what's coming at them? You gotta believe, he thinks. Believe you can win *and* save Joan. There's got to be a way.

You know you love Joan, whatever happened on that damned island between you and Sheila, and Sheila can try until kingdom come to own you, but you'll love Joan all the more. So you commit to Sheila. Not the most direct way to show affection for Joan, sure, but Christ, the world might as well yield up some favorable contradictions once in a while. I mean love can't be all suffer-suffer, pine-pine.

You love Joan, which is your shield against Sheila. Meaning you can double-cross her, you noble bastard. To save the world of course. Things are starting to go your way. You make your commitment on the surface, knowing deep down (where it counts) you're committed elsewhere, take over the team, go all out to win, and what happens? You cop the Series, and she says Joan goes to hell. Gets the ultimate punishment, beyond imagination. But who says that's for sure? Who says she's not lying to save her own skin? You play to lose and the world goes to hell. That *is* for sure; we're halfway there and careening fast. You have to put Joan's potential punishment out of your mind. Give her up, to give her a chance.

You can't trust Sheila as far as you can throw her. She wants you on the field because she thinks when the time comes, you'll do what she tells you to. The Devil's work. Raoul's. Thinks she has you under her spell. Screw that. Play to win. Bluff her like your mom, the old poker champ, would do.

"Okay. I'm yours," says Eliot to Sheila.

"Good boy," says Sheila. "I'm glad you've seen the light."

. . .

As dawn breaks on the day of the seventh game, Eliot finds himself in a taxi, headed for Yankee Stadium from Newark Airport, where the Dugan jet landed. Driving up the New Jersey turnpike past the oil refineries and chemical plants churning smoke into the smoggy sky, he marvels at the band of red that spreads across the Manhattan skyline. Still standing, he thinks. It didn't sink into the sea as he imagined it would. Maybe he's survived the worst.

He flew out of Kennedy, to the east of the city, and came back to Newark, in the west, giving him the sense of having orbited the earth. He's not sure how he got diverted, or whether it was always the plan, and not sure what really happened in between. But he's still wearing his Burger Boat outfit, which he figures he can toss in the trash when he reaches the locker room. Never going back to that miserable job, where the nightmare began. Wash the rest of that nightmare off in a nice hot shower, put on those Yankee pinstripes, and get on with the task of winning the Series, winning back Joan.

Sheila thinks she owns you, he tells himself, which is why she let you ride solo, but she's got another thing coming. Your soul's intact, your mission's clear. The world may look at you differently, may expect something different from you, but as far as you're concerned, you're just exchanging one uniform for another.

The cabbie, a Vietnam vet from Tupelo named Tommy, has his own story of transformation, which he relates to Eliot. His helicopter was shot down during the Battle of Hamburger Hill, and he fell into a rice paddy, where he thought he died. But then, unconscious, he was pulled out by a Vietnamese villager and nursed back to health. Up to then, he was a rabid anti-Communist who totally bought into the war and the whole domino theory behind it, believing Ho Chi Minh was a devil and his regime needed to be decimated to ensure America's future. But witnessing from ground level the American bombs falling during his convalescence, seeing the devastation they caused from what he called the other side of the looking glass, he came to believe it was the Yankees who were devils, and he swore he'd do everything he could to stop the carnage. That's why, when he finally made his way home, he became an ardent member of Vietnam Veterans Against the War, which he urges Eliot to contribute to, handing him a pamphlet.

Eliot doesn't need any convincing. The cabbie's story sobers him up. He happily hands Tommy from Tupelo a $1,000 bill he peels from the wad in his pocket, trying to remember how it got back there. The money comes and goes, he thinks, the only constant being that it continues to lose value at an alarming pace. He can't believe how fast the taxi meter is racing ahead. Feeling the cab shift gears as it veers into the passing lane, he thinks he's probably still in the Dream Dimension, but getting closer to reality, even if it's a grim one. The war grinds on. The depression endures. The planet keeps getting polluted. Violence abounds. Nixon's still in power. His parents are dead. The Bronx, when he gets there, will still be a wasteland.

Watching the smoke rise from chemical plants, he tries to decipher which way the wind is blowing now, how it will affect fly balls in the stadium. That'll factor into the decisions you make, he thinks, like where to position the outfielders. While he doesn't know much about baseball, he probably knows enough to manage . . . with a little help from his coaches. With a little help from my friends, he thinks, remembering the Beatles tune. Can't wait to meet them, to meet Swannie and Angel in the flesh. To meet the other guys, whatever their names are. You'll have to learn fast.

Still, it feels good to be part of a team. He hums the Beatles song, alone and sad no more.

It was horribly lonely down there on Gulliver's Island, the dark night of your soul, he thinks. Joan was awful, crueler than she ever was in real life, drugged beyond belief with some super-bad crap, and his father was no help whatsoever. The wrong guy in the wrong place, trying to apply logic to a profoundly illogical world. And he has to admit that the woman who blithely turned him into a jackass was in fact his real beloved, not her evil twin, but Joan as he projected her under Nightmare's influence. The Joan he must have always suspected lurked below the surface. Okay well that's out in the open now, he tells himself. She has the power to torment you. Can you love her all the same? Yes, for life, he remembers thinking as the punishment rained down, determined to pass the test. But no, not the same. There's no going back. As that Greek philosopher Heraclitus he studied in college once said, "You can't step into the same river twice." All being is becoming. You can't fight change. You've got to build a new relationship with her, one better able to withstand the wild swings.

Back in the old days, he recalls, you didn't fight much. What's the worst fight you ever had? Maybe the one at the very beginning of the relationship, when you bought her that green velvet dress from the vintage clothing store on Avenue B. No occasion. Just saw it in the

window and thought she'd look good in it. Wanted to give a sponta-
neous gift to show your affection. But she thought it was the ugliest
thing she'd ever seen. "How could you possibly have imagined me in
this old rag?" she said. "Can't you see it's not me? Don't you have eyes? I
can't believe I'm going with someone with such a poor aesthetic sense.
Such a lack of vision. We are totally not for one another. Go way, just
go way."

They didn't see one another for a week after that. But then she
called to say she forgave him, just never buy me clothes again. Best
call ever. "You have vision," she said. "I know you have vision. You just
don't express it the same way as I do. You paint in words and ideas, and
I'm down with that, even if you're color-blind. You inspire me, you're
my muse! I mean I'm really into you, Eliot. You must know that, and
I know you do. I just panicked a little because we got so close so fast."

It felt so good to hear her say that. He'd never had such a sense of
relief. And then she defended him fiercely when they went to see her
mother off to Florida a few days later. He'd brought an umbrella to that
meeting outside her Upper East Side apartment, with the moving van
being packed, even though it was a bright sunny day, because he'd left
it in her room before their mini-breakup and planned to take it back to
his. No big deal. But to her disapproving mother, the plastic lady, it was
an ominous sign. "What kind of man carries an umbrella around when
there's not a cloud in the sky?" she'd said. "Does he have a personal dark
cloud that always hangs over his head? I'd be careful with this dreary
guy if I were you."

That really set Joan off. "He's a poet," she declared. "Something
you'll never understand, because it requires thought. It requires looking
for meaning in life, instead of just skimming along the surface like you
always do, rocking out on your crazy-ass conspiracy theories. I don't
know why I ever came here, why I thought it was worth saying goodbye. You have no right to judge me, or the choices I make."

And with that she ushered him off, never to speak to her mother
again. Thinking of his own mom, he felt sad she'd made such a definitive

break with her parents. Still, it felt great that she'd defended him. More than that, she defined him: as a poet, as her lover, as her muse. "With a little help from my friends," he sings to himself.

Still, there was something about what her mother said that struck him as true. His personal dark cloud, his sense of self-doubt, his premonition that as strong as the bond with Joan was, it wouldn't last forever. The negativity he inherited from his father. That's what opened the astral door to Raoul, to Nightmare. That's what exploded into last night's storm. He had to go through that storm to get where he needed to go with his mind, with his spirit.

Which is here, now, hopeful, he thinks, rolling down his window and breathing in the polluted air. The stink of these industrial plants is so powerful it has to be real. The sky is clear though, and so is his head. The threats are still out there. You haven't won anything yet. And even if you win, what then? You still have to confront the possibility that winning will be bad for Joan. Maybe she doesn't die, but she gets punished in other ways. Like not being able to have kids. So what, as long as you're together. Whatever the world slings at you, you have the power to manage. With a little help, a little help . . .

Looking in the taxi's rearview mirror, he sees that his beard, full again, now has streaks of gray. How long were you down in that underworld, after all? You've aged, he thinks, beyond your years. Is this permanent? Is Joan's transformation into Frenchie permanent? That would complicate things for sure, especially if she still has the drug habit. He hums a little louder, tries to put the thought out of his mind.

Hearing him hum, Tommy from Tupelo asks if he wants some music. And in the next minute, there she is on the radio as Frenchie, belting out "Me and Bobby McGee."

"Don't you love her?" the cabbie asks. "She makes me feel like I'm Bobby, and it makes me want to cry."

"Makes me want to cry, too," says Eliot.

27

WELCOME TO PARADOX

"Here," says Spillage, in his sleep. "Here. Got to win here."

"It's okay, baby," says Joan, dreamily, running her hand through his golden curls in the Coney Island fun house Raoul has transported them to. "Momma's here. It's okay."

But it's not okay, she thinks. Her orders are clear: seduce the Swan, corrupt him, make him throw the Series, bring New York down. And while you're at it, bring down New York's biggest fan, its mayor, the presidential hopeful, who'll somehow be implicated in the scheme. She doesn't know exactly how, but she knows it's part of the puzzle, because the Devil's ultimate goal is to keep Nixon in the White House so he can keep driving the country deeper into hell. Why else would he have the architect of Nixon's past two victories on his team?

The Satanic Vanguard is just a ruse, Joan thinks, just another bogeyman for Nixon to run against. His campaigns are always based on fear. That's Big Daddy's genius. But what's so genius about involving you? What special sauce do you bring to this concoction?

In another world, you might think that the Devil kidnapped you to force Big Daddy to support his cause. But that would imply the Mad Man cared one teeny bit about you, when the one absolutely certain thing is that he never did. No, you were targeted because Big

Daddy wanted you here. He put you in this place because he knew he could count on you to defend his interests when the chips were down. Because you *did* defend him in the divorce against Dear Mother's accusations of child molesting.

You saved his career by not going along with her, she thinks. And with that second lease on life, he created Nixon! So depressing to think you indirectly helped. And why should he not assume you'll do it again, helping the tyrant extend his reign?

Because you're onto his game now. You know you didn't create this mess. It was forced on you! There's a great conspiracy afoot—the Russians, Cubans, Chinese, and Nixon are all involved, probably the CIA and Mafia too—and you're just a pawn. It's so much bigger than your little love interests. You couldn't be the cause. You hate to admit it, but maybe Dear Mother was right about the Kennedy assassination, right about Big Daddy, too. You should have kicked him out of your bedroom sooner. You need to resist now. But you're weak. Too dependent on Raoul's stuff. And the fun house is burning all around you.

You were targeted, no question, she thinks. Big Daddy dragged you into this, but that doesn't absolve you of responsibility. On your own you became obsessed with the Swan, set out on this insane journey, fell in bed with the first actor you met, left your loving boyfriend for roadkill, rushed headlong into oncoming traffic, and didn't fight hard enough against the Devil's evil needle. All bad shit you'll have to live with for the rest of your life, if you call this life, which is still an open question. You wanted more and got more than you wanted. They should write that on your tombstone. But it was beyond you, too. So much went down that you couldn't help.

Eliot could help, could've helped, if you kept him at your side. If only he were with you now, instead of the dreamy pitcher. He *was* with you here, remember, in this very fun house, back in the days when you could still have fun. Walking the boardwalk, riding the Wonder Wheel, ringing the bell with that big hammer in the contest of strength. Wily Eliot, your guide through Brooklyn, could figure a way out of this nightmare. Which is precisely why Raoul wants to burn the place down. Reduce to ashes all traces of your prior existence. Make you totally his.

Spillage wakes with a start in the raging blaze. The warped mirrors surrounding them are filled to the brim with what seems like a stadium full of newborn babies, wailing and screaming at the tops of their lungs. "We've got to get out of here, Frenchie. Fast. Before this blazing infirmary burns us to a crisp."

Seeing no obvious exit, he scoops her in his arms and plunges straight ahead, protecting her as best he can as he bursts through the glass and out of the fun house, running so hard he can feel himself lifted, up over the boardwalk, over the sand, and into the bracingly cold waters of the Atlantic, where the flames are quickly doused but the current sucks them out with a force he's no match for, holding tightly to the woman of his dreams and trying with only intermittent success to keep their heads above the surface until a huge wave crashes over them and washes them out onto the shore.

Coming to his senses, he can see in the predawn distance the spray of the firemen's hoses trying to get the boardwalk blaze under control, while closer in, beside a single warped mirror stuck up like the *2001* obelisk in the sand, his dog Gemini is licking Frenchie's cheeks in an effort to revive her. The red sun, reflected in the mirror, is just beginning to rise, while the beach in the mirror, unlike the strong Coney Island surf, is strikingly calm, the water more clear and turquoise blue, with a flock of snow-white gulls feeding at the edge. Like a tropical island, he thinks, as Frenchie wakes, shakes, and coughs out salt water.

"Welcome to paradox, Frenchie," he says, reaching out to pet his dog. "How do you feel?"

"I feel like shit," says Joan, between heaves. "Where's Raoul? I need my fix." Her head is pounding, her stomach is churning, and her tracks itch so bad it's like she has vermin crawling across her body. And this is what you traded your soul for? Blech.

"He's not here. We ditched him."

"He's here. Don't worry." She stares into the rising sun, thinks she sees his eyes, his snaky grin. "Raoul! Stop playing games."

"Frenchie, I've got to talk to you about something."

"No. Don't," she says, grabbing hold of the Dalmatian and pulling him toward her like a shield. Gem, she thinks. Oh, Lord, what do I do? You're my bestest friend, tell me. You and me, man, we go back, we go all the way back to when I was pure, had this love for your master that was so unreal, like just the thought that I was as close to him as his dog had me dizzy with excitement, you remember? Now that I have him, I can't get up for him. He's fallen for me like I'm some kind of goddess, though I'm really just the reverse, but he's so damned young and headstrong he still trusts his instincts like I did, like Choice told me I should, but I can't. It's so hard to go against Raoul, you've got to understand that, Gem. I need him so bad, I need him this instant, why can't you make me not need him, why can't you, why can't you?

"Don't cry, Frenchie. It's not the end of the world. You're better off without that guy, and the god-awful drugs he put you on." He crawls toward her and the dog in his drenched, clamdigger-length torn jeans and elbow-sleeved, equally torn, untucked Yankee shirt.

She hunkers down behind the Dalmatian, hides her face in her trembling hands while she feels the remaining bits of blue ebb from her burning eyes in bittersweet droplets that make a beeline down her wrists to the tracks on her arm that she needs to expand right now if she's to cope. She's tied to the tracks, to Raoul, and this boy can't cut you free any more than his dog could. "Go way," she says between sobs.

"I'm not going away. I'm going to help you get through this. I'm your antonym. Sister Sabrina told me."

"You mean antidote, you dumb jock. But there is no antidote. I'm done for, can't you see? And you can't save me. You can't even talk straight."

"I can pitch, though," says Spillage. "You've got to let me make my pitch. I always put it where I want it. Don't you know who I am?" He looks in the fun house mirror as if to make sure himself, and likes what he sees, but wonders when his clothes shrunk. Were they like this when he was on tour with her?

"Of course I know," says Joan, sniffing loudly. "Who doesn't know, for Christ's sake? I've seen to that, been singing your damned praises across the country. Sick to death of hearing myself sing." She gags, takes her hands from her face to try to throw up, but nothing comes out and she flicks her head back with a second loud sniff, wipes gunk off her nose with her shaking right hand, then seems at a loss what to do with the hand.

Spillage hastily hauls his Yankee shirt over his long neck and head, reluctant only to lose sight of her for the instant it takes. "Here. Use this," he says, and when his Dalmatian snaps at it as though it were a plaything, he rudely pushes him away and adds, "You had your ups, boy. My turn now. Go find us a ride to the ballpark or something."

"No," says Joan, lunging for the dog and catching him by the leg. "He's my only friend." Feels good to stretch out—well, better, for the moment.

"He's my friend too, Frenchie, and I'm your friend," says Spillage. "I mean I want to help you."

"Sure you do." My winged stallion, thinks Joan, caressing the dog. What doesn't he get about my desperate state? Good thing he doesn't have to think to pitch. That's my job, right? To give him ideas. "Know what, Gem?" she whispers to the Dalmatian. "I think he's already got them. Took his shirt off and I didn't even ask."

"I thought maybe you needed it," says Spillage, wondering how it got stained with blood. His memory was never as great as his arm, even before the collusion, but now he's conscious of more holes than before.

"You give everyone everything they need?" says Joan, running her fingers along the dog's white underbelly. Stay still now, Gem.

"I do my best," says Spillage. "Say, is your name really Frenchie?"

"Might as well be," says Joan. "I've gotten used to it, you know?"

"But it's not your real name." Spillage stretches out beside her. "You want to tell me your real name?"

"Nah."

"How'd you get here, Frenchie? How'd you get in this state?"

"Don't probe, baby." Joan rolls away, still holding on to the dog. "My story's like too gruesome to hit you with."

"Hit me. I don't get hit often enough to get hurt." Or see sand that glimmers like precious lodestones in a woman's alive and kicking red stresses. Would she mind just a touch? And what would that do to you? Be yourself, said the gypsy.

"You've never been threatened," says Joan. "You've never come close to losing, have you."

"Sure, I've come close. I come close a lot, when I don't get support. Almost lost the first game of the Series. Did you catch that?"

"I thought you were beautiful."

"What changed your mind?"

"Nothing. I still think you're beautiful, baby." But young, so young.

Spillage moves his pitching hand within a fraction of an inch of her hair, lets the sea breeze—picking up now and causing the fun house mirror to waver—bring him to fleeting contact. "Then why won't you look at me?" he says.

"Because I'll ruin you," says Joan. "I'll make a loser out of you, like I make everyone I come into contact with a loser."

"The only one you've got to lose is that manager of yours," says Spillage. "He's bad news."

"I wouldn't be here with you if it weren't for him."

"Not true. I've been looking for you my whole life. I would have found you."

"Course you would." She coughs, tries to vomit again, but again comes up dry.

"And you wouldn't be in such sorry shape."

In the fun house mirror, she sees Eliot at the mound in his Yankee pinstripes, chatting with the umps, who all look like Raoul. Think he has a chance, Gem, against those guys? She hugs the dog tightly. No, no, no, smart dog, or is that yes? You're heaving so, is it the heat? Well it won't get any cooler, Gem, wish it would myself. But look at Eliot, he's sweating through his pinstripes and it *has* to be cooler there, the game hasn't started yet. They don't fit him any better than his clothes ever do, always hang so loose, man some people never change. And then some people change so much you can't recognize them, they can't even recognize themselves, like me.

Come on, Gem, quit trembling, why are you so scared? My one true friend, don't quit on me now. You know how this came down. You were everywhere with me, even in the graveyard, you led the friggin' way. Saw bony Eliot ball phony Sheila, what was that about? You heard me cry out for him, right? You're my witness. He didn't respond and never will. Wily Eliot be damned. He missed his chance. What's he wearing now, zero? Least that fits. Shit, it's thirty. Well, I never wanted thirty anyhow, always freaked me out. Rather die than be thirty. Eliot, you're dead. Tell him, Raoul. You can't win.

A wave of nausea surges through her as she thinks about the punishment that awaits if the Yankees, with her boyfriend at the helm, somehow manage to win it all. So much worse than she's suffering now, she can hear Raoul say, worse than you can possibly imagine. Eliot needs to understand. Tell him.

You have to put me first, boyfriend, top of the order, the way you always did, and lose. Let the world go to hell, it was bound to sooner or later. Besides, there are levels of hell, as many levels as there are to any relationship. It just depends on the parties, and their levels of involvement. There are levels, and I'm at one, but you can send me still lower because there's always room for one more fall. The Devil runs a fine house. He's always having new additions dug, like there's no foundation, you've never seen such frenetic activity, but he expects the place to be overflowing soon so his minions have to hustle and that includes me.

I'm the one he depends on, see, like you once depended on me. I'm a woman of experience, right? And according to my ability, according to his needs (which are mine by virtue of being hooked), I keep his body and soul together by keeping mine split up. So you know what I'm finding? I'm divisible as all hell. There are as many parts to me as there are pores on my skin and they're all hot and they all itch. Yet when he pumps that stuff into me, Eliot, even though there's no direct contact (he does it through his man), there's this incredible impact and it's—Lord, I want it now.

Only now I have to do this trick with the pitcher, you know, the one in your lineup. In your lineup! You're whacked out, bro, on wishful thinking, always were, but this is ridiculous, come on. Thinking like the kid that you can win *and* save me. I don't believe you, Eliot. Why do you look so happy? Do you think like all this unreal shit happening with the world is gonna make me *more* ready to believe in you? The Swan is gonna throw this Series and you're gonna let him because *I* am Mother Earth and I say so. I'm all the forces of your nature pulling in different directions so you can't make the right moves, can't win to save your life, much less mine. You've got to understand. This is serious, man. I'm in serious shit and you could make it much worse if you don't watch out.

But then, maybe you're being too hard on him, she thinks. Maybe he knows something you don't know. I want to believe in you, Eliot. I really do, like I once did. Believe you can save me from myself, from this self I've become. Believe in Nick, Angel, your whole team. Go Yanks! But I just don't know if I have the courage, not in the state the Devil has me in. It's not going to be easy, boys. You've got to know that. And the risk is so great it's making me sick.

"Let's talk about your manager," Joan says to the pitcher. "What gives you such confidence Howie Love can do the job?"

"Love? I don't get it. What happened to Casey?"

"Where've you been, baby? Casey died. Sheila went with Love. Look in the mirror, don't you see?"

Spillage looks, sees the stadium, wishes he was there already but knows he has business to take care of first. "I'm okay with Love," he says. "Howie's always been good for me."

"Good for me too," she sighs. "Once upon a time. But not now."

"You know him?"

"I lived with him, before he got into baseball."

"You sure have gotten around, Frenchie. I'd love to hear a liturgy of the places you've been. I probably never heard of a tenth of them."

"Wouldn't surprise me."

"What would?"

"If you'd stop coming on to me. Can't you see I'm wrong for you?"

The sand shifts, and the mirror tilts toward them. Nick holds out his arms to stop the fall, while the dog breaks free of Joan's grasp and runs toward the boardwalk, where the firefighters seem to be finally getting the blaze under control. She can't help but look at him now, straining to hold up the mirror. Gorgeous beyond belief. My Samson. Time to snip those curls? Maybe not. What if you let them flow?

You've got to summon your power to believe. All of it, and more. Never mind the risk, just give it a shot. Everything up to now has been a bad dream, just like Salem. The Swan kisses you, you wake, and the world is set right. That's the kind of power he had when all of this started. The power you saw in him, before Raoul had his way. Sure, you made your deal with the Devil, but remember, you were forced into it, drugged. And besides, this was NOT the deal he promised, not the rotten way you feel now. You know, if he wanted you to stay loyal, he should have stuck with you, kept sticking it to you, instead of letting you fall apart like this.

"Frenchie. Trust me."

"Stop. Don't say a word. I'm like trying to concentrate my energies here, see if we have a chance. Would you want the catcher to get personal with you just when you're trying to dig in at the plate, your team down one, two men on and two men out, two strikes called before you even see the balls and only this one last shot to go against a guy as friggin' phenomenal as you?"

"Don't know what you mean exactly."

"Forget it. We can't talk."

"Don't get angry with me, Frenchie."

"I can't help it, baby. I'm bad!"

Spillage, looking in the mirror, sees in the Yankee locker room the whirlpool bath his pitching arm could use at this point, certainly before he goes into action again. The weight of the mirror feels more like the weight of the world the more he holds it, but he can't summon the strength to push it off. She needs to give him that strength with her kiss, he thinks, while he gives her the strength to throw off her tormentor. But how can he get her to see that?

"Believe me," he says, "the two of us were destituted for each other. The gypsies told me."

"What gypsies? Where?"

Funny how you thought she knew. "The ones in Sister Sabrina's kitchen, arguing across the table. They bounded back and forth between languages, talking a blue streak about things it seemed like I ought to have known something about but couldn't put my finger through— you, for instance, and your manager, who come to think of it looks like a lot of guys I know. The Wo brothers for one, they're the umps in this Series, and this guy I put a bullet through in this childhooded dream I had that you were in without your hair, and guys in scores of other dreams I've had about you, Frenchie. Sometimes it seems like I dream about you more than I stay awake. Thrown some awful bad pitches with those Woes out there, you talk about coming near to losing, but fortunously I've gotten away with them like we've always gotten away in my dreams, and now that we've really gotten away from it all, Frenchie, I just wish you'd lean over and kiss me so I can throw off this mirror and make your Wo disappear for good."

Sabrina, thinks Joan. The Good Witch of SoHo. Wasn't much use when you went to her for guidance, but maybe it was just her way? And who's this? The superhuman pitcher, or the leprechaun newsboy? "Combination of the Two," she thinks. Janis's song. Nick's shrunken clothes. It all fits together. The great conspiracy, where you're just a pawn. In the mirror, she can see Raoul striding across the sand, rifle in hand, ammo belt across his shoulders, preparing for war. He knows you're thinking of changing sides.

"We haven't gotten away from anything. He's here," she says.

"You haven't kissed me yet."

"Look into the mirror. Tell me what you see."

Spillage looks, sees a group of firemen coming toward them from the boardwalk. The flames are out. There's nothing but smoke now. He stares directly at her. "I see your eyes," he says. "And they're even more spellblinding than they were in my dreams. I think it's 'cause they're so red from crying."

"My God, Nick, look!" With her hands on his golden-fuzzed cheeks, she steers his face back toward the mirror. "He's here, right? Coming right at us. And he's mad as all hell I've been thinking about betraying him."

"I don't see him, Frenchie. Honest. All's I see is a bunch of good guys, the guys who put out the boardwalk fire. They want to help us. But you've got to kiss me first."

What is he talking about? She only sees Raoul, more menacing than ever. "You're not seeing things right," she says. "You don't know who you're dealing with."

He's swimming in her watery, bloodshot eyes. "I'm about to take a dive."

"Damned straight. Seventh game." She can't resist, leans in for the kiss.

"Let's forget about baseball."

"Mmm."

As their lips make contact, Spillage feels his elbow pop. Ignoring the pain, he throws back the mirror and takes her in his arms.

"All right, kids," says Raoul, standing over them. "Party's over. Time for the big game. Let's go to the car now. Got to hustle."

The firemen arrive a moment later, accompanied by the barking Dalmatian. "Swannie, Frenchie, come with us," says the lead guy, with a ponytail hanging out from under his helmet. "We'll get you to the stadium in no time flat."

Spillage scrambles to his feet, dusts off sand. "We're going with them," he says firmly to Raoul. "She's done with you. You're fired."

Raoul looks amused. "Frenchie? You let him do that?"

She's still seated on the sand, head between her knees. Her skin still tingles, but the head-pounding and nausea have lessened somewhat. The nightmare's not over, but she's willing to believe there's hope. "Yeah," she says softly, almost inaudibly. "I'm going with Nick."

She glances up at Raoul, expecting a sharp rebuke, but he just wags his head and frowns in disbelief. You've done it, she thinks. You've made the break. It's a tepid break, for sure, one filled with fear of the terrible consequences that may very well come, but it's definitely a break. You're done doing the Devil's bidding. Time to put your faith in your better angels.

Nick's arm is killing him. He tries to shake it off.

"Suit yourself," says Raoul. "You did what you needed to. Just remember how you suffered, cause it can get worse." He flashes his snaky grin. "Mucho worse."

28

THANK YOU, ANGEL!

Dispirited, Raoul digs a flask out of his green fatigues and removes his cigar to take a swig of rum as he looks over Art's shoulder in Joan and Eliot's charred apartment.

In life, he was a mean drunk, and now he knows the booze will make him even meaner. But someone's got to be mean, he thinks, to get the job done. Can't let these people defy him like this, just because Señor Satan went soft, swallowed the mush his old flame fed him. He's not out on the front line, can't know what the struggle's like, can't see the danger of losing precious gains if we don't stay on top of situations, smother resistance before she surfaces. Let them throw off their mirrors and next thing you know they think they look good. Next thing you know they think they feel good, think they can do good and get away with it. Next thing you've got a plague of runaway goodness, and how's that supposed to help spark the revolution?

She's dreaming if she thinks she can just walk away and abandon the cause. Your fires still burn in her, and they won't die so fast. They're ready to leap up and consume her at your command. You're just not in the mood to issue the order yet. In the mood for another stiff drink.

He takes another gulp, as Art keeps working.

The *Mercury* story reads:

THANK YOU, ANGEL!
YANKEE OUTFIELDER HELPS PUT OUT FIRE

Slugging Yankee outfielder Angel Guerrero proved his humanitarian chops again as he volunteered to help firefighters put out
the raging Coney Island fire that refused to die until he entered
the scene, giving new hope to the beleaguered city just as his
beloved Bronx Bombers prepared to face off against the Phillies
in their do-or-die World Series finale.

"Rip it up!" shouts Raoul. "I don't want to see it. Whose side do you
think you're on?"

Art reluctantly yanks the page out of his Hermes typewriter, tears
it into little pieces. "Your side, of course," he says. "You think I'm a
glutton for punishment?"

"Think you're a tool. My tool. And you better write what I want if
you know what's good for you."

"Sure thing, chief. But the boss says we need to balance things out
to keep the advertisers on board. Thinks readers will lose interest if we
go too far. Didn't you get that message?"

"Don't you get my message?" He gives him a cigar burn to the neck
to make his point. "Nobody knows better what advertisers want than
me. I'm the best there is at this. You better believe it."

"Hey," says Art, rubbing the spot. "I'm just reporting the facts."

"The facts are what I say they are. You report to me. Maybe Señor
Satan blinked, but we keep fighting."

. . .

"How 'bout that," says Yankee sportscaster Al Deep on the pregame
show for the Series finale. "Like they say in the Good Book, 'Ask and
ye shall receive.' Well, I asked. You heard me asking. Been asking all

week, ever since Game One when our stars disappeared, when the city blacked out and the Brooklyn fire started, poor Admiral Dugan going down for the count and his team going down with him—down, down, down—down three games to one before you know it and looking like there was no tomorrow down in Liberty Bell Creek.

"But what do you know, outta nowhere Daffy Allatime twirls a gem and we live another day, return to the Bronx for some home cookin', and then the no-names hold on until Angel arrives to swat that mammoth walk-off winner and we're even, but not really, still with one big missing piece. And then it's Angel once again, this time with a hose instead of his big bat, putting out the fire and finding Swannie on the beach!

"I'm telling ya, how many heroics is this guy capable of? We'll find out soon on this beautiful day to play ball, the Yankees' big stars all in place to make new manager Howie Love's job a whole lot easier. What a sight for sore eyes it was seeing New York's Bravest cruising up Fifth Avenue with Angel, Swannie, and hot-rocker Frenchie Jones in tow. Sure had the feel of a victory parade but let's not jump ahead of ourselves, these Independence Hallers are still tough."

· · ·

In the Yankee locker room, a man who could pass for the team's regular right fielder (though an inch smaller and ten pounds lighter, with riveting green eyes instead of deep-set blue-green, with an even bigger smile and less hair all around unless you count the ponytail wig) rolls over on the rubdown table to address his trainer.

"You're pressing too hard, my man. Just need a little tweaking to loosen up," he says.

"Why'd you go to Brooklyn?" says the trainer. "You almost messed things up. Good thing she ruined him before you arrived."

The outfielder shrugs. "Just had an impulse. Couldn't help myself. Saw a chance to help and took it. That's me." He rolls back over onto his stomach.

"Which me is that, Choice?"

"There's only one me. I'm in the part now, Raoul."

"Don't get too carried away. We don't need no more showboating."

"But showboating's who I am! You can't put me on the big stage and not expect me to showboat. The fans want me to showboat, they're eating it up. If I don't showboat, they won't believe I'm Angel. And you need them to believe that, don't you, bro?"

"Don't care what they believe. Just care about the end result." His hands move around the outfielder's shoulders and neck, looking for pressure points. "You better start caring about that too, if you know what's good for you." He pinches between the blades.

"Ow! You're hurting. Go easy, my man."

"Nothing compared to the hurt I'll give you if you go against me in the game. You don't remember the Tombs?"

"Sure. How can I forget? But I've got to be me out there. You've got to let me be me."

"Me again! I don't want to hear that word no more coming from your lips." He pinches harder, lower down the spine. "Me is what gets the world into trouble, what the Free Market God feasts on. Me-ism's what we got to overthrow. You got rid of all me when you joined the cause. The revolution has no me."

"You lost me there, Raoul. That's not what I signed up for."

"No need to sign. You gave me your soul."

"You had me in a bad place. Lied about Mirlanda."

"Mirlanda's come around. She's back on our team now. You'll hurt her too, and Junior, if you go off script."

"Right. Now I'm supposed to care about hurting Mirlanda, after you just about had me blow her to smithereens? I shimmied down that rabbit hole as far as I could take it. But the explosion knocked some sense into me. I'm seeing things different now."

"Close your eyes. Tell me what you see. It's your future for all time if . . ."

"Ain't going to play that game. Going to play my way. Something inside's telling me you don't have the control you pretend to have. Got some pretty bad tricks, sure, but not my soul. Something inside says you don't have Mirlanda or my bald momma neither."

"Angel."

"Maybe."

"He lies."

"Maybe. Not saying I believe him, but I got his power. Who knows what else? Trust me, Raoul. I don't want to go against you, don't want to take the risk and all. But on the other hand . . ."

"There's no other hand." He presses down hard with both palms.

"Look." The outfielder rolls over, manages to sit up. "We're done here. I'm going to see the ball and go for it. If it's down and away, maybe I chase it. Gonna improvise, make it up as I go along, just like the jazz greats, just like I do on stage. I'm playing like I have soul, see, whether I got it or not. And I'm flying across the field, making whatever catches I can. Maybe I miss some pitches. Maybe I drop some flies, make some wild throws. Maybe in the end I get hurt real bad, by you or by the Phillies, don't matter to me which. I don't know how the game's going to turn out, my man. There's no predicting. I just know I'm going to give the fans a great show. I'm in the moment. I'm in the role. And I'm up for it."

He smiles his megawatt smile, swings off the table, and snaps his towel at Raoul. "Just watch me play."

29

LAND OF THE FREE

Standing at home plate, trembling as she grips her mike, bloodshot eyes scanning the jam-packed Yankee Stadium crowd as they take off their hats and place their hands on their hearts, Joan wonders if she has the strength to deliver the national anthem they've all come to hear.

She thinks of Jimi Hendrix at Woodstock, playing the most electrifying "Star-Spangled Banner" ever played, turning his guitar into so much more, a profound act of protest against the Vietnam War, the distortion and feedback bringing forth the sounds of bombs, airplane engines, explosions, and human cries, rage flying out of the amps in every direction, with a little taps toward the end for a dying empire. That was a moment, a defining moment for the greatest rock concert in history, and she was there, with Eliot, having survived the deluge! It was early Monday morning, she remembers it clearly, having endured a torrential downpour the day before by huddling with a dozen people in a makeshift shelter that was built for maybe four. The crowd had dwindled, but they made it and were so proud. This was a moment, they were sure, that would change America forever. Set it free.

And now here you are at another moment, another turning point, which could be even more consequential, but the script has been flipped. You're the one on stage, about to make history. But if the Devil has his way, it's the wrong kind of history, not the one you ever wanted to make. This moment feels less like Woodstock, more like Altamont, where the '60s crashed and burned in a West Coast Stones concert that led to deaths. What do you expect when you turn security over to the Hells Angels? Now it's their distant cousins, the Satanic Vanguard. You can see Raoul's clones everywhere as you look around the stands. There's violence in the air here at Yankee Stadium, for sure, and you're supposed to be the warm-up act that will help precipitate it. No way!

Looking around the stadium, she sees ads for Burger Boat everywhere. "Don't miss the Boat!" they proclaim. Big Daddy's slogan. He's conspiring with Raoul, for sure. He *is* Raoul to some degree; they share the same kind of snaky grin. This is Big Daddy's ultimate revenge, trying to turn you into the ultimate fake, with a voice that's not yours, a mission you can't identify with. You can't let him do it. You can't be the Devil's slave. You've made the break. Stick with it! No matter how bad things get, and they could get awfully bad, you've got to find the strength to be your own person, reclaim your soul.

She remembers the last time she and Eliot were in the Bronx together, visiting the zoo as a prelude to a night of subway graffiti making, fantasizing about going on an African safari. Standing by the lion's cage with her Leo beside her, she saw a crazy woman make her way inside and do a dance to taunt the beasts. The woman almost got herself killed before the guards pulled her out, kicking and screaming. "Let me go! Let me die! I want to die!" she called out. It was around the time the economy crashed. A lot of people wanted to die in those days and a lot of people did, the suicide rate rising to heights not seen since the last Great Depression. Even their cabbie on the midnight ride home, after the subway had broken down, said he'd considered suicide after losing his fortune speculating in currencies, just like Big Daddy did. But unlike Big Daddy, Jean-Luc from Lyon cared too much for his teenage daughter to abandon her.

At the time, Joan thinks, suicide was the farthest thing from your mind, or Eliot's. First off, you didn't have much to lose. Big Daddy's meager checks, which you always cashed with guilt, went away, but so what? Your little art studio went too, that was the biggest blow, but you found new spaces to create in—the apartment, outdoors, underground. And most of all you had each other, you had your love, which was still pure, and that love gave you strength. You can find that strength again, she thinks, locking eyes with him, and maybe even a more profound love, given what you've been through.

He's aged, she can see it. He has his beautiful beard back, but there are streaks of gray around the chin, giving him kind of a chipmunk look. Alvin, she thinks, remembering the Good Witch of SoHo. There are bags under his eyes too, but maybe that's just from lack of sleep. All this time you've been down in the underworld, he's been chasing after you, trying to bring you back. He's communicating something to you now, with his stare. The eyes aren't begging anymore; they're weary but wiser, newly confident. He's giving you strength, the journey's almost over. He's going to save you, save the Yankees, save America. Look, his hand is over his heart, he swears he will. Can you believe it?

And there, towering beside him, is the pitcher you ruined with your kiss, your baby-faced pitcher, looking equally stalwart. He wants to save you too, with all his puppy love. And his lame arm. My darling Swan, I can't believe I did that to you. Trust me, I never wanted to. But did I really ruin you, or did I just transform you? We've all been transformed, so what's a little elbow trouble, when it comes down to it. You've still got enough spirit to win, just have to do it in a different way.

"Isn't that right, Angel?" she silently asks the ponytailed slugger to Spillage's left, who's smiling his grand smile the way Choice did when they first met. He's a man with no doubt. No doubt whatsoever. That's what she always loved about him, and that hasn't changed one bit. He's just a little more muscled now, a little more sculpted, a little hairier, unless that's a wig. Maybe when this is all over, you'll get your little studio back and he'll pose for you. All will end well, isn't that right?

Angel brought you here, in a parade up Fifth Avenue, he stole you away from Raoul and put you on this stage. You're doing his bidding now, not Raoul's, singing this anthem, celebrating this country for all its faults. You can do it. You can sing this song. It's a song of independence, after all. Not just a celebration of America, but a celebration of freedom itself. Make it a statement of your will to be free. Make it yours.

She remembers the time Eliot brought her to Prospect Park in Brooklyn for a picnic lunch. The very spot, he said, where the colonists fought their first battle with the British after declaring their independence. The fight for freedom against King George, another bullying father, she thinks. Maybe less evil than her own, but still worth fighting. Sing for beating back bullying fathers everywhere!

Sing for America, too. It's okay. You may not be the All-American girl Raoul's tried to paint you as, but you don't hate this country either. You went to the bicentennial celebration after all, watched the parade of tall ships sail up the Hudson from the Christopher Street pier, marveled at the fireworks, got inspired by Eliot reading Walt Whitman that night in bed. No one delighted in America like Whitman, Eliot said. Sure it's screwed up, she thinks. Sure your parents' generation made a total mess of it. Sure you reject its rampant materialism, which Big Daddy relentlessly fed on. But you've never been into the idea of revolution, except in culture, except in art. This country, this city can still be redeemed. Just like you.

Sing it. In your own voice.

.   .   .

"Alrighty then. Here we go," says Yankee announcer Al Deep. "Fifty thousand Yankee fans on their feet cheering as hot-rocker Frenchie Jones whips them up with as stirring a national anthem as you're ever going to hear. I'm here by the dugout with new Yankee skipper Howie Love and I want to tell you, the way Frenchie blasted that last line, stretching out the land of the freeeeeeee as long as any human possibly could, until her haunting voice cracked under the strain, and then into a minor key for the home of the brave, why that was really something else, wasn't it, Lovey?"

"Someone else," says Eliot, about an inch shorter than the former pitching coach, hair a little darker and without the gray, ten pounds lighter and ten years younger but no one seems to have put it all together.

"How's that?" asks Deep.

"Reminds me of someone I used to live with, someone I have a message for, Al. And the message is this: I forgive you, Joan, forgive you everything if you can forgive me. I know we were stuck, and you needed to break free. I needed to break free too, though I didn't know it at the time. It's been like a long, strange trip, if you know what I mean, and I know I did some weird things, even if I don't know how much of it was real. But I never meant to hurt you, that's for sure, and I don't mean to hurt you now, no matter how it looks. You mean the world to me, and I'm determined to win you back. We're on the same team. And we can pull this off, I know it!"

"That's great, Lovey. But can we just focus on the game for a sec? I like what you did making Dick Trowgin your bench coach. Taking the old workhorse out of the bullpen, where he was coaching the pitchers, helping the no-names hold the fort while Swannie was MIA, and putting all those years of accumulated baseball wisdom right at your side. Deceptive Dick Trowgin, as dependable a stopper in his prime as you could find with that sneaky sinker just a wee little greased and that big breaking gem of a curve—what a pitch it was! Trowgie should help you big-time."

"Yep. I'm going to count on old Trowgie."

"Big comfort blanket. But not so big as Swannie. Bet you're glad to have him back!"

"Yep."

"And Angel Guerrero too. How about the way he called that walk-off homer in his last at bat? A great ballplayer, and great humanitarian too, the way he helped put out one of the biggest fires this city's ever had last night between games. I mean the guy is everywhere, working wonders."

"Amazing."

"If only he could field." Deep chuckles. "But anyway, it's good to have the stars back. Should make your job easier, which is maybe why you don't look worried. In fact, you're looking real loosey-goosey, Lovey, for a guy in the hot seat, facing a do-or-die moment. Like you've sipped a little something from the fountain of youth. Is that a new hair dye or what?"

"Thought I'd try something different."

"Good move. But let me tell you another move I'd make, if you don't mind my suggesting. I'd take Amdeeprist out of center. The kid's been in a slump the entire series. Maybe give him a break and put DeJoy in. Sparky'll cover more ground out there, give you more speed on the basepaths too, which will come in handy if the game is tight. What do you say, Lovey?"

"Sure. Why not? I'm down with DeJoy."

"I like the way you think. So would my brother-in-law, Lieutenant Gus Berkley, who died out at Kennedy protecting the mayor, who looks like he's having a grand old time in the stands with his new family and Frenchie, pressing the flesh and drumming up votes for his 'Save the Cities' campaign, which would certainly get a boost if New York wins. Gus always liked DeJoy. And I know he's looking down on us as the Yanks get set to take the field for this seventh and deciding game. Buckle your seat belts, here we go!"

．　．　．

"What the hell is he talking about?" Raoul asks Sheila in her luxury box high above the field. "What's he think he can pull off? You've got control of him, right? He'd better make the moves we tell him, follow our signs."

"Don't worry, darling," says the Yankee owner, taking a drag of her cigarette from a long silver holder. "He's just dreaming. Dreaming out loud. He knows I own him."

"Don't sound like he knows. Think you need to send him a message." He takes a swig of rum from his flask, wipes his mouth with the back of his hand. "We don't need no more defectors."

"Done," says Sheila, waving her cigarette holder like a wand.

Eliot feels a pain in his head so sharp it doubles him over, as his players trot past him tapping him on the shoulder, back, and rump with their gloves.

"You okay, skip?" asks Spillage as he passes by.

"Sure, sure, no problem," says Eliot, straightening up. He looks up at the owner's box and sees her blowing smoke. She gives him a little wave. Remember when you thought you could turn her around? She was Circe, who started off an enemy, but in the end helped Odysseus ward off the Sirens, chained to the mast of his ship. His men all had wax in their ears. He alone could hear their deadly songs, because he needed to hear them, to prove he could withstand the worst.

"Again," says Raoul. "You've got to keep prodding this jackass. Make sure he knows who's in charge."

She waves her wand again and Eliot winces. You can take it, he thinks, whatever she dishes out. Have to take it, if you want Joan back. Be your own man, make your own decisions.

"Again," says Raoul.

"Darling, he gets the point. If I do it too often, he'll just build resistance. Trust me, I know how to handle him."

"I don't trust no one." He takes another drink. "Not since Señor Satan gave in to the old witch. Supposed to be both sides stepping back, but I don't see Angel stepping back none, just me. And now everyone's got ideas. Choice, Frenchie, Señor Ensign. Maybe you've got them too, for all I know."

"Now that you mention it, I do have one idea."

"What's that?"

"I want Art. I need him here, at my side."

"The reporter? You kidding me? What do you see in that fat slob?"

"I see what I want to see in Art. A big lovable teddy bear who saw the beauty in me when it was nothing but makeup. And I can still change him into something more presentable, if I choose. But I don't know for how much longer. I can hear my mother's voice, calling me back. Her power persists, you know."

"Damn that old witch." He takes another swig. "Okay. You get Art. But that's the last thing you get. And no funny business, either, or you'll both suffer bad." He pulls the cigarette holder out of her hand as she moves it toward her black lips, grabs her by the wrist, and squeezes hard. "Just remember, I've still got power too, and I'm itching to use it."

*　　*　　*

"Well, that didn't take long," says Yankee announcer Al Deep. "The Phillies filling all the bases here in the top of the first, a rude welcome back for Nick 'The Swan' Spillage in this do-or-die seventh game, and things won't get any easier for him as Vernon 'Big Tree' Washington lumbers to the plate.

"The big guy's having a heck of a Series, an MVP candidate for sure if the Independence Hallers take all the marbles, twelve ribbies overall on seven hits and four of them homers, all walloped real good, but the longest and maybe most crushing blow a three-run blast to win Game Four.

"Now Washington's set. Swannie looks in, takes his sign from catcher Dert, talks to the baseball, goes into his motion, and here's the pitch to Big Tree—ball one. Another one that could have gone either way, looks like it caught the corner to me, but home plate ump Manny Wo says no, as he has all inning, his strike zone the size of a donut hole.

"Swannie shakes his arm like he's trying to get the stiffness out. His time away didn't help at all. Control a little off, even with that tight strike zone, and maybe not the same zip either, as Big Tree rips a bullet foul outside of first. Boy, he got around on that one, didn't he? Manny tosses a new ball to Swannie, who turns his back toward the batter and walks a few steps behind the mound rubbing it up, glances over to Frenchie in the stands for inspiration, then back to the rubber, the windup, the pitch, and BOOM!

"This one's high, this one's deep, Angel looks up but there's no way he can get this, it's gone, a grand slam for Washington, and just like that the Liberty Bell Creekers are up 4–zip. And that'll bring new skipper Howie Love out to the mound to talk to his young star, who's definitely off his game today. Catcher Dert walking to the mound as well, and here's Angel flying in from right to join the conversation."

.   .   .

My boys, thinks Joan, watching Eliot, Nick, and Choice gather at the mound with Dert from her front row seat just past the Yankee dugout with the mayor and his entourage. The fog in her head has lifted some, though the nausea persists and her voice is gone from having given her all with the national anthem to open the game. Nothing like the thrill of hearing everyone in the packed stadium clap and whoop and cheer, a thrill she never asked for and senses will never have again. Just another fan now. She claps and calls hoarsely, "Come on, boys!"

Can they come up with something to turn the tide? It's going against them and it's her fault, she knows, from having screwed up the pitcher. But what's done is done, she thinks, there's no going back, even though the temptation to go back, all the way back under the covers with Eliot like before things started, has never been greater. She got all this going, launched a thousand ships, but now that the war's raging, she wants to say never mind. Didn't mean it.

Yeah, I got obsessed with Swannie, but so did a million others, she thinks. Look at them out here. They're all crazy about the guy. Can't believe what's happening to him, getting knocked around like this.

They deserve better. And they're not gonna let him lose, no way. We're all going to pull together, all us Yankee fans, and with our collective might help him get his groove back. She claps again. It's not just me.

Just think of the stakes, it's so beyond me. I mean this potbellied guy next to me is running for president, trying to save the country from Nixon's ruin, and there's a grand conspiracy working against him. I'm just one little fan in the stands who wants her old boyfriend beside her again so we can sit back and enjoy the game. Come on over and watch with me, Eliot. You've got no business out there, like you don't know what you're doing. Turn it over to Trowgin, let him fight the war. He's got tons of experience you'll never have. What do you think you know that he doesn't? Swannie was doing just fine without you. Why do you think you can make him better?

But can they make you better, your boys at the mound? That's the real question. Sure, you broke with the Devil, and he didn't try to stop you, but that doesn't mean he's done with you. Just because Raoul is gone for the moment, just because his stuff is fading and you're not crying out for more, doesn't mean he won't come back, try to get you hooked again. Doesn't mean he won't ask you to do another little favor or two to ensure the Yankees lose. And can you really resist, when the game is on the line? Remember the graveyard where you reigned as his queen, flying high, so damned high, could you get any higher? What can life offer that compares? He'll whisper that this discomfort you're feeling now is only the tug of reactionary forces. Crush them and you're golden, immortal, supreme. He'll hint at the unspeakable torture that awaits you if you desert him when he needs you most. Just because you dare to imagine you can live with a Yankee victory doesn't mean you can.

And yet you do dare even to think beyond, to marrying Eliot, bearing healthy children, like this cute little green-eyed baby at your side. Is there one inside already? She feels her belly. Didn't think of that when he shoved the needle in you. But that was just a bad dream, right? You thought the baby was gone, if there ever was one, in the car crash. And he forced you into it, forced the whole thing. You never invited it, never consented, not in your right mind, no matter what he says. Besides, it wasn't you. It was that body double in the stands with you now, the mayor's aide, Ms. Jones, who has no soul to begin with. Your long-lost half sister, your evil twin. Not really. It *was* you, Frenchie. But maybe, miraculously, it did no damage to the baby. Maybe you both come out of this in decent shape. No harm in hoping.

"Sí," she can hear Raoul say inside her head. "That's exactly where there's harm, chiquita. Hope is the Free Market God's false promise. Hope gets you nowhere while oppression rules. Come back to me while you can." She looks around but he's not in the stands. He's all over the field in umpire garb. Then she hears the Good Witch of SoHo say, "Rest assured, my dear, you've escaped him, can live happily . . ."

She's here! Not just in spirit, she's really here, Joan thinks, standing up to see if she can find her. There she is, just a few rows up the right-field line, folded wheelchair at her side, black cat in lap pawing at her popcorn. She's looking at you, smiling as if she sees something, which you know is not obvious because what's right in front of her she never sees. She's seeing something inside you. Something she likes. She's beaming, her smile much bigger than you thought her ancient face could muster, reconfiguring every one of her countless wrinkles, blinding in its brightness, with teeth too white and straight to be real. If you could just see what she sees. Your baby? Your soul? It's making you dizzy, staring into her smile, trying to decipher what it means.

Exhausted by the effort, Joan collapses back into her seat and lets her lids grow heavy, fall shut. She's asleep the moment they touch bottom, dreams she's drinking borscht in Sister Sabrina's kitchen. It's a love potion that will make her feel a divine passion for the first person she sees upon waking. And in her dream that's Eliot, who's been counting the stars over Yankee Stadium with the diligent air of a Methuselah trying to keep pace with his constantly multiplying descendants. One foot in, one foot out of the dugout, neck craned. From the pitcher's mound she calls to him, is dying to tell him he has reasons to consider the heavens his, that she and he have been blessed and this is only the beginning. Yes, she is going to have his baby. And she's going to love that baby with a passion she's never had for anything in the world before, which is saying something. But before she can express any more than his name, the mayor jostles her awake.

"Call of nature," he says, mistaking her for his aide. "What say we take a look for the restrooms while the action is stopped."

"Wrong person, sweetheart," says Mirlanda. "This is Frenchie, your warm-up act. That's your aide over there."

Ms. Jones jumps to her feet and escorts the mayor up the steps.

30

BASEBALL WISDOM

"What's this?" asks the pitcher, as his manager hands him a little bag at the mound.

"It's a gift from Trowgie," says Eliot. "A resin bag. Says it gives him good luck."

"It's a bag of glop," says Spillage, throwing it to the ground. "You know I can't use this, Skip. It's against the rules. Wo would throw the book at me if he caught me using this glop. Eject me, lickety-spit. Besides, it's not who I am. Not the way I want to win."

"I know, I know. But I didn't want to go against Trowgie's baseball wisdom. That's why I got him on the bench with me, right? He says it's safe to use. Everybody does it."

"Well, I'm different from everyone. So let's focus on other optics."

Eliot casts about for inspiration. Glancing toward the sky, he sees Sheila in her luxury box gesturing for him to give Spillage the hook, but that's not an option he's willing to consider. A sharp pain goes through his skull, doubling him over.

"You okay, skip?" asks Spillage, helping him up.

"Sure, sure," says Eliot. "More to the point, how are you? How's your arm?"

"Okay," says Spillage, giving it a shake. "Little tightness in the elbow but nothing I can't play through." Actually, it's killing him, but he's not going to let on.

"Problem's not your arm, my man," Angel interjects. "It's up here, in your head." He taps his temple. "You got too much damned crap going on up here. You're worried about your red-haired momma in the stands, I can see that. Love her too and so does Lovey here, but trust me, she's okay. The Devil's done his worst and she's still standing. You're worried about politics, where you got no business being. Forget it. Mayor Mumbo Jumbo can save the cities without you. You're worried about all your fans and what they expect. Can't let the weight of that drag you down, bro. Surprise them, like I'm doing, and all your teammates too. So what if those Phillies score, we're going to score more. The fans love high-scoring games. It's what this show is all about. Your stuff's still amazing. Just float it out there and give us a chance."

Eliot looks over at Joan, who seems to be looking adoringly at Mirlanda's baby. Gives him a lift. She wants one. She wants yours. You're going straight back home after you win this game and make a baby with her, okay? He thinks he sees her nod, just a little, but enough. She hears him! It's okay. We're going to emerge from this together, with a stronger bond than ever before. Do you hear me? She nods. I won't let you down. I'll never let you down. I'll stick with you no matter what. I'm not going to let old Nightmare win. And then he catches sight of the first-base umpire furtively stealing a sip from his flask. "Hey, he's drinking!" he says, pointing.

"Women problems," says Angel. "More than he knows. All the women he's done wrong are rising up against him."

Dert pulls Eliot's arm down. "Don't point, Lovey. They'll think you're going to the bullpen."

"Give me the ball, Nick," says Eliot, thinking he's had this conversation before. Not that it's helpful, but it does add to his confidence.

"You're not thinking of taking me out, are you, Skip?" says Spillage. He actually believes you could, just like you imagined he would.

Remember, he's just a kid, an impressionable kid. How could you ever have seen him as a threat? You need to be his mentor, a better mentor than your father ever was to you. Show you believe in him. Help him believe in himself. "Nah," he says. "I just want to rub it some myself, give it my own luck. They're grooving on your smoke, Swannie. You've got to change things up to fool them."

"I'll reach back for something extra."

"No. Take something off. Give 'em junk." Another shot of pain strikes home. He looks up to see Sheila gesturing more frantically. And who's the James Bond look-alike standing beside her? New boyfriend, no doubt. So much for her commitment to you.

"Lovey's right," says Angel, grabbing Spillage by both shoulders and staring intently with his riveting green eyes into the pitcher's baby blues. "I want you to visualize this, my man. You're the craftiest pitcher that is, experienced beyond your years. You're all movement and deception, arm angles and split seams. Sliders, cutters, knuckleballs, screwballs. Here." He takes the ball from Eliot, demonstrates some different grips. "Experiment out there. Your method is no method. See the ball going smack into Derty's glove, no matter where he places it. That's all you need to think about. Block out the rest."

He hands the ball back to Spillage, who nods, says, "Gotcha. Derty's glove. Mix it up."

Eliot sees the home plate ump walking toward them. "I got an idea," he says. "Forget the whirling dervish stuff. Go with no windup. They're not prepared for that. Mess with their timing."

"Good idea, Lovey," says Angel, slapping him on the back.

"I like it," says Dert, adding a slap of his own.

"I knew we had you out here for a reason," says Angel.

"All right, kids," says the ump. "Hate to break up this party, but you've been out here long enough. You making a move or not?"

"We're sticking with Nick," says Eliot, brushing past the ump as he heads back to the dugout and smelling the alcohol on his breath. He smiles and waves to Sheila, who looks none too happy in her box with her Bond. "You're committed to me, my pet," he can hear her saying inside his pounding skull. "You owe your presence at this stadium, in this uniform, to me. I can fire you as fast as I hired you."

Aside from his splitting headache, he's feeling pretty good about himself. Go ahead and fire me, he thinks, giving her a final wave. See if I care.

. . .

Raoul sneaks up behind Mirlanda in the stands, parts her braids, and gives her a kiss on the nape of her neck. "Remember me, dollface?" he says. "We've got business to talk about."

Mirlanda calmly hands her baby over to Joan, saying, "Can you hold him for a second, hon, while I take care of business?"

"Happy to," says Joan, feeling a rush as she takes him in her arms. This is a feeling you could really get into, she thinks. What would it feel like to have him at your breast? To have someone who literally depends on you for his existence? Or hers. Do you have a preference? A boy. A little Eliot. It feels good to be grooving on Eliot again. Look at him, managing. He's going to be a great dad. And now look back down to the baby, with his twinkling green eyes. Give me a smile, a big one like your father's. That's it. You want your baby to have Eliot's eyes, which you've found a way to love again. Whatever possessed you to look for fulfillment further afield, when it was right there under your nose, in your womb? How could you have just dumped him like that?

A wave of nausea passes through her. Big Daddy, of course, she thinks. Big Daddy the Devil, whose snaky grin is now so apparent on Raoul. You'd smash it if you could but your hands are full. He was afraid you'd find happiness, true and lasting happiness, with Eliot. He made you panic, gave you nightmares, like he always used to. Even when he was there with you, kissing you on the forehead late at night, you knew he wasn't really there, not in his heart. Because he never had a heart, he was a fake at love. And you knew he'd run away, you knew he'd abandon you, sooner or later. Not like Eliot, forever loyal. Of course, there was Sheila, but you can forgive him that, if he could forgive you everything else. You forced him into it, by abandoning him first. And his heart wasn't into it, you're dead sure of that. How could you have left him to fend for himself?

You panicked, that's all. Big Daddy made you panic, just like you did at the beginning of your time with Eliot, when you were afraid of getting too close, too fast. So now it's having a baby too fast. But what's fast, what does time matter? The baby will come when it's time to come. As long as he's Eliot's, he will be fine. Or she. You don't have to worry about passing on Big Daddy's bad seed. Eliot's will supersede. Just look at him, managing. I'm proud of you, man.

And I'm done with you, Big Daddy. I'm really done with you now. Thought I was before, but I guess I needed one more big push. Face it, he abused you, mentally *and* physically, just like Raoul. Reached down under your nightshirt and touched you where he shouldn't have. Pretended with that snaky grin that he was just being playful, then got mad when you pushed him away, kicked him out of your room. "Don't you ever say anything about this. It never happened," he hissed, sulking off. Frightened you so much you had to block it out. It never happened, he insisted, and you repeated it, over and over, lying to yourself as well as to Dear Mother and the rest of them. But it did happen! It was real! More real than any of the shit that's gone down this week. You need to confront that truth to move on. I'm done with you, Big Daddy, and I'm done with you, too, Raoul. Wish I could wipe that grin off your face.

Then she watches Mirlanda twirl around and do it for her, socking Raoul hard in the jaw before his rum-riddled reaction speed gives him time to deflect the blow. "Don't you ever try nothing like that again," she says.

And up the right-field line, Joan sees Sister Sabrina clap her hands, still smiling. Easy to see what she's smiling about now. The Good Witch likes what she sees in Mirlanda, and Joan does too. She feeds on her strength. If Mirlanda can stand up to Raoul, there's hope for you too, she thinks. She can't imagine what it was like being married to him. Toughened her up, for sure. She'll make a great First Lady. Just what the country needs to get out of this mess.

"Thought we had a deal," says Raoul, touching his jaw. Doesn't hurt, but it does make him think. Can't trust no one no more.

"Deal don't include kisses, skunk. You gave up that right a long time ago."

"Here's the deal, dollface. This is the way it's going to go down." He fishes an envelope out of his fatigues. "You're going to expose your new hubby with these pictures, show him for the pervert he really is. You go on national TV, tell the country how he abused you. Tell how he bet a fortune against the home team, took dark money from the Satanic Vanguard, and would stoop to anything just to gain a little edge, pull one over on the people. Make him a monster, sink his campaign for good. Demoralize his supporters, just before we deliver the final blow. That's the way it goes down, you got that?" He shoves the envelope into her bag. "You got any trouble thinking up his abuses, just remember when things went bad with us. You got any trouble remembering that . . ." He grabs the baby from Joan. ". . . just think about how bad things will get if you don't."

"Why do you keep dragging Junior into this? Give him back right now." She reaches, gets a hard shove in the chest.

"Maybe I'll give Junior a treat, take him up to Sheila's box to watch the game with me. Teach him what luxury is, what riches can buy. Maybe that'll help you remember what your job is. What do you think, Frenchie? Do I take Junior with me?"

"Give him back, Raoul," says Joan, hoarsely. "You're not gonna win by making stupid threats."

"You go, girl," says Mirlanda. "Tell him what's what."

"I tell you what's what," says Raoul. "You think your lame-arm pitcher wins? Frenchie did her job, Mirlanda. She destroyed the Swan. Soon it'll be your job to destroy Comrade Mayor. Comprende?"

"Only thing I comprende is that you're drunk, skunk," Mirlanda says. "Give me back Junior or I'll scream, expose you and all your crazy schemes."

He hugs the baby tight. "So, you're not going to do your job? You're out of the deal?"

"Didn't say that." Remember: play along. "Just don't want Junior to be a pawn. Whatever's in store for me, I want Junior to be safe. You promise me that?"

"Sure, dollface." He smiles his snaky grin, stands with the baby. "I'll keep him real safe up in Sheila's box."

She lunges for him, screams, "Stop! He's got my baby!" But he side-steps her and starts up the aisle, only to be met by a tall security guard with a ponytail.

"I think the lady wants her baby back," says the guard.

Thinking better of making a big scene in the stands, Raoul hands Junior back to Mirlanda. "Just do your job," he says to her, shoving the guard aside as he makes his way up the stairs.

. . .

"I think we've got a problem," says Art to Sheila in her luxury box. He tears the story he was writing out of his typewriter, balls it up, and throws it in the trash basket. It reads:

SPILLAGE FLOPS!
YANKED IN THE FIRST AS NEW YORK GOES DOWN

Pitching the biggest game of his life, former Yankee phenom Nick "The Swan" Spillage had the candle-burning-at-both-ends "good life" he was living with hot-rocker Frenchie Jones catch up with him as he failed to get a batter out, giving up four quick runs on a monster grand slam by Vernon "Big Tree"

Washington to put the Yanks in a big hole and prompt a quick hook by new skipper Howie Love . . .

"I'm afraid so," says Sheila. "I used all my precious powers to transport you here and transform you into this beautiful hunk. Couldn't help myself. I needed my Art." She gives him a kiss. "You like your new look?"

"Sure. But I don't like thinking about what Raoul's going to do to us when he gets back. He's going to be in a foul mood. Nothing else you can do?"

"Nothing I can do about that jackass manager. I thought I could make him jump, but he's just too stubborn."

"Yeah. He's a jerk. But I didn't think he was strong enough to go against the plan."

"What plan, pet? There is no plan, you know that. The Devil made it up as he went along, any means to his satanic ends. And now he's checked out, leaving our man to his own devices."

"Which I don't want to face."

"Nor do I. Let's go to my island, Gulliver's Island. If we disappear there, perhaps the Great Powers will lose sight of us. I have oodles of money, you won't need to work. I'll put the Yankees in a blind trust. It'll be just you and me, off the grid, away from it all."

"I could get into that." He embraces her. "Maybe I can write spy thrillers under a pseudonym, now that I look the part and know what true villainy's all about."

"Perfect. I hated to see your talent polluted by all that satanic propaganda."

"And I hated to see you making it with that idiot Eliot."

"He's history, pet." She takes his hand, leads him to the door. "You mean everything to me, Art."

31

ON YOUR OWN

Raoul returns to Sheila's box, finds it empty, and marches to the open section at the front. "WHERE ARE THEY?" he screams into the sky in a voice that reverberates throughout the stadium.

He took away my troops, that fat little Russian pig. Gave in to all the old witch's demands. Go fight the revolution, he says, but you're on your own. How many hands can he tie behind your back? No matter, just keep fighting. Can't trust no one, got to do the job yourself.

He turns his attention to his bow and arrows, a classic red cedar set that once belonged to one of his favorite nineteenth-century opponents of American imperialism, Apache Chief Cochise.

. . .

"Where are they?" says Yankee announcer Al Deep. "That was the chant we heard back in the first, after Skipper Howie Love decided to leave his reeling pitcher in the game, and now, here in the sixth, the meaning of that chant is becoming clear. Where are those Philly bats? They've gone silent after that first inning outburst, with Swannie looking like a young Dick Trowgin out there, throwing nothing but junk from all kinds of angles and that new no-windup delivery which I hear was Lovey's brainchild, another nice move for the Yanks' rookie skipper.

"Not a whole lot of control for Swannie as he experiments with his new style, eight walks so far in this game as ump Manny Wo refuses to give him an inch, a couple of singles for the Phils but nothing when it counts, eight runners left on base as the young phenom works out of jam after jam, helped by his crew of Guardian Angels, led by Angel himself along with Lovey and Dert, who gather at the mound whenever Nick gets in trouble, once every inning so far, which is all the visits they're allowed, and don't look to the Wo brothers to cut them any breaks by bending the rules. No siree. The Woes are not on the Yanks' side, that much is clear. Every close call is going against them.

"The Bombers up 5–4 thanks to Angel's big bat, two long home runs to bring his team back, one better than Vernon 'Big Tree' Washington who's up against Swannie now, all the marbles at stake and the count's been full forever. Spillage behind the mound with his back to the batter, having an animated chat with the baseball as always, the one thing he's done consistently all game. Tree waiting patiently, never leaving the box, passing the time in conversation with Derty while Manny Wo gets agitated behind the plate, calls to Spillage to quit stalling and how many times has he done that this inning? Almost as many times as Tree's hit fouls, and here's another one.

"It's a high twisting fungo off a no-windup Swannie screwball and this one's way up there, behaving like a kite in a swirling cross-breeze. Looks like it's heading toward the mayor and his gang, down the first-base line just past the dugout, first baseman Stretch Notnuf heading toward it but here comes Angel, ponytail flying, waving off Notnuf and jumping into the seats to nab it. Does he have it? He has himself a soft landing, that's for sure, right into the laps of Mrs. Mayor, Mirlanda, aka the Haitian Hell-Raiser, and her companion, Swannie's flame, hot-rocker Frenchie Jones. And looking like he's enjoying it, too, but where's the ball?

"Oh there it is. It just popped out of his glove. Right into the hands of the cute little baby on the mayor's lap. Don't put that in your mouth, son, don't know what's on it, not with the way Swannie's got that ball dancing. Angel's claiming he tossed the baseball to the babe after the catch but the Woes say no. They're ruling it a drop and Big Tree stays alive. Tough break for the Yanks. Don't want to give Washington too many chances.

"Angel lingering in the stands, giving kisses to the ladies, and that's got Manny Wo mighty upset. Looks like the ump is trying to wrestle the outfielder back onto the field. Some sharp words exchanged, don't know what Wo's so angry about, but Notnuf, DeJoy, and Evert step in to break things up and Manny goes back behind home to await Swannie's next pitch. Full count for Tree, who's been Nick's nemesis in this Series, got the only two hits off Swannie in the first game and the grand slam in this one. I'd just walk him like he did in the third, take my chance on Adams, with Jefferson to follow, but the kid has other ideas, still nursing a slim lead without his usual heat, a close contest here in the Bronx . . ."

*   *   *

Plastered, Raoul fools around with his bow and arrows, loading up, stretching the bow, setting his sights on intended targets. He could take out Spillage and his Guardian Angels right now in rapid succession as they gather at the mound, but the moment isn't right, he thinks. The score is tied, 5–5, after Washington used his reprieve to blast a solo shot down the right-field line, just inside the foul pole.

He lays his arrows out in a neat little row, considers his new plan. This little piggie is for Choice, the bastard. This one's for the lame-armed pitcher. This one's for his lame-brained manager. This one's special, for Comrade Mayor. If you can't expose the blowhard, then just eliminate him. It's simpler, cleaner. The plot was always too complicated. Nixon wins either way, and that's all that matters. Violence helps him. As the ad goes, "He can keep us safe!" (Love that line, one of your best.)

These two here are for your unfaithful ladies—the mayor's new missus and his warm-up act, Miss American Dream. Face it: you expected more from each. You loved them both in your own special way, whether they realized it or not, for a time. You never thought they would do what you told them of their own free will, but you thought you could still seduce them with that hypnotic power of persuasion that served you so well over the years. That plus the drugs, which had also worked before. So what went wrong? You refuse to believe your lack of power was to blame, even with your wings clipped. Must have been the drugs, not what they were cracked up to be. Maybe Angel screwed with them. Not beyond him.

Do you let the baby live? No way. He's got to go. The product of Mirlanda's original sin, which put you through hell in the first place. (He laughs, knowing that's not true.) This arrow's for him. And the rest of them are just to rain down everywhere like balls of fire so the panic is total. Maybe then you can recapture Señor Satan's attention.

He puts the arrows in his batch of buffalo leather quivers, covers the weapons with a blanket and uses them as a pillow to rest his head. Maybe catch a few winks so he's fresh when he needs to be. This game's so slow, he thinks, so boring. For the time being.

. . .

"Ouch," says Deep. "This one's gotta hurt. Angel in an awful collision with DeJoy in right center as they both go for Hancock's blooper, the ball popping out of DeJoy's glove and that brings in two runs here in the top of the seventh. The Phils lead it 7–5 and you gotta hold Angel responsible for this one. Totally out of position. It belonged to DeJoy. But Angel giveth, and he taketh away—his two bangers accounting for all the Bombers' runs but this is his second big mistake in the field and it's a costly one.

"He could have a chance to redeem himself in the bottom of this inning, but before that, don't go way. We have a treat for you during the seventh inning stretch—Mayor Lightly and his new wife, Mirlanda, aka the Haitian Hell-Raiser, coming to the booth to talk about their vision for America and address some nasty new rumors that could sink their campaign. Wouldn't want to miss that as Swannie gets Hamilton to ground weakly to third to end the inning, but not before the damage is done. The Boys From Liberty Bell Creek with 7, the Bombers from the Bronx with 5 as we head for the stretch."

. . .

"Hold him for me, would you, honey?" says Mirlanda to Joan, handing her baby and a bottle over. "I've got to go save the mayor's fat ass."

"You trust me with your baby? All alone?" says Joan. She doesn't trust herself, not fully, not yet. Glancing up the right-field line, she sees that Sister Sabrina is gone. I guess if you know the outcome, she thinks, why bother to stick around until the bitter end? Just have to imagine her continuing to smile your way.

"You won't be alone." Mirlanda gestures toward the ponytailed security guard. "You'll be safe."

"But I've never like taken care of a baby before."

"You're expecting, right? Might as well get some practice."

"Who told you that?"

"Angel."

"You mean Choice."

"I mean Angel, before he got mixed up with Choice. Said you've got a beautiful soul too, which I can see for myself. And you never traded it away, no matter what that skunk Raoul told you. He was just trying to mess with your head. You're gonna be okay."

"You think? He messed me up pretty bad. Look at these tracks." She holds out her arm.

"What of them?"

"That stuff he had me on couldn't have been good for the baby, if there ever was one, or is now."

"Huh. Don't know nothing about that. All's I know is what Angel told me, which is that you're gonna be okay. And I believe him. So have faith. And make sure Junior drinks the whole bottle. I'll be back soon enough." She kisses the baby on the forehead, then heads up the steps with the mayor and his aide.

He's got Choice's green eyes, thinks Joan, looking toward the dugout, where Angel's talking with Eliot. Definitely belongs to Choice, who'd better do something this inning in his role as slugger. Time's running out.

32

LUCKY MAN

"I want you to play more conservative, Angel," the Yankee manager tells his right fielder, standing on the dugout steps. "Deeper, closer to the line. Give DeJoy more room out there. Stay in your zone."

"I love you, Lovey," says the outfielder. "But don't tell me how to play." He catches sight of Joan feeding the baby in the stands, smiles his megawatt smile, slaps Eliot on the back. "Look at that, my man. Don't she look fine? Congratulations, Dad."

"What are you congratulating me for? That baby's not mine." She looks radiant holding him, like there's a special glow behind her setting her off from the crowd.

"Course not. He's mine. But yours is inside her. You're a lucky man."

For real? Angels don't lie, Eliot thinks. How awesome is this? He has the urge to bolt over to the stands to give Joan a hug, raise her and the baby high into the air. But he resists. Got a job to do, man.

Spillage interjects. "I didn't know you were connected with Frenchie, Skip." Yes, you did. Just didn't believe it. And you knew she was pregnant too, from that childhooded dream where she wore the turban. So much for romance. But at least she's safe, no sign of her tormentor. Just focus on finishing, getting the win.

"I lived with her," says Eliot. "But that feels like ages ago. Don't know if we can like put it back together after all the shit that's gone down."

You're being too modest. If you win, you're in, he thinks. Just focus on winning, and she'll be there.

"Hey," says Angel. "If you're thinking about me, forget about it. That was an impulse play, nothing more. She was just testing her limits."

"It's a lot more than you," says Eliot. A whole lot more. All behind you now, though, as family life beckons. Where are we going to keep the baby? Do we need a new apartment? Don't get ahead of yourself. You're still behind on the scoreboard.

"All's I did was kiss her," says Spillage. But the kiss had meaning, he thinks.

"How you feeling, Nick?" says Eliot.

"Okay." His arm is a dead weight.

"Think you can go the distance, get six more outs?"

"Sure thing."

"I think maybe you should rely less on the screwball, go more with the cutter and change."

The bench coach, Trowgin, interjects. "You're overthinking things, son. Too many instructions. What are you panicking for? You've got everything going your way. Let it go, for Christ's sake."

Eliot glances toward home, sees ump Manny Wo sneak a drink, watches the crowd rise to its feet for the seventh inning stretch. "How's it going my way? We're down by two, the last I looked."

"We got the top of the order coming up," says Trowgin. "We got the crowd on our side. You've got a baby coming. I feel good about our chances."

"We are such stuff as dreams are made on," says Angel, remembering an old line.

. . .

"I told you we had a treat coming," says Yankee announcer Al Deep. "But I didn't know the full extent. Happy to have hot-rocker Frenchie Jones joining us in the booth, along with Mayor and Mrs. Lightly, as we all take a stretch. Frenchie, I just loved the way you belted that 'Star-Spangled Banner' to open the game. Talk about a stretch, the way you bent that last line. I'll never think about the 'land of the free and home of the brave' the same way."

"She's not Frenchie," says Mirlanda. "Looks like her, but don't have her soul. That's Frenchie in the stands there, with my Junior."

"How 'bout that," says Deep. "Could be twins. But Mr. and Mrs. Mayor, we're real happy to have you here. Hope you're enjoying the game. It's a doozy."

"It certainly is," says the mayor. "But New York's been down before, and we'll come back. I know we will. We're a beacon of hope for all the cities in America, for all our countrymen and women of all races and creeds. If we can just unite, seize this moment, imagine the possibilities!"

"Speaking of which," says Deep. "I hear the *Mercury* has new pictures coming out of you and the missus that leave nothing to the imagination. Unspeakable perversion. Horrible abuse. And what's more, they've got you dead to rights placing bets against your home team, an unpardonable sin in my book, working in cahoots with the Satanic Vanguard to wreck New York's chances. Want to give you a chance to address those nasty rumors before we discuss your promise to the nation."

"Nonsense," says the mayor. "Utter nonsense. Don't you know by now you can't believe anything you read in the press? I'm not an abuser, I'm a healer. I can heal America's great divide, restore our great promise. And I'd never bet against New York in a million years. I have faith in this city, faith in its future, faith in . . ."

Deep cuts him off. "What do you say, Mirlanda? What about those pictures of you all bruised up? I hear you're prepared to tell all."

"Huh," says Mirlanda, staring into the camera with her piercing brown eyes. "You hear wrong. That stuff never happened."

The mayor's aide grabs an envelope out of Mirlanda's bag, extends it toward Deep. "Here's the evidence," she says.

"Give me that," says Mirlanda, grabbing the envelope from her. "What do you think you're doing, invading my space like that?"

"I'm just trying to protect you," says the aide.

"Well, I don't need your protection, honey." She tears the envelope in half, stuffs it back in her bag, says to the mayor, "You need to make this bitch disappear, sweetheart. She's not adding anything. Just confusing things."

The mayor does as he's told. "You heard the lady. You're done. We'll take it from here."

The aide leaves the booth.

"Now as I was saying," the mayor begins again, but Mirlanda stops him with a hand on his knee.

"This mayor's a good man," she says. "He's got a big heart. Took me and my Junior in when we were in big trouble. Treats us with respect, like he'll treat all of you, unlike someone I know who'd make your lives a living hell, just like he made mine until I gave him the boot. Trust me, I know what real hell is. I came from Haiti, under Papa Doc. And my no-good skunk of an ex-husband is the living, breathing spirit of that evil monster. He's the true Baby Doc. You talk about perversion, talk about abuse. The boob in charge now who calls himself Baby Doc is a pale imitation."

"Brave Mirlanda," says the mayor.

"Well, speaking about babies," says Deep, "there's some that would say the mayor here is just fulfilling his basic responsibility in taking in his, and that he only did it because he was dragged into it."

"Now listen here," says the mayor, "I've taken responsibility from the very start, total responsibility. I'm accountable, and I'm transparent, the way I'll always be. The buck stops here and that's all you need to know. From the moment I learned . . ."

"You learned wrong," says Mirlanda, resting her hand on his shoulder. "I hate to break it to you, sweetheart, but you ain't the father. The father is Choice. You're the godfather, which Choice thought he was, but the role fits you better, since he's too much of a free spirit to provide for us like I know you will."

The mayor looks shocked. "Do I know this Choice?"

"He goes by Angel now."

"You don't mean our Angel, do you?" asks Deep.

"The guy playing right," says Mirlanda. "Too shallow, if you ask me. But he plays the way he wants to play 'cause that's who he is. I know he can bring us back."

"He'll have the chance this inning," says Deep, "if the Yanks can get a runner on. Sparky DeJoy getting set to lead things off here in the bottom of the seventh, Yanks down by two."

"Be careful, Angel. Raoul's still dangerous," says Mirlanda.

"Raoul?" asks Deep. "You mean Revere, the Philly pitcher? Paulie with that nasty slider."

"Raoul Wo, my ex-husband. He's got a nasty scheme."

"Ahh. The noted underworld figure, no relation to the Woes on the field," says Deep. "Explains a lot."

"Don't know about that," says Mirlanda. "The way those bozos are calling this game, he could be related. He's got a lot of tricks."

"So he was your husband? I'm beginning to understand . . ."

"You ain't never gonna understand the depths he can sink to. He pretends his Vanguard wants to set us free, when what he really wants is . . ."

"Chaos," says the mayor. "Chaos and despair. That's what all these extremists want, left and right. But we can't let them have their way. We must steer a sensible course, a course that benefits all, lifts all boats. We must move beyond the hatred, the bitter divisions, and it all starts with saving our cities, above all New York. Our great melting pots with their teeming masses, the heart of our democracy, on the verge of calamity, in need of a helping hand. That's what I'm offering, with brave Mirlanda beside me. For my wonderful godchild, for all God's children. We can't just be like my heartless opponent and tell the cities to drop dead! We can't let them go to hell! No, that's unconscionable. The very soul of America is at stake! We must rise up, marshal the resources of this special land, meet the challenge at hand."

"Sure, sweetheart," says Mirlanda, brushing his bushy gray mane. "And you're just the man to do it. He's just the man to do it, Al."

"I take your word, Mirlanda," says Deep. "And DeJoy takes the first pitch from Revere for a strike. It's been real enlightening to have you both here in the booth, glad we put those rumors to rest so you can continue your campaign as New York looks to rally here, just two innings to go in this do-or-die seventh game. Sparky diggin' in again, my family's favorite, having a nice game as I knew he would, save for that costly collision with Angel which wasn't his fault, two for three with two runs scored and there he goes again, a slap single through the middle and the Yanks have got it going. Tying run at the plate now with Toomich coming up and plenty of baseball left to play."

. . .

In Sheila Dugan's luxury box, asleep on his weapons, Raoul dreams he's given the order to drop the big one on New York. He's so ecstatic he gives his Russian comrade a bear hug that almost pops the chubby fellow right out of his pink skin. Then he boards his hijacked Dugan D-2 bomber and takes off for the stratosphere, breaking the sound barrier in no time whatsoever.

It's all fine and good to play sniper at the stadium with your flaming arrows, but true satisfaction will only come when you make a more emphatic statement, he thinks. Grind God's free market to an immediate halt by taking out its nerve center in one mighty blow. Strike fear into the heart of every surviving American. As the Mad Man in you knows, fear's what sells best. The time for playing games is over.

Up to now, you've been too cute. You can't end God's oppressive rule by being cute. Half measures won't do. You've got to throw everything you have at him, everything imaginable, swing for the fences, bombs away. It makes no sense to bank on Nixon winning, and then losing later. You don't owe nothing to that prick, Tricky Dick. Take the whole thing down now.

The point of impact will be the SoHo building where your archenemies live, God's special agents who foiled the original plan. More precisely, the kitchen where the old gypsy witch got the Russian to blink. That cost you a lot. But now you can make up for it.

He zeroes in, past interfering clouds, opens his hatch wide, watches skyscrapers take shape, releases his tonnage, feels the heat, sees the light, hears the hum of the ancient refrigerator at Joan's place and then Frenchie taking the edge off with a soft, touching "Ring Around the Rosy," sung as though she were playing with the baby he ruthlessly took from her. Not something a father should do, but justified in the big picture (always one of his favorite rationalizations). His biggest regret is giving it back, allowing a glimmer of hope she could escape unscathed. All ancient history. He'll take all their babies from them now—firstborn, secondborn, down the line. He'll take them all from themselves in one big searing mushroom blast. Diving headlong into the heart of it, he experiences a surge of extreme bliss.

The Gates of Hell are open. You did it! The revolution can begin.

• • •

Mercury reporter Art Popov files his final dispatch before boarding Yankee owner Sheila Dugan's private jet.

ANGEL PUTS YANKS ON TOP! ART BIDS FAREWELL

Yankee slugger Angel Guerrero slugged a three-run homer in the bottom of the seventh, his third of the topsy-turvy World Series finale, to give the Bronx Bombers an 8–7 lead and New York City a new lease on life as I pen my final words.

Making his signature prediction with a point of his bat to dead center field, the same spot where his "main mommas" and

baby boy were pointing from the stands, the ponytailed outfielder drilled a tape-measure shot to the spot that was unques-
tionably gone from the moment it left his bat. And with Nick
"The Swan" Spillage, a shell of his former self, working in and
out of a jam in the eighth to hold the Phillies scoreless, the
Yanks are just three outs away from a come-from-behind win.

Angel, who's been carrying the Bombers on his broad
shoulders since he magically reappeared at the end of Game
Six, started New York's comeback with his mammoth walk-off
homer in that one to another predicted spot. But when we look
back at this Series, my bet is that the moment we'll say mattered
the most was off the field, when Angel helped New York's Bravest extinguish the fire that was threatening to consume all of
Brooklyn. That's when the tide really started to turn, when the
city and its home team could finally dare to dream big things.
Who will ever forget that cavalcade up Fifth Avenue—with
Angel, Swannie, and hot-rocker Frenchie Jones, flanked by our
hero firefighters, headed for their date with destiny? What New
Yorker wasn't touched by the sight?

Baseball immortal Yogi Berra once said, "It ain't over till it's
over." Yet this afternoon, as we head into the ninth inning of
the deciding game, a once-again self-confident Big Apple is
responding, "Nuts to that, Yogi. It ain't over but *it is over*."

It's over, at any rate, for the much ballyhooed Satanic Vanguard, which hoped to turn a New York defeat into a spring-
board for revolution. The Vanguard is a spent force, its members
scattered, its plot exposed, its big benefactor gone, its capacity
to create mass hysteria crippled. It's been reduced to little more
than a mad, lone-wolf terrorist and some family connections,
still capable of doing damage, but overthrow the system? Not
a chance.

Win or lose, this much is clear: despite all Satan's efforts,
the Yanks are not going to throw this Series. Their stars will not

take a dive. They're going to give it their all, even if it's tough to lift their arms over their shoulders, as seems the case with their former pitching phenom.

Spillage should have been pulled in the first, when it was obvious he had nothing, digging a 4–zip hole for the Bombers before he could get a batter out. But goofball skipper Howie Love showed some mettle by sticking with the pitcher, and the kid has gutted it out with an assortment of no-windup junk to put his team in position to win. His stats are ugly but his spirit's intact, and no doubt Love is going to give him the chance to finish what he started.

Love has come to the rescue of Mayor Lightweight too, in the form of a rousing defense by his new missus, the Hell-Raising Mirlanda, in a nationally broadcast interview seen by fifty million. His promises are as empty as ever, but his poll numbers have shot up, and he's not about to resign in disgrace no matter what new mud gets thrown at him. Watch out, Tricky Dick. With brave Mirlanda beside him, this guy's become the Teflon mayor. So sit back and enjoy the game, Mr. and Missus Lightweight, your fortunes are rising along with New York's.

Signs of the city's renewal are everywhere. Crime is going down, the boards are coming off the storefronts, the garbage is being collected again, and young artists are moving into abandoned buildings all over town, a sure sign that a renaissance is at hand. These young artists are the true Vanguard, the Vanguard of better times, and I wish I could stick around to see the fruits of their creations. But for old Art Popov, the time has come to depart the scene.

It's been a great ride being your faithful correspondent, and I've loved every minute of it, until the last week when I've been forced under threat of unending torture to spout nonsensical Satanist propaganda. But I saw my chance to get away and I'm taking it. I will no longer be their tool, and a critical tool I was, if I must say so. No revolution can succeed without controlling the flow of communication. And with no Art at their disposal to spread their evil gospel, they might as well call it quits right now.

They won't, but I will. That's it, my friends. See you on the other side.

33

BIG OUT

Raoul wakes, grabs his bow, loads an arrow, lights the tip with a snap of his fingers, and sets his sights on the Yankee right fielder, who he sees is playing a little deeper, not that it matters.

. . .

"Ball four to Adams, and that loads the bases here with two outs in the ninth for Nick 'The Swan' Spillage as he tries to protect the Yanks' one-run lead against the Liberty Bell Creekers in this do-or-die seventh game," says Yankee announcer Al Deep. "Twelve straight balls called by home-plate ump Manny Wo, and you gotta believe at least half of them were strikes, just the latest in a string of outrageously bad calls by the Wo brothers goin' against the Yanks. Maybe Missus Mayor Mirlanda was onto something when she suggested not everything is up-and-up with those guys.

"New York has a case to make that this game was robbed if it goes the wrong way for them now, and here's Dick Trowgin jumping out of the dugout all excited to make that case, but he better watch himself jawboning with Manny, who's got no patience for this kind of stuff, and oops! There he goes! The old workhorse is outta here, Trowgin ejected by ump Manny Wo, and that'll leave Yankee manager Howie Love

272 I MICHAEL GROSS

without the protection of his trusted sidekick as Yankee-killer Vernon 'Big Tree' Washington steps to the plate.

"No place to put him, Phillies on every base, Big Tree with the chance for a second grand slam and a surefire Series MVP honor if he comes through here, though it's the Woes who made it all possible and Baseball Commissioner Mo Schtick, who we see chatting up the mayor in the stands, is going to need to look into this if you ask me. Yup. A Philadelphia win would come with an asterisk, the way this game has been called. But that's a scenario Nick Spillage can still prevent as he talks to the ball behind the mound, back to the batter, and takes a deep breath. It's been a long, long game for the Yankee pitching wonder whose dream season is on the line. Needs one more out, but it's a big one.

"Lovey's got the shift on, Angel playing shallow in right, though he takes a few steps back out of respect for Washington's power. Here comes the pitch, and Big Tree gets under it, skies one way high up in right-center gap, way up there, but with these tricky winds will it have the distance? Angel on his horse, really flying, long ways to go but what a jump he got! DeJoy running for it too, but he's not going to risk another collision with Angel, who's goin' full tilt and whoa! What's that streak? A flaming arrow! More! Angel dancing through them like he's tiptoein' through the tulips. DeJoy holding up, he won't go near. The ball still hanging, Angel nearing the fence and no! He's hit! Staggers, leaps. There goes his hat, there goes his wig. Glove over the fence and he's got it! He's got it! Crashes into the wall and goes down in a pool of blood and flames. Can he hold on? Yes! Lifts his glove and the ball is in it. Big megawatt smile! The Yankees win!

"But no, say the Woes, all signaling the safe sign, as fans react to the arrows racing to the exits. More arrows flying. The mayor takes cover. Where are they coming from? There. Sheila Dugan's luxury box. We've got a camera on the sniper now, in green fatigues, fighting on the floor with a fierce dog, looks like a Dalmatian. It's Raoul Wo, the notorious underworld figure and Satanic Vanguard leader, with a whole stash of weapons in the Yankee owner's box but it looks like the big dog's getting the better of him. The bow's knocked free, kicked aside, and here come New York's Finest to finish the job. Trying to get the cuffs on him and would you look at that? What a sight for sore eyes! It's my dear, departed brother-in-law Lieutenant Gus Berkley, who must've faked his death to put the Vanguard off the scent, now waving to the camera and here's to you, Gus! How 'bout the way DeJoy worked out!

"Bedlam here in Yankee Stadium as the Phils continue to cross the bases, but the commissioner's signaling that Washington's out, overruling the Woes, and this one's in the books. No doubt about it. The World Champion New York Yankees in a comeback 8–7 win as Angel makes the big catch when it counts! Looks like he was hit in the leg but that doesn't stop him from rising to his feet, pulling out the arrow and taking one last bow before he's swarmed by grateful fans. What a showman!

"Meanwhile, back in the owner's box, the police are scratching their heads wondering where Wo, the madman archer, went. Looks like he disappeared into thin air, leaving only a piece of his green fatigues in the mouth of the hero Dalmatian who stopped him cold. The umping Wo brothers have disappeared from the field too. All the Woes are gone, and good riddance, I say. Swannie gets the hard-earned victory, not pretty, but it counts all the same. New York wins!"

. . .

Shortly after liftoff, a voice emerges from the cockpit of Sheila Dugan's private plane. "You think you can get away so easy?" the pilot cackles. "Really?"

. . .

Outside Joan and Eliot's East Village building, a red-haired newsboy with a Yankee cap backward on his head and his left arm in a sling, holds a *Mercury* high above his head with his right hand and shouts, "Miracle in the Bronx! Wounded Angel Saves the Day! Yanks Win Crown on Schtick Overruling! Full Color Series Pix, See 'Em Right Here!

"Ugly Win for Swannie, Who's Not Himself!" shouts the newsboy. "Will Face Knife to Repair Damaged Elbow! Won't Be Lightly's Vice! Will He Ever Be the Same? Sister Sabrina Says Better! SoHo Seer Predictions Right Here!"

The dog beside him barks, and the newsboy continues. "Frenchie Says Bye-bye to Rock and Roll! Angel Says Hello to Broadway! Mayor and Mirlanda Barnstorm Midwest as Lightly Looks to Balance Ticket! Gives Medal of Honor to Hero Dalmatian!"

The dog sits up and barks again, shaking his head.

"Sheila Dugan Plane Crashes in Atlantic!" the newsboy bellows. "Follows Uncle's Footsteps Without the Fire! Cops Search for Missing Woes! Read Last from Art Popov Right Here!"

"World Champ Yankees Placed in Trust!" He wags the *Mercury* at Eliot. "Will Love Return to Skipper Team? Depends on Trust!"

"No way," says Eliot. "Too much pressure." He peels a hundred off the wad he finds in his pocket, hands it to the newsboy and takes a paper.

"Say," says the newsboy. "Are you Howie Love?"

"Nah," says Eliot.

"You look just like him. Could be his doppelslanger."

"Doppelganger? No." Eliot gives the boy a quizzical look. "Are you Nick Spillage?"

"Yeah," the newsboy chuckles. "In my dreams."

*   *   *

Arriving home to a restored apartment, the walls stripped bare of clippings and freshly painted, Eliot finds Joan in bed watching television with a bowl of popcorn on her lap.

"You were great out there, babe," she says.

"You were, too," says Eliot.

"I dunno. It felt a little off. And that ending. Ugh!"

"I thought it was perfect."

"You would."

She puts the popcorn aside, lifts her Yankee nightshirt to reveal her belly.

"C'mere," she says. "I want you to feel something."

He jumps onto the mattress, confident there's nothing to fear underneath.

THE END

ACKNOWLEDGMENTS

It's been quite a ride for my efforts to write fiction—from early promise, to despair, to redirected ambition, to the pivot back. I'm grateful to all those true believers who offered encouragement and support along the way.

When I retired, early in the COVID pandemic, I returned to my abandoned office to retrieve my remaining personal items, including an early version of this book. New York was still a ghost town, Broadway closed, most skyscrapers empty, my favorite restaurants boarded up. The virus had slowed the city to a crawl—the exact opposite of the frenetically chaotic 1976 Big Apple of my imagination that I tried to capture in the novel.

I spent the better part of my twenties writing *Spillage*. When I started it, I had just fallen in love with the woman who became and remains my wife, three kids and three grandkids later, though at the time it all seemed so tenuous. My father had just died—suddenly, from a heart attack—and in the book the dead come back to life. But in reality, without a father to confide in, I was rudderless, not at all sure where life would take me. I loved New York in all its graffiti-ridden, bankrupt, burning-Bronx squalor. And my mind was exploding with a fractured fairy-tale vision of this magical melting pot that I just had to get out in a way that matched the moment.

I was not able to get the book published in its original form, and going back to it, I could see why. It was unreadable, even for its author—far too long, too disjointed, too many characters darting in and out, too many improbable twists and turns, just too much altogether. But buried within, there was still much I loved about it. It was, after all, a statement of who I was at the time in all my youthful, anarchistic fervor, an expression of how I viewed the world at the height of my imaginative powers.

So I've reworked the novel with the perspective of age, tempering its excesses while trying to maintain its original vitality. I am happy to have reached the point, nearly fifty years later, where I feel comfortable sharing it with others.

I want to thank the great mentors who got me started on this long pursuit, including Donald Barthelme, Isaac Asimov, Stephen Minot, Hugh Ogden, Drew Hyland, Franklin D. Reeve, Mark Mirsky, and Faith Sale. I'll always appreciate your wisdom and guidance. Special thanks to the Thomas J. Watson Foundation for the faith you showed in me and for giving me critical time to find my voice.

Thanks to my wife, Barbara, for sticking with your poet through thick and thin. Your passionate love of reading continues to inspire me. Thanks as well to my other early readers, including my brother Chuck, who read every draft; my daughter Gilda, son Max and daughter-in-law Mia; and my friends Jack Frishberg and David Roochnick.

Finally, many thanks to the people who have helped me take this project over the finish line, including my editor Andra Miller, my publisher Josh Raab and his team at Raab & Co., my daughter Willa for her art direction, James Scott for his cover illustration, Beattie Carothers for his photograph, and Brian Phillips for his book design.

Made in United States
North Haven, CT
28 March 2024

50617940R00171